I had just finished my daily labor report when the phone rang.

"Sil-Trac, this is Harley speaking."

"Miss Harley..." said a weak voice on the other end. I could hardly hear over the sound of traffic in the background.

"Hello...Hello...Who is this?"

"Miss Harley, it's Rebecca." It sounded like she was sobbing.

"Rebecca, what's wrong?"

"It's Miroslaw." More sobbing.

"Rebecca, listen. Take a deep breath and then tell me what's wrong." I could hear engine noise in the background. "Start with where you are."

"I am at the petrol store. I went to Miroslaw's home. I am feeding Lech while Miroslaw is with his cousin." She went into another siege of sobbing. At this rate, it would be next week before I got the story out of her.

"Rebecca, if you can't tell me what's wrong, I can't help you." I had a sudden vision of Debbie Dayshift arriving at Mike's while Rebecca was feeding Lech. "Are you hurt, Rebecca?"

"Not me. Miss Harley, I think Miroslaw is dying."

ALSO BY ARLENE SACHITANO

Quilt As Desired

Quilter's Knot (2008)

CHIP AND DIE

BY

ARLENE SACHITANO

ZUMAYA ENIGMA   AUSTIN TX

2003

This book is a work of fiction. Names, characters, places and incidents are products of the author's imagination or are used fictitiously. Any resemblance to actual persons or events is purely coincidental.

CHIP AND DIE
© 2003 by Arlene Sachitano

ISBN: 978-1-894942-35-5

Cover art and design by April Martinez
Cover painting by Sidonie Caron

Look for us online at http://www.zumayapublications.com

National Library of Canada Cataloguing in Publication Data

Sachitano, Arlene
        Chip and die / Arlene Sachitano.

ISBN 1-894942-35-3 I. Title.

PS3619.A23C44 2003 813'.6 C2003-911225-X

DEDICATION

Dedicated to the late Gordon DeMarco, who always said: "If you just write a page a day, in a year you will have a book."

ACKNOWLEDGMENTS

I'd like to thank my critique partners, Katy King and LuAnn Vaughn, without whom it would have been hard to keep going. Thanks also to the wonderful people at Zumaya Publications: Tina and Liz, you made my dream come true.

Thanks to Sisters in Crime for the invaluable support and information you have given me.

I would never have been able to type my manuscript if it weren't for the skillful application of knife to hand by Dr. Anton Eilers— thank you, Dr. E.

Thanks to all my friends, who now know more then they ever wanted to about dead bodies.

And of course, thanks to my family: Jack, Karen, Rueben, Malakai, Annie and David— the true believers.

CHAPTER ONE

I SAT IN THE large, dimly lit conference room. The chairs were comfortable, and if the waistband of my skirt hadn't been biting my side I'd probably have been asleep. I listened to the quality assurance manager argue endlessly with the purchasing manager over the quality of wafers we had been receiving from Japan. I actually welcomed the interruption when Mary motioned me out of the room. I followed her back to her desk.

"I'm sorry, Harley, this guy won't say who he is, but it sounds urgent." She handed me the phone.

"Don't say anything," the voice said in heavily accented English. "If you ever want to see Miroslaw again, be at the Blue Whale tonight. Nine o'clock."

"I think you have the wrong number. I don't know what you're talking about."

"Yes, you do. Be there."

The receiver went dead.

"Anything I need to do?" Mary asked. She had been my secretary for a number of years and most of the time had the uncanny ability to know what I needed before I did.

"That person was talking about someone named Miroslaw. Wanted me to meet him at the Whale to talk about it. I tried to tell him I didn't know what he was talking about, but he wasn't buying."

"Of course, you know Miroslaw. That's Mike's real name." Many of my workers were from other countries, and they often Anglicized their names. You usually only knew their real name if you dealt with their legal documents on a regular basis.

1

"Get him for me. I need to talk to him now."

"I'd like to get him, but he's out sick today."

"Did he call in himself?"

"As a matter of fact, he didn't. His brother called and said he had stomach flu and couldn't come to the phone."

"Mary, Mike doesn't have a brother. Don't you remember? When he filled out his insurance beneficiary form, he told you he has no brothers or sisters. You brought it to my attention. You worried about how alone he was."

As a supervisor, I had faced many employee problems. Most often, it had to do with wages. No one is ever happy, no matter how much money he or she gets. In fact, usually the more you give a person the less happy they are. This was something entirely different.

The meeting ended without a conclusion, and I spent the next two hours tracking down my part of the quality data. I worked long after everyone else had gone home for the night.

My office is one of those modular affairs created using padded dividers in colors designed to soothe agitated employees. Dozens of identical cubicles surround my cube. It enhances that mole-like feeling you get working twelve hours a day in a windowless environment.

The swing shift manager was in the clean room with his people. I picked up several copies of an article on solvent recycling and headed for the other end of the maze. I had promised to distribute them before tomorrow's meeting on chemical handling. My feet made clomping noises on the linoleum, followed by a faint echo. The echo got louder and faster.

Someone else was in the cubicles.

I looked around. I was in a dead end created by three desk areas. I stopped to listen, but the footsteps stopped, too. There was only one way out, and it would take me right where I'd heard them.

I looked at the desk nearest me, picked up a large, hand-thrown pottery mug. I heard a rustling noise and charged toward it into the hallway

"Harley," a voice shouted as I raised my mug, ready to slam it into the figure bent over the first desk in the corner cubicle. Steve, the swing shift manager, dropped a handful of Hershey's Kisses he had just extracted from the jar on Jose's desk. "What are you doing?"

"Jesus, Steve. You scared me. I was handing out the solvent recycling report. Why aren't you in the lab?"

"I had a chocolate craving. So shoot me. Or should I say, 'club me with a mug?'" He laughed.

I returned the mug, dropped my last report and went back to my desk.

A slow drizzle had been falling all day and was showing no signs of letting up. I could have walked to the Blue Whale Tavern, but a few minutes before nine, I drove across the street.

The Blue Whale was like a home-away-from-home for all of us at Sil-Trac. Electronics factories are never small; but computer chipmakers like Sil-Trac, with their air and water purification needs, need more room than most. The Sil-Trac plant is located in an industrial park in the middle of rural Washington County, Oregon. The locals call it the Sunset Corridor, named for the Sunset Highway that carries Portlanders west to the beach.

The Blue Whale set up shop across the street from the plant, correctly guessing that people would overlook a lot if a place were convenient. The Whale's gold-flecked wallpaper and dark paneling gave it that Texas whorehouse feel. Executives in Armani suits and Gucci loafers sat side-by-side with production workers in Levis and Nikes, sipping cheap beer and eating the Whale's surprisingly good fried chicken.

By nine most of the day crowd had gone home, and the swing shift lunch rush was over. I had just gotten my raincoat from the dry cleaners; I wished I'd left it in the car. The smoke was thick, and my clothes would be full of it by the time I left. A few more trips to the Whale, and I will have paid for the first year of college for my dry cleaner's kid.

I looked around through the haze. There were a couple of people playing pool; a big rip in the felt was giving them fits. I recognized the Implant maintenance man. The poor guy was going through a messy divorce and spent most of his spare time drowning his sorrows in an ocean of Budweiser and playing pool.

Normally, I wouldn't be caught dead in a place like the Blue Whale, but it was such a tempting illusion. We all pretend we're getting away from Sil-Trac at the Whale. I don't think three non-Sil-Trac people have walked through the door in the last five years. In reality, the Blue Whale is the only food place for at least five miles in any direction, a little parasite on our industrial giant.

"Hey, boss-lady," the bartender called out as I entered the tavern.

"How ya doin', Skip?" By the time I retire from Sil-Trac, I will have spent enough time with Skip to become functionally illiterate.

Skip dressed in a uniform of white pants and a white button-down shirt with the sleeves rolled up. He tied a stained chef's apron proudly to his skinny waist to let the uninitiated know he was a serious cook. His premature near-baldness made it difficult to guess his true age. He could be twenty-two or forty-two.

"Same ole same ole," he answered. "How about yourself?"

"Has anyone been asking for me?"

"Nope. Been pretty quiet tonight. You expecting someone?" he asked as he set a large diet cola on the bar in front of me.

"I'm not sure." I picked up my glass and walked to one of the booths. It was darker there, but I had a clear view of both doors to the place, and I felt somehow more secure with my back protected by the scarred wood.

I had just about decided I'd been the victim of a prank when a group of men walked through the door. The rain was falling in buckets now, and the men took a few minutes removing their wet hats and coats by the door. I knew they were here to see me.

Skip started toward the group. An older man with a big belly, coarse features and thick white hair froze him with a glare, causing him to retreat to the far corner behind the bar. The little bit of security I'd felt slipped away.

A baby-faced young man with a bad haircut took up a post by the front door. Another guy went back by the restrooms. You could tell by looking that he was a recent immigrant from Eastern Europe. European men have a flair for texture in their clothes that has escaped the American fashion scene. This guy's wool pants looked like he could use a good dry cleaner, though.

I did not intend to buckle to any demands they might make; but if they played their cards right, I might reveal the name of my cleaner.

The older man and the third young man came over to my booth. I could smell the cheap grease in their wet hair. The old guy squeezed his way into the booth opposite me; the younger man sat in silence beside me, blocking my escape. He picked up my paper napkin and started ripping the edges.

The older man wore an ill-fitted tweed sport coat over a worn sweater. He leaned forward.

"You want to see Miroslaw alive again, you listen good. Give to me four thousand, two hundred dollars. Bring— how you say?— no writing dollars."

"He means unmarked bills," the young man said with only a hint of an accent.

"Unmarked bills, yes." The old guy continued. "You bring to phone booth. Thursday."

He gestured to the young man. The young man stopped shredding my napkin and handed me a slip of paper with an address on it from his suit pocket.

"Don't tell no one," the old one finished.

"Wait. What about Mike? How do I know he's okay?"

The older man started to get out of the booth, but his stomach pinned him in like a pregnant woman in a phone booth. The young man jumped up and pulled the old guy by the arm, freeing him.

"Wait a minute. You mean to tell me you're holding a guy for four thousand, two hundred dollars? My dry cleaning bill is more than that."

The group headed for the door. The one with the wool pants looked back, but the old guy pushed him on out the door.

"Who were those dudes?" Skip asked as he wiped imaginary crumbs from my table. He had materialized as soon as the door shut on my "friends."

"I don't know. Kidnappers, murderers, all-purpose thugs, I guess."

"That old dude looked really mean."

"Yeah, Skip, he did. I really appreciated your show of support."

"Well, did you see the way he looked at me?" His face turned red thinking about it.

"I'll forgive you if you get me another Diet Coke."

I followed him back to the bar.

"Are those guys really murderers?"

"I don't know who or what they are, but I have a feeling I'm going to find out."

I finished my Coke then drove home. I kept going over and over the night's developments. As intimidating as the men seemed, I just couldn't believe someone would plan a kidnapping for forty-two hundred dollars. But then again, the *Oregonian*, Portland's daily paper, runs stories almost every day about people getting stabbed or shot for pocket change.

I live in an older neighborhood in northeast Portland. The sidewalks are cracked and most of the basements leak, but on a sunny day you can see young mothers pushing baby strollers past old folks leaning on walkers. Teenagers drive by in their stereophonic cocoons. At night, you see their parents walking patrol in twos and threes, trying to prevent the drug dealers from coming any closer.

Locals call my house a Portland Bungalow. That means it's over sixty years old and has two bedrooms. It was one of the spoils from my divorce. That and my teenaged stepson Noah were all I had to show for five of the most exasperating years of my life. Noah was in a prep school out-of-state, but he called my place home whenever he wasn't at school.

I had been married for two years when Sam came home from an overseas trip one day with Noah in tow. He lived with us for the next three years. When the marriage broke up, he just stayed on with me. His mother was "out of the picture," according to Sam.

Noah could only remember living with a succession of relatives. He started at a military prep school last year by Sam's decree. Legally, I had guardianship, but that really just let me take him to the doctor. Sam remote-controlled his future — for now.

I was surprised to see all the lights on in the house. When I pulled my car into the garage, my frantic housekeeper met me.

"Mrs. Johnson, what are you still doing here?" I live alone. Mrs. Johnson was a gift I gave myself after my marriage broke up. She cleaned the house, did the laundry and cooked. It only took her a couple of hours a day. Her husband Henry had retired a few years ago, and I think her escape to my house was the only thing that kept their marriage intact.

"I feel so terrible. Sonny has escaped." She began sobbing.

"What do you mean, escaped?" Sonny was my ill-tempered dachshund. I kept him inside most of the time to prevent him from terrorizing the neighborhood kids. His only redeeming feature was his absolute devotion to Noah.

"I put him in the backyard while I was washing the kitchen floor, just like I always do. When I went to get him, he was gone." Mrs. Johnson buried her face in the hem of the apron tied around her ample middle. "My Henry came over and drove around the neighborhood, but no one has seen nothing."

"You go on ahead and go home. I'm sure he'll come home when he gets hungry. He can crawl right back through the hole he probably dug to get out. I'll call the pound in the morning and see if they have him."

Frankly, I would be lucky if they didn't call me first to find out if he was current on his rabies shots after he bit someone. A small part of me hoped he would stay lost. In his six short years on this planet, he had been more trouble than any ten dogs with long legs.

All things considered, it took me a long time to fall asleep that night.

CHAPTER TWO

THE NEXT MORNING STARTED like all mornings at Sil-Trac. First, all the production people met with their supervisors then all the supervisors met.

"Where's Mike? Or more to the point, where's the data for the audit?" asked Debbie, the day-shift photolithography lead operator.

I have six Debbies in my production group, so I developed nicknames to keep them straight. One is Debbie Red; another one is Debbie C. There is no real logic to the Debbie System.

This one I call Debbie Dayshift. She got that distinction when we hired her. She was our second Debbie, and the first one worked nights. More Debbies came after her, but the name stuck. This Debbie has a voice that reminds you of big trucks driving on deep gravel and hair that looks like she just walked out of a cheap salon.

"I'm not sure where Mike is right now," I answered.

"I said you would be sorry if you promoted Mike. I knew he would be nothing but trouble." Debbie didn't want anyone promoted to her level or beyond.

"Get a grip, Debbie. Just because he's gone for a day or two doesn't make him a problem. Besides, he only has the logs from test on through to the end. He finished yours and put them on my desk."

Manufacturers across the country were all scrambling to gather documents and put procedures in place to meet an external quality audit called ISO 9000. This standard requires companies to demonstrate that they are following repeatable processes in everything from training to the actual manufacturing of products, and that they document their results as they go. Sil-Trac was due for its final inspection in four days.

In most areas, my people are really good. Basically, we take people off the street with a high school education then ask them to handle million-dollar pieces of equipment with a degree of precision most people cannot comprehend. They do that and more.

Most of the work areas at Sil-Trac are Class 10 clean rooms. This means no more than 10 half-micron particles can be in the air under certain controlled conditions. A half-micron might not sound like much, but computer chip circuits are so small a tiny particle of dust getting on one is like a meteor landing on the interstate.

To accomplish this level of cleanliness, we construct special rooms with massive HEPA filters cleaning the air. All the workers are required to wear head-to-toe coverings called bunny suits. A bunny suit is made of a woven polyester or nylon fiber and includes a coverall, a hood that tucks into the coverall, and booties. Sil-Trac added particle masks, which protect against spit, as well as beard bags for people with facial hair. With the gloves and goggles for chemical protection, you end up with virtually no exposed skin.

With all the difficult tasks my people handle with ease, their inability to do the simple task of counting output stuns me. No matter what their education, years of experience or other background, this simple task eludes them all. Sometimes, I wake up in a cold sweat in the middle of the night thinking about this. With ISO 9000 looming large, it was at the top of my worry list.

"Okay, how many of you team leaders still have problems reconciling count?" I asked this question every morning. In all my years of supervising, the answer had never been "No one."

"I don't know if my problem is fixed. I haven't seen my records since Mike took them." Debbie Dayshift said.

"We've already talked about your records. Thank you, Debbie. Tommy, how are your die prep counts?"

"My count agrees between test and laser scribe."

Tommy Chan is one of my better lead people. He is slender and has a haircut that is popular with the young Asian crowd. The top is long and combed straight back with the sides shaved to the skin. The young single women at Sil-Trac consider him the number-one catch. He told me right after he came to work at Sil-Trac that his parents would arrange his marriage with an Asian woman of his class. I hadn't shared this info with my group.

Tommy was the only son in his family. He had been raised to have little tolerance for anyone who wasn't of his race, sex or class. He was caught between his parents' Old World values and his American education and lifestyle. I didn't envy his position.

"Great, Tommy, so your own areas agree. But do you agree with the area before you and after you?"

"I start my count with the die that pass test."

"You mean you don't keep track of the wafers coming in?" Integrated circuits start life on a thin slice of single crystal silicon known in the business as a *wafer*. A series of photographic steps and heat treatments result in microscopic circuitry that shuffles electrons in a controlled fashion. This enables them to do everything from telling time in a two-dollar watch to launching the Space Shuttle.

Depending on what the circuit size is, anywhere from fifty to one hundred-fifty or more designs are printed on a single wafer. When the basic processing is complete, the wafer is tested and then cut up to provide the individual circuits. At this stage, we refer to the pieces as *die*.

"Not really. I'm just going to bust them into pieces anyway."

"How do you think we calculate yield? We compare the die count to the wafer count. You know that."

"The test machine counts that automatically," Tommy said.

"From now on, I want you to log the wafers in when you get them and check what you receive against what Debbie says she sent to diffusion."

The diffusion process is a lot like baking cookies. The area consists of row after row of long, tubular furnaces. High temperatures drive impurities into the surface of the wafers and influence how the electrons move around.

"Shannon, how are the packaging numbers?"

"My numbers were fine, they matched with Tommy's. I hope I don't have to show any proof, though. Mike took my records on Friday to change the format of my log, and I haven't seen them since."

It always came back to Mike. You'd think he was the only one who worked here.

"Can you reconstruct the information from the labor sheets?"

"Well, I've never thought about it. Does payroll keep them?"

Shannon asked. She is one of those naturally graceful people. Her clothes never wrinkle; her hair always falls back into place perfectly. Most of us come out of the bunny suit area with flat sweaty hair. Shannon's shoulder-length auburn locks bounce right back into place no matter how long she wears her suit. I'd be willing to bet money she could walk out of a tornado and not have a hair out of place or a wrinkle in her perfectly creased pants.

"Yes. They won't like it, but payroll batches, boxes and keeps all the labor cards for a year. Ask Mr. Nakata where to find them."

All people who are involved in any direct labor at Sil-Trac are required to fill out a document reporting how much time they spend on which batch of what product. We managers compile all the information weekly so we can tell if we are meeting the expected labor costs. They are the cornerstones of some really delightful meetings.

Every day, each lead person was supposed to check the die and wafer counts of their area. They matched them against deliveries from the previous area and receipts of the area after theirs. Mike was the lead in charge of the overall ISO 9000 project in the clean room. He had been working for days trying to reconcile everyone's counts.

I didn't like the way this was shaping up. Everything kept coming back to the one guy we couldn't find.

CHAPTER THREE

WAS ABLE TO get through the supervisor meeting without having to publicize my problem, thanks to Jose Flores, the DRAM product supervisor. At our meeting, the person called on first faced the closest scrutiny. If their area had enough trouble, they could consume the whole hour and spare the rest of us. Poor Jose had lost several of his experienced people to the competition recently, so his logs were a mess. After the meeting, I spent a few minutes with him. We agreed Tommy would spend a couple of hours this afternoon with Jose's test and scribe people to help them untangle their problems.

As soon as Jose calmed down, I headed for the Human Resource Department. HR is located in an area away from production. They sit in cubicles, too, separated by taller, thicker dividers in even more muted shades than those in production. Their furniture is plusher and trimmed in real wood. Since people tend to be pretty volatile by the time they reach HR, it makes a certain amount of sense. Personally, I always feel like I'm entering a library. Everyone seems to whisper, and their desktops are artful arrangements of books and coffee mugs.

You can smell Karen Hatcher's area about three cubes before you get there. Karen loves herb tea and always has her little electric pot brewing.

"Hey, Karen, what kind of tea is that?" I asked.

"It's apple cranberry. You want a cup? Pull up a chair."

One of the things I like about Karen is her ability to tell the difference between a tea moocher and a person with a purpose. It saves a lot of small talk.

"What's up?"

"Well, you aren't going to believe this, but I think Mike Wyzcek has been kidnapped."

"You're right. I don't believe it. You'd better start at the beginning. What makes you think that?"

I adjusted the waistband of my plaid Pendleton wool skirt and wished I were thinner. I tried to think of how to make last night's events sound credible. Finally, I just told Karen everything that had happened. She listened without stopping me and sat silent in her chair. Her close-cropped gray hair matched the fabric of the divider behind her. I wondered if she had planned it that way last time they decorated the area.

"Well?" I asked, "What do you think? Is it a prank? Are they serious?"

"For Mike's sake, I think we have to assume they are serious," Karen finally said. "Have you tried calling Mike's house?"

"No, I haven't done anything," I admitted.

She looked up Mike's number on her computer and dialed. She handed me the receiver.

"Is this his voice?" she asked.

He had the usual stiff answering machine message. "Yeah, that's Mike, all right."

"If he's there, he's not answering." Karen took the receiver and hung it up.

"What I don't get is why only forty-two hundred. The penalty for kidnapping is the same whether you ask for that or forty-two million."

"Well, Harley, maybe that's all they thought you could afford. Did you think of that?"

"I assume they thought I'd go to the company. I don't get it."

"I think we need to call the police. If there is any chance that someone really has Mike, the police need to handle it."

"Something doesn't add up. Not just the money. I would swear the old guy I talked to was Polish or at least East European. The Polish community in Portland is small enough I can't imagine they would tolerate something like this. For that matter, I can't imagine word wouldn't be out immediately if someone turned on one of their own." I was thinking aloud.

"Harley, don't even think of going off on your own. This should be a police matter."

"Think about it, Karen. Don't you remember when we had the bomb threat? The local police sat a safe distance away and waited to see if the building would blow up. This isn't Portland, after all."

"Just because they didn't have a bomb squad doesn't mean they aren't trained officers."

"Give me a break, Karen. I was the one who had to go back in the building first. Jose and I were in here looking for bombs while the police sat sipping Cokes in their command post across the street. It didn't do a lot for my confidence."

"I'm going to call them," she said. "I imagine they'll send someone over to talk to you. Don't do anything crazy. Just wait for them to get here."

"Oh, don't worry. I'll be busy helping my leads try to reconstruct the data Mike took home over the weekend. The ISO 9000 auditors are coming Friday, which means I've only got four days to either get Mike back or make new records."

As I got up to go, Karen handed me a folder.

"You can get started on an incident file. Remember, you need to record dates and times and everything you can remember. If anything else happens, record that, too. And please, Harley, wait for the police."

"Don't worry, Karen. Just give me a call when they get here."

"See you later, Harley."

I could tell I'd made her day.

The clean room area is at the opposite end of the building from personnel. The walk back gave me time to refine my plan. My workers are the typical group of people you find in any company. They do specialized tasks with specialized jargon and unique working conditions. They tend to socialize with others who speak the same jargon and understand their own special stresses.

The net result is about three serious romances and an equal number of messy breakups in progress at any given moment. Mike, being twenty-four years old and single, is currently involved in one of each.

Debbie Dayshift is about eight years older than Mike and had chased him hard when he first came to Sil-Trac two years ago. I think he was grateful for all the help she gave him in the beginning. He had just emigrated from Gdansk. As he became surer of himself, though, Debbie was not willing to relinquish any of her control over his life.

Still, if Rebecca hadn't appeared, Mike might have stayed with Debbie out of misplaced loyalty. He didn't seem to notice that his blue eyes, blond hair, flawless skin and well-muscled physique could provide him a lot more options than a well-used truckstop cowgirl. Then again, maybe that was just what he wanted for a while.

About two months ago, Rebecca Valenta arrived from Chicago. She was originally from Gdansk, too. Rebecca was everything Debbie isn't. She is twenty-one, petite and, most importantly, Polish. It took Mike about a nanosecond to dump Debbie and claim Rebecca.

I was pretty sure Rebecca wouldn't have a key to Mike's place. I could almost see the white scarf around her head and the Bible in her hand. It looked like she had never cut her long brown hair in her life. She didn't seem to understand the concept of makeup. On the other hand, I was sure Debbie had made a copy before returning Mike's key to him.

When I got back to the area, I called Debbie out. There was no sense in broadcasting my plan to the whole clean room. She sat on the edge of the upholstered chair next to my desk. Her faded flannel shirt was unbuttoned over a pink T-shirt that had cartoon pigs doing obscene activities on her ample chest.

"Debbie, you know how we're missing the records from Tommy's group? Well, Mike left me a note saying he came in on Saturday and picked up all the records. As you know, that puts us in a bit of a bind. Mike is home sick. I called his house and got no answer..."

"Excuse me, boss. If you want me to go look at Mike's place, just say so."

"Debbie, I think you know, as your boss, I can't ask you to do that. If you happened to come across the records on your own...well, that would be a different matter."

"Consider it done."

CHAPTER FOUR

I SPENT THE NEXT COUPLE of hours working with Shannon, going through the labor cards for her packaging area, trying to remake the missing records.

"Is Tommy back from Jose's area?" I asked her.

"Not yet. I called over there, and they said he left quite a while ago. They said he's probably in the cafeteria solving someone's problems and forgot what time it was. Hieu was looking for him before lunch. He seemed pretty agitated. I think he said something about his daughter. Maybe he's talking to Tommy about it."

"If he's not back in another ten minutes, would you go get him? We need to know which lot number his records start with. He can check the computer on his test system."

"Harley, do you ever think maybe we just aren't meant to pass ISO 9000?"

"We have no choice. Once Micro Tech got the Betty Crocker stamp of approval, it meant we all had to. That or go out of business."

Mike lived in southeast Portland, not far from his uncle's family. It took Debbie Dayshift just under an hour to make the round trip. She said she did a thorough search and found nothing but a hungry cat.

So far, none of Mike's fellow workers knew about the alleged kidnapping, and I was hoping I could keep it that way until I found out what was going on. Besides, with the ISO inspection breathing down my neck, I didn't need Debbie, Rebecca or anyone else going crazy on me.

I thanked Debbie for her trouble and sent her back into the

clean room to help Shannon with her record reconstruction. I was alone at my desk a few minutes later when the phone rang. Karen Hatcher identified herself.

"Hi, Karen. I don't suppose you're calling to tell me Mike has called in, are you?"

"'Fraid not, Harley. The police are coming to talk to you. They'll call my desk from the lobby. I thought maybe you could walk them over to the Whale and avoid arousing the suspicions of the whole building."

"You're not suggesting I manipulate them, are you?" I asked. "Our fine, upstanding boys in blue? I think I'll just head on down to the lobby now and catch them before they even come in."

Karen spent another minute or two giving me a pep talk about cooperation and discretion. I rang off and headed for the front of the building.

Walking into the Sil-Trac lobby is like stepping through a portal to the future. There is lots of glass. Everything that is not glass is chrome. Samples of Sil-Trac products are on display in futuristic cases, a sort of high-tech museum. The tinted floor-to-ceiling windows leave the lobby dark, except for the recessed lights over the displays and one little podium light at the reception desk.

I loafed around and pretended to look at the product exhibition. There are groups of gadgets that contain Sil-Trac chips. Some clever designer did something with mirrors and wires that makes them appear suspended in air. In one section, the wafers themselves glow eerily, like some kind of high-tech house of mirrors. I avoided the seating area. To be honest, I'm afraid of the chrome and teakwood contraptions that pass for chairs here. You cannot convince me they will hold a full-grown human.

While I waited, I used the lobby phone to call the animal shelter, and then Mrs. Johnson. There was no sign of Sonny.

A few more minutes passed before I saw the police car approach. I walked out to the entrance of the visitors' parking lot and flagged them down. They were willing to meet me across the street at The Blue Whale. It was not a doughnut shop, but I think they liked the idea.

The officers were getting out of their patrol car as I crossed the lot to the entrance of the Whale. They reminded me of Officer Friendly. I loved those little stick-on badges they gave out when he came to school. These two had the same kind of nightstick he did—

you know, one of those long wooden ones with a handle— and those gun belts with loops for individual bullets. I guess they don't know about telescoping nightsticks and speed loaders.

I introduced myself and led them inside. We sat at the scene of the crime, so to speak. Skip came over, poured coffee for the two officers and brought me my customary diet cola. He lingered, doing his wipe-the-table routine.

"Skip, if we need anything else, we'll call you."

Sometimes he can be a bit obtuse. This time he went back to his bar without comment.

Officer Hunt seemed to be the senior of the two. He was a good twenty years older than Officer Ward, and he had less hair. He did all the talking.

"Tell me exactly what happened," Hunt said. "Don't leave anything out."

I told them everything. They listened without speaking.

"Well, what do you make of it?" I asked.

"Let me get this straight. These guys you don't know called you up, met you and then left without talking to anyone else?" Hunt asked.

"That pretty well sums it up." I was getting an uneasy feeling about this.

"And you're not related to this guy, right?"

"Well, no. Not unless you count my being his boss. I probably see Mike more than his relatives do." I couldn't decide if the "Hunt" and "Ward" on their badges were first names or last names. This didn't seem like the time to ask.

"There's no reason for you to go getting smart with me, young lady."

"I'm sorry, you're right," I said, though I didn't really mean it.

"This young man lives in the City of Portland, right?" Hunt asked.

"Well, yes."

"And the phone booth where you drop the cash is in Portland, right?"

"That's true." I was beginning to see where this was going.

"The way I see it, this is a problem for the Portland police. And I'll give you a tip. Right now, all we have is your word that anything has happened. Without a ransom note or any other supporting evidence..."

"Oh, I get it. They'll think I am some kind of crackpot," I said, my face turning red.

"Now, don't get upset. All I'm saying is in Portland they have to deal with all kinds of people, and they won't know you like we do."

"What are you talking about?" I could hear my voice rising. "I just met you."

Usually, I am a lot more composed, but this guy was getting on my nerves.

"Now, come on. You know what I mean," Hunt said.

I didn't know what he meant, but I could see this was no longer a productive conversation.

"Call us if anything happens out here. And you call the Portland police when you go home tonight." Hunt obviously was dismissing me.

"Good afternoon, ma'am," Officer Ward said as they got up and left.

Skip materialized almost immediately.

"Are you in some kind of trouble with the police, Harley?" he asked.

"Not here. Just ask the officers. They don't have trouble here."

I got up and handed him a couple of dollars. As I walked back to Sil-Trac, I tried to remember all those TV movies where someone would disappear. If real life were like those shows, Mike had to be missing twenty-four hours before they would investigate. Today was Tuesday, and we first knew he was missing for sure Monday night; so we probably would have to wait until tomorrow before anyone would listen.

When I got back, I went directly to Karen Hatcher's area.

"How did it go?" she asked. "What are they going to do?"

"You want the short version? They're doing nothing."

"You're joking, right?"

"Karen, I wouldn't joke about a thing like this."

"No, really," she asked again, "what did they say?"

"They said it sounded like a problem for the Portland police. If I could get them to believe me."

"Surely we can do something?"

"The first step is to get him officially reported as missing. We need to find out if the company is able to report him gone or if a family member is required."

"I can take care of that," Karen said. "If we need a relative, his personnel file should list at least one. If not a relative, at least a close friend or sponsor or something."

"Okay. While you do that, I've got to check my group. Call me as soon as you hear something."

I left and went directly back to the clean room. Getting through the air shower that leads to the bunny suit dressing room can be a bit tricky in a skirt. Air jets wash any dust particles off you with air from all angles, including the floor. The marketing manager, who insisted we dress professionally at all times in case a customer might visit, had obviously never tried this maneuver in a skirt. I felt like a high-tech Marilyn Monroe.

When I got into the dressing room, I made sure no one was looking, hiked my skirt up and climbed into my suit. I checked the output for each area then checked in with the lead operators. Our daily output had met the target numbers, and the leads were still frantically reconstructing the missing logs. At the rate they were going, they wouldn't finish by the Friday inspection. I was going to have to figure out a better plan if Mike didn't show up pretty quick.

The clean room is divided functionally into enclosed rooms joined by a common hallway. I headed for the photolithography room looking for Rebecca. The yellow lighting in the room bothers some people— yellow light is necessary to protect the photosensitive liquid plastic that is spun on the wafers to create the circuit patterns. I'm so used to it I don't even notice anymore.

I stepped into the black entrance drum and spun the opening to align with the room side of the doorway. You would think it would be difficult to identify people when everything but their eye area is swathed in white. I guess your senses just shift or something, because those of us who work in the room don't have any trouble.

Some of us look like that dough guy on the canned biscuits. Rebecca didn't. She looked more like the Virgin Mary. I found her aligning wafers with a projection stepper.

"Rebecca, can I talk to you for a minute?"

"Of course, just a moment." She finished aligning the new pattern to the ones already on the wafer and pressed the expose button. The machine began stepping through its exposures.

"Rebecca, have you seen Mike lately?"

"Not since Friday."

"I don't mean to pry, but is that usual?" I asked. "Don't you do things together on the weekends?"

"Usually he takes me to church. You know St. Stanislaus on Interstate Street? They are the Polish Catholic Church. They have the Polish service at nine and eleven. Sometimes, Mike, he has to help his uncle. On those days, I go with Father and Mother."

"Is that where he was this weekend? Helping his uncle?"

"No, I don't think so," she said. "He said he was going to visit his cousin. Some city in the south of Oregon."

Finally, we were getting somewhere. "Do you know his cousin's name?"

"No, I only know Uncle Andrush."

"Do you know his last name?"

"I'm sorry. He didn't tell me." Rebecca looked down and blushed. "Is Miroslaw in some kind of problem?"

"If he is where he said, with his cousin, he should be okay."

I left Rebecca aligning her wafers and went to find Tommy. As I was coming out of the photo area, I saw him enter the test-and-scribe area and followed him.

"Hey, Tommy," I asked, "did you get Jose's people straightened out?"

"I did what I could. They have some real problems. They haven't been zeroing their machine when they start a new work order, for one thing. I can't do much about that now. I showed them how to do it right for the future. And, of course, their log entries don't match from area to area. What's new, huh?"

"At least they have logs to mess up."

"Come on, boss. I can make a set of logs that will pass any inspection. You just say the word."

Tommy is the unofficial leader of the Asian production workers at Sil-Trac. His parents are prominent members of the local community. His whole family is involved in helping Asian immigrants resettle in the Portland area. As the only son of the Chan family, he commands a lot of respect. Whenever any of the Asian workers has a problem, they go to Tommy.

"Thanks for your generous offer, Tommy, but I have this strange need for the logs my whole career hinges on to be authentic."

"Suit yourself, boss. If you change your mind let me know."

"I'll keep it in mind, Tommy. Until then, will you help Shannon try to figure out her counts from the labor sheets? See if anything they are getting matches with what you got off your machine."

"Sure, boss, whatever you say."

Tommy went off on his appointed task, and I spent the rest of the shift questioning my workers on their processes and procedures. The ISO 9000 inspection was not just a review of documents. The inspectors would ask assemblers questions to insure that they were trained and used the posted procedures. I spent an hour running each group through the suiting up routine in the dressing room. When you put on a bunny suit, there is a specified order for donning each piece with no part of the suit touching the floor. It is not as easy as it sounds.

When Debbie Dayshift's group finished and went out she stayed back to talk to me.

"I saw you talking to Miss Perfect Rebecca earlier," she said. "Does she know where Mike is?"

"She says he went to see his cousin out of town. Do you know who that might be?"

"Well, I know his mother's cousin lives in Eugene. I don't know their names or anything, though. You know, Harley, I think Rebecca knows more than she's saying."

"What makes you say that?"

"Mike would never leave Lech without anyone to feed him. And when I went there he was hungry, but not like he'd been without food for days."

"Who on earth is Lech?"

"Mike's cat. I always took care of him when Mike was gone before Miss Polish Perfect came along."

"Well, she didn't volunteer anything, and I didn't ask if she was feeding his cat, either. I don't see what difference it makes, anyway. She says she hasn't heard from Mike since Friday."

"Harley, for a boss, you can sure be naive."

"What are you talking about?"

"The logs, of course. I'll bet you anything young Miss Rebecca has the logs. That's why they're not at Mike's apartment."

"Why on earth would Rebecca take the logs?"

"Don't you see? She'll do anything to make me look bad. If we flunk ISO 9000, the assemblers won't feel the heat. It will be us leads."

"Listen to what you're saying, Debbie. If the leads look bad, that includes Mike, too."

Being her supervisor prevented me from saying any more.

"You just wait and see." Debbie stomped off to her room. If the door to the dressing room hadn't been under air pressure, I'm sure it would have slammed.

When the shift ended, I went to the packaging area to review the progress Shannon was making on the log reconstruction. Unfortunately, it was not enough to make me feel better. She assured me she would work on it first thing in the morning.

I came out of the clean room and went to the cafeteria. All the supervisors in my division had an unofficial group nervous breakdown at the end of the workers' shift. It helped us put our own problems in perspective. The caffeine also rejuvenated us for the additional two to three hours we put in after our work teams went home.

I left feeling much better than when I arrived. If the inspection started with the DRAM area or the EPROM group, I would be in good shape — we would have flunked ISO 9000 long before they discovered my missing logs. Of course, there was always the chance they would start with my microprocessor group, in which case it would all be my fault. I decided not to dwell on that thought.

When I got back to my desk, I found a note that Mrs. Johnson had called. There was still no sign of Sonny, and my cat, Cher, was on a hunger strike. I didn't know why she was upset. She hates Sonny. I made myself a note to pick up some of that deluxe cat food in the foil package she loves.

I had just finished my daily labor report when the phone rang.

"Sil-Trac, this is Harley speaking."

"Miss Harley..." said a weak voice on the other end. I could hardly hear over the sound of traffic in the background.

"Hello...Hello...Who is this?"

"Miss Harley, it's Rebecca." It sounded like she was sobbing.

"Rebecca, what's wrong?"

"It's Miroslaw." More sobbing.

"Rebecca, listen. Take a deep breath and then tell me what's wrong." I could hear engine noise in the background. "Start with where you are."

"I am at the petrol store. I went to Miroslaw's home. I am feeding Lech while Miroslaw is with his cousin." She went into another siege of sobbing. At this rate, it would be next week before I got the story out of her.

"Rebecca, if you can't tell me what's wrong, I can't help you." I had a sudden vision of Debbie Dayshift arriving at Mike's while Rebecca was feeding Lech. "Are you hurt, Rebecca?"

"Not me. Miss Harley, I think Miroslaw is dying."

"Rebecca, tell me right now where you are and where is Mike!" I stood up and looked around the cubicle area. There was no one in sight. I'm not sure what anyone could have done to help at that point, but it would have made me feel better.

"Tonight I am going to Miroslaw's home. I am to feeding the cat. I open the door, and he is on the floor. And there is blood...and it smells so bad, and poor Lech, he is crying...I couldn't stay. I shut the door. I ran to the petrol store to call to you."

"Okay, listen carefully. First, tell me the address where you are. Look at the door to the office and tell me that number." She told me the address. It was not far from the neighborhood where Mike lived. "Now, you need to dial nine-one-one...Yes, after you hang up from me. Dial nine-one-one and tell them to send an ambulance to Mike's house. You wait right where you are, and I will come pick you up. Do you understand? Okay, I'm going to hang up, and I will be there in about fifteen minutes."

Rebecca was upset to the point her English was failing her. I couldn't tell if Mike was still alive or not, but it didn't sound good.

CHAPTER FIVE

T TOOK ME TWENTY-TWO minutes to reach the address Rebecca had given me. It was one of those gas station/mini-mart combos. Rebecca was inside, crying. The clerk was trying to press a cup of coffee into her hands, but she was shaking too much to hold it on her own. I was thankful for her petite size, since I had to half-carry her to my car. I belted her into the passenger seat and drove the few blocks to Mike's apartment.

Mike lived in an old brick building. The single-story structure faced a quiet side street. Tenants found their own parking spaces along the crumbling curbs. Police cars and a big fire truck blocked the street in front of Mike's apartment.

I've never understood why you have to have the big truck every time you call for a paramedic. It's not like the paramedics ride in the big truck. They have their own special vehicle. There was no sign of fire; an ambulance was backed up on the lawn near Mike's door. We could see a police officer stringing yellow crime scene tape from the end of the apartment building to a shrub near the curb.

There was no place to park, or even pull out of the way, so I drove past and parked in the next block. Rebecca began sobbing again as we got out of the car. She was shivering in her thin sweater so I grabbed my raincoat from the backseat and put it around her shoulders. My coat still smelled like the Whale, but Rebecca didn't seem to be in any shape to notice.

"Rebecca, I'm going to try to find the person in charge and find out about Mike. Stay with me and don't say anything."

The fact no one was rushing around the ambulance probably

said all we needed to know, but I didn't tell her that.

"Yes, Miss Harley," Rebecca said. "I don't say nothing."

By the time we arrived back at Mike's apartment, they had blocked the entire front area with tape. We went up to the enclosed area. I called to the police officer, and after a few minutes, he came over.

"I'm sorry, miss. You can't come in. This is a crime scene." He turned back toward the apartment.

"Yes, I know. I need to speak to whoever is in charge. My friend is the one who called nine-one-one."

"You mean she discovered the body?" he asked.

Rebecca had lost her ability to speak English, but she understood just fine. She fainted. I broke her fall but couldn't keep her from sliding down onto the cement. The officer called the ambulance attendants. While they administered smelling salts, I took a minute to grill the policeman.

"Am I correct in assuming Mike is dead?"

"If that's the guy in the apartment, yeah, he's dead. Been that way for a while, if you ask me."

"What do you mean?"

"Well, I'm no expert," he said, "but a body doesn't get rigor mortis until about four hours after death. And this guy is stiff."

"How did he die?"

"You need to talk to the detectives about that," he said. "While we wait for them, I need to get your name and the girl's."

I gave him our names then went to wait with Rebecca by the ambulance where the attendants had taken her. She was conscious, but her face was so pale her skin looked translucent. They kept her seated, in case she fainted again. She cried quietly.

"Is it true, Miss Harley?" she asked. "Is Mike...gone?"

"I'm afraid it looks that way. I'm really sorry, Rebecca."

While I sat with her, I saw two people in street clothes drive up, leave their car in the street and duck under the yellow tape. The woman looked like someone you would see in a management meeting at Sil-Trac. She had the thin, wiry frame that looked good in a wool blazer. My blazer made me look like a linebacker. She did her hair in one of those miniature cornrow styles that look like short dreadlocks.

The guy, on the other hand, was an advertisement for Goodwill.

His tie stopped about six inches short of his belt buckle, and his white sweat socks would have been stylish had they had been paired with almost anything except polyester.

Two guys in white coats came out of Mike's apartment and joined the new arrivals. They all went back to the apartment door where the patrolman was standing guard. He turned toward Rebecca and me and nodded then back to the group. A few moments later, the pair in street clothes came over to the ambulance.

"I'm Detective Green and this is Detective Harper," the man said, pointing to the woman beside him. His voice was straight out of an old-fashioned gangster movie. His zipper gaped open about an inch where his pants strained to cover his waistline. It was hard not to stare.

"I'm sorry about your friend," the woman said. "I understand you found the body."

She was looking at Rebecca. Rebecca nodded and sniffed, trying to avoid open sobbing.

"Does she speak English?" she asked, looking at me.

"Sometimes," I said, "but usually not very well after she finds her boyfriend dead."

"Look, lady," Detective Green said, "we're sorry about her boyfriend, but we need to ask you both a few questions, and it will go a lot easier if you cooperate."

"I'm sorry," I said. "No one will tell us anything. What happened to Mike?"

"Why don't you start by telling us everything that happened tonight," Detective Harper asked.

I recounted Rebecca's call and my response. Rebecca confirmed that she worked, ate an early dinner and stopped by to feed Mike's cat on the way to church. I asked again if someone would tell us what had happened.

"All we know at this point is we've got a dead man that appears to be your friend Mike. He appears to have a single gunshot to the head. We won't know any more until the medical examiner finishes her work," Green told us. "We can't rule anything out yet. He might have committed suicide — we just don't know."

Rebecca stiffened beside me. "Mike would never do such a thing," she said hotly.

I put a hand on her arm. "Come on, Rebecca, they just need to check everything out. Don't get upset until we know something for sure."

"Rebecca," Detective Harper asked, "can you tell me about the last time you saw Mike alive?"

Rebecca went into another fit of sobbing. I was beginning to worry she would need an IV if she didn't stop crying like this. I didn't want to discuss my Monday night visitors in front of her — in fact, I really didn't want to mention it at all. I just couldn't think of a good justification not to.

Rebecca was telling Detective Harper about Uncle Andrush and the cousins. I tried to signal Detective Green that I'd like him to come with me, but he wasn't getting it.

"Detective Green," I finally said, "could I talk to you alone?"

Rebecca looked at me as if I'd stabbed her in the heart.

"I'll be right back, Rebecca. This will just take a minute. I don't know how to say this — " I began after he and I were a few feet away.

"Look," Detective Green interrupted, "just tell me what you've got to say." So much for the pleasantries.

"Okay. Some guys contacted me last night and said if I didn't pay up I wouldn't see Mike alive again."

"Wait a minute, sister," Detective Green said. "Did you report this?"

"Well, sort of."

"What do you mean, sort of?"

I explained my encounter with the smalltown police force from the Sil-Trac community.

"You realize this guy might be alive right now if you had called us?" Green twisted the knife in my gut a little.

"Yeah," I said, "I just didn't think you would believe me. We were trying to contact his relatives and see if they thought he was missing. Rebecca said he was supposed to be gone, so I figured it was a prank or something."

"Well, next time you leave it to the professionals," he said. "We know how to deal with this kind of crap."

"What would you have done different?"

"That's none of your business," he answered and walked away. "Don't go anywhere," he called back over his shoulder as he joined

Detective Harper.

After a moment, she came over and had me tell *her* the story. She asked a few questions, clarifying details, and took notes.

"Why do you think they wanted forty-two hundred?" she asked.

"That's the part that made me think it was a prank. I can't imagine why anyone would go to all that trouble for such a small amount of money," I said. "And I don't understand why they would kill him today if the money drop was going to be Thursday. Oh, my God! I wonder if the old guy confused Tuesday with Thursday. A lot of my people do that."

I was feeling worse by the minute. Maybe they expected the payoff today, and when they didn't get it, they killed him. I don't have that kind of cash lying around the house, but it wouldn't have bankrupted me to find it.

"Your partner mentioned suicide. Is there any chance my visitors were just an unlucky coincidence?"

"Anything's possible," Harper said. "We won't really know until the medical examiner finishes. From what I saw, I wouldn't bet on it, though. When someone commits suicide with a gun, he usually touches the gun to his head, or close to it. I'm guessing it will turn out to be farther away than that. It's hard to shoot yourself from any distance.

"That's just my opinion, though. We'll have to wait until the experts are done to know for sure. We're probably going to need both of you to come downtown to make a statement. We might want to try to make a sketch of the guys you met, too."

Detective Green had taken Rebecca back to the paramedics. He came over to Detective Harper and me. I wished someone would tell him about his zipper.

"Any witnesses to your alleged meeting?" he asked.

"What do you mean, alleged?" I protested. "Do you really think I would make something like this up?"

"I don't know, honey, you tell me."

"Does the word *discrimination* ring a bell with you?" I asked. "How about *sexual harassment?*"

"Come on, Harley," Detective Harper said. "Let's have a time-out. Green, back off. This isn't going to get us anywhere."

I took a deep breath. "Skip, the bartender at the Blue Whale, was there."

"Did he hear the threat?" he asked.

"Well, no. He didn't actually hear anything. But he did see the guys."

"Don't worry. We'll check with Skip and everyone else you know. When we're done, we'll know more about you than your own mother."

"Look, Detective, I've got a big inspection that means a lot to my company coming up on Friday. Mike is the key to my area passing, which makes him just about the last person I'd like to see gone right now."

"Is there anyone who would benefit from you not passing?" Detective Harper asked.

"Not that I know of," I said. "Everyone is trying to pass, but we're all pretty much in the same boat right now. You hear about sabotage and stuff like that happening in Silicon Valley, but not here."

"I'm afraid Mike's not gonna be much help now," Detective Green said.

I went back to Rebecca. She seemed a little calmer. Maybe she'd just run out of steam.

"We must find Lech," she said. "He can't stay alone."

I walked to the taped area and spoke to the policeman. He said they'd shut Lech up in the bedroom. No one would be able to enter the crime scene area until the criminalists were finished. At this point, Detectives Green and Harper had only looked in the door themselves.

I guess only TV detectives get to tromp through the crime scene while the criminalists take samples. They were the ones who processed the crime scene, taking pictures and videotapes and samples of everything. The officer said Green and Harper wouldn't go in until all the possible evidence had been gathered and Mike's body transported.

A white-haired woman in a pink sweatsuit came from the apartment next to Mike's and asked Rebecca and me if we wanted a cup of tea. She led us back to her place. Detective Harper was talking to someone at the apartment manager's door; I didn't see Green anywhere.

The pink lady explained she and Rebecca had developed a nodding acquaintance over the last few days while Rebecca was feeding the cat. Her kitchen smelled like a cross between fresh-baked cookies and mothballs. The chairs had quilted pads covered in calico. It reminded me of my grandmother's farm. Except for the angels. There were images of angels everywhere. Little porcelain figures filled the knickknack shelves and tables. Framed needlepoint renderings of angels hung on the walls. And little doll-like angels— soft sculpture, I guess they're called— sat around looking at us from chairs and shelves and any other space they could fit in. I couldn't help but stare.

"Oh, you noticed the angels," she said.

"Uh, yes, you have quite a collection."

"That's what I wanted to talk to you about." She lowered her voice to a whisper. "I've seen Mike."

"What do you mean?" I asked. "Did you see who killed him?"

Rebecca began sobbing again. I pulled a fresh Kleenex from my pocket, stuffed it into her hand and sat her down in a padded rocker in the front room. The pink lady handed her a cup of "restorative" tea. It smelled like old sweat socks, but Rebecca didn't seem to notice. When she calmed down, I went back to the kitchen.

"Now, tell me what you meant earlier," I said. "What do you mean, you saw Mike? When?"

"I am an angelologist, you see," she said. "I saw his angel. It was much sharper than usual. And the colors — I can't tell you how brilliant they were. It was hard to look at him, it was that bright. I knew right then something had happened. Usually, I just see people's guardian angels. This was different. He just came floating in."

"What do you mean?" I asked again. "You saw his *angel*?"

"I haven't always had the gift. It wasn't until my Geoffrey passed on that I started seeing them."

I was afraid to ask. "Who was Geoffrey?"

"He was my firstborn. He had golden hair and big blue eyes, just like his dad. He just didn't have his daddy's strong heart. He lived about a year, but there wasn't anything they could do for him. 'Course, it would be different now, but back then you just prayed.

"When he first left, I was inconsolable. All I did was cry. My Daniel didn't know what he was going to do with me. I didn't care. My little angel was gone. And then it happened."

"What happened?"

"I saw Geoffrey. He was a beautiful angel." Her face glowed at the memory. "He told me he was happy, and he didn't hurt anymore. He said it wasn't my time yet, but he would be waiting when I came. He also told me I was going to have another baby soon, and it would be healthy. And he was right. Since then, I've seen angels." She ended with a shrug.

"Uh, how did you know it was Mike's angel? Couldn't it have been one of your other visitors?"

The pink lady stiffened. "No more likely than mistaking you for that brother of yours."

It had to be a lucky guess. Half the population probably had a brother.

"What did he say?" I asked. "Did he tell you who shot him?"

"They don't talk like we do," she said in that tone older people reserve for simple children. "I could tell what he was saying just the same. 'Neva Dean Willit,' he said, and he was looking right at me with those ice blue eyes, 'don't you forget,' he said. Just like that."

"Is that all?" I tried to pick my words carefully.

"He wanted Rebecca to know he was okay, and then he was kind of agitated, like he wanted to say something but couldn't."

"Great. If he says anything else, let me know, okay?" I handed her my business card. She looked at my name.

"Oh, Mike told me about you."

I wasn't sure if that was good or bad.

"I can't quite remember what he said," she mumbled to herself. "I just know he talked about you."

Being a supervisor, I had seen more than my share of eccentric people. When I first joined Sil-Trac I inherited a woman who periodically saw space aliens. Only when the Pacific Rim volcanoes were active, though.

As we walked back into the front room, I could see out Neva Dean's partially drawn drapes behind Rebecca. It looked like the paramedics were loading Mike's body into the ambulance.

"Come on, Rebecca," I said when the doors to the ambulance closed. "I think we can get Lech now."

As we went out the front door, the two detectives walked up. I wished I could be a mouse in the corner while Detective Green tried to talk to Neva Dean.

"Good luck," I called with a smile as we passed.

Rebecca and I walked over to the taped-off area, and after a brief discussion, the patrol officer permitted us to come under the yellow-and-black crime scene tape and enter the apartment. It was typical young man's decor. Unremarkable furniture stood in a symmetrical pattern in the sterile room. There was nothing personal in evidence, only a take-out food bag. Unless you count the blood.

They had found Mike's body lying on the floor in front of the sofa. The landlord would probably have to replace the carpet. Here and there, you could see traces of the gray powder the fingerprint people had used.

Rebecca went directly to one of the two doors that opened off the living room area. I followed her into what turned out to be Mike's bedroom. A black cat was sprawled on the bed casually licking its paw and covering the hand-crocheted bedspread with black hair.

This room was a surprise after the living room. A carved chest held a gilt-framed picture of a woman who was probably Mike's mother. Over the bed was an ornate crucifix and, on the opposite wall, a reproduction of the Black Madonna, Our Lady of Czestochowa. I'm no expert when it comes to obscure Catholic lore, but Mike had always worn a pin with the same image on his jacket. He had explained the significance in great detail when I asked. On the nightstand was a creature made from a cut-up bleach bottle and fuzzy yarn. Debbie had sold them at a Christmas bazaar.

I looked in the closet to see if there was a box or something to carry the cat. I picked up the freshly polished dress shoes Mike would never wear to church again, and I felt tears fill my eyes. They were the only shoes he owned besides the Nikes he was probably wearing when he was killed.

While I was in the closet blubbering, Rebecca got up and walked to Mike's dresser. I heard her open one of the drawers.

"Miss Harley," she called softly, "you must look at this."

I wiped my eyes on the corner of my sweater and came out of the closet. Rebecca had the missing production records in her hands.

"It is the missing records, yes?" she asked, and held the book out to me.

"It sure looks like it," I said as I leafed through the pages. I had imagined these records in my dreams. The numbers looked like they were in close agreement. The pile of raw data was still in the drawer.

"Finally, we can pass the inspection. Miroslaw wanted that," Rebecca said.

"Unfortunately, I don't think Detective Green would like our taking them," I said. "Mike's apartment will be sealed. Actually, it already is sealed. That means nothing can be removed until the police finish their investigation."

"Do you mean we must fail the inspection?" Rebecca asked as the tears began filling her eyes again. "Miroslaw worked so hard so we could pass."

"It *is* hard to believe this notebook could have any bearing on...on...what happened here today," I said. "It was just in here with Mike's socks. On the other hand, if we take it, we could be arrested."

"I don't care," Rebecca sobbed as she grabbed the notebook from my hands. "Nothing else matters now."

"Well, I do care," I said as I took the book back. "I'm sure after a few days in jail you would, too."

"Can't you do something?" Rebecca begged.

She looked so pitiful. I hesitated, then opened the book and removed the pages. I lifted my sweater and tucked them into the waistband of my skirt. When my sweater was back in place, you almost couldn't tell anything was there. I put the notebook back in the drawer and adjusted my skirt. For once, I was thankful for my constricted waistband; those pages weren't going anywhere.

CHAPTER SIX

EBECCA WRAPPED THE CAT in my raincoat, and we headed out of the apartment. I worried about the papers in my skirt, but everyone watched the squirming cat in Rebecca's arms. Detective Green stopped us as we were going under the yellow tape, but the cat started growling and was trying to get away so he let us pass.

The cat hooked a claw in Rebecca's shoulder and tried to launch himself off her back. I was able to grab him by the scruff of his neck while she wrapped him tighter in the coat. We finally reached my car and dumped him into the backseat. I drove Rebecca to her house without further incident.

Rebecca's parents met us at the door. Her father wore tan slacks and a Ralph Lauren polo shirt. Mom was dressed in a white silk blouse with a lace collar and a navy gabardine skirt. Both were thin and looked fit, as if they had a more than passing acquaintance with the local gym. I guessed they were in their mid-forties.

Rebecca had told me her mother was a schoolteacher in Poland. Her father was an accountant. He had taken the CPA exam when they first got to Portland, and he worked for a business that was trying to expand into Eastern Europe. They watched as she led me to a small bathroom. I waited to remove the papers until the cat was safely locked inside. If they thought it was odd, me pulling papers from my shirt, they kept it to themselves.

It took a while to explain why I had driven Rebecca home, during which time she again became hysterical. I assured them it was okay if she wasn't at work tomorrow. I hoped they understood me. It was after ten before I was able to leave.

I drove home thinking of Mike. He and I had had our differences of opinion. Like many of my workers, he had been born and raised in a communist environment. He reveled in the fact that in America you could argue with almost anyone. The worst that could happen was you might lose your job if you were rude enough. Most of the time Mike's arguments were of the good-natured sort. He liked to argue all sides of an issue for the pure joy of it. I just couldn't imagine anyone taking his arguments seriously enough to kill him.

I experienced a sense of deja vu when I pulled into my driveway and got out of the car. All the lights were on, and I could see Mrs. Johnson in the kitchen.

"Mrs. Johnson, what are you doing here again tonight?" I asked as I entered from the garage.

"I thought someone should be here in case Sonny came home," she replied. "And it's a good thing I was."

"What now?" I was afraid to ask.

"Dog control came by." She waved a pink paper in her hand.

"Did they find Sonny?"

"Well, not exactly."

"What do you mean, not exactly?"

"I mean, someone found him, but not like you think. He bit someone, and they reported him. The man said he tried to grab him by the collar, and the collar came off in his hand. He tried to grab him again, but Sonny bit at him. The guy turned in a complaint because he had Sonny's collar and tags."

"Let me see the notice." I said. I read the paper. A citation. I had to pay a fifty-dollar fine within ten days and send proof of current rabies vaccination status. I had thirty days to upgrade my fence.

"What do they mean 'failure to control animal?'" I screamed. "I don't even have the dog! How can I control him if I can't find him?"

"At least we know he's okay."

"Not for long."

🦴 🦴 🦴

At Sil-Trac, managers can choose their own arrival time. Some supervisors feel they should be privileged. They start at nine a.m.

The rest of us believe we shouldn't ask our workers to do something we weren't willing to do.

I came a few minutes before the seven a.m. start time. My crew was in the breakroom having their pre-work lattes. I was amazed at how efficient their gossip line was. I had heard nothing on the morning news before work, yet they were debating the finer points of what had happened to Mike.

"I bet it will turn out to be drugs," said the red-haired Debbie. She looked like a person who might know about such things. In her tight black jeans, cropped sweater top and with rings hanging out of her ears and nose and navel, I could imagine there were a lot of things she could teach the group.

"Why on earth would you say that?" Debbie Dayshift asked. "Mike never touched drugs. Just because he isn't American doesn't make him a drug dealer." She looked pitiful. Her black T-shirt trimmed in Holstein cow print was probably her idea of mourning dress.

"Yeah, but did you really know what he was saying to his friends?" Debbie-Red countered. "He could have been doing transactions right under your nose and you wouldn't have known. Besides, why are you defending him? He dumped you."

"For your information, we were getting back together. We just needed a little more time. We were working it out."

"In your dreams," Debbie-Red said. "Why would he want a retread like you when he could have undamaged goods?"

Debbie Dayshift got up and threw her napkin down. "I can't listen to this." She stalked away from the table. She said nothing as she brushed past me.

"I think you guys need to get your imaginations under control," I said to the group. "I need to see all the leads in the small conference room before the morning meeting. Shannon, go after Debbie and bring her back."

While the group was gathering, I made copies of the records I had taken from Mike's. When they were all assembled, I handed out copies of the relevant sections to each leader.

"Here are the records Mike was working on," I said. "I want everyone to check what he has for your area and see if you have any problems with it."

"Harley, do you know what is happening about Mike?" Tommy

asked. "Is there going to be a memorial service?"

"Can we all get time off to go?" Shannon asked.

"I don't know anything yet," I said. "We'll have to see what his family wants to do." I made a mental note to ask Karen Hatcher to arrange for a grief counselor from our Employee Assistance Program.

"We were all thinking maybe we could collect some money and bring Mike's mom here," Debbie Red said. "Mike was trying to save the money so she could come live here. Rebecca could call her for us."

"I think that's a good idea," I said. "I'll check and see if Sil-Trac can contribute anything. His family is probably entitled to some kind of benefit."

Everyone filed quietly out of the room and then reassembled in the clean room for the general morning meeting. I can't remember what we said. After the meeting, Shannon stopped me.

"Harley, I've been looking at the records," she said. "I've been comparing them to what I had reconstructed."

"Is there a problem?" I asked. "I'm not sure I want to hear this, but tell me anyway."

"Well, the problem is, there is no problem — and there should be."

"What do you mean?" I asked. "Wait, let's go out to my desk. I think I need a Diet Coke."

On the way there, I bought a Diet Coke for myself and a cappuccino for Shannon from machines in the hallway.

"Okay, Shannon, tell me what the problem is."

"You know how we always start an extra wafer on new product designs for destructive testing?" she asked. "Well, with the new masks there's unpatterned space on all the wafers. Min has some way to do the test on the good wafers. He has that new piece of Fuji equipment that's replacing the old ball bevel. It really is neat; the die aren't harmed at all."

"That's good. Did you turn that idea in to the quality improvement committee?" I asked. I was getting a little impatient. I wished she would get to the point.

"No, not yet. The problem is, we've been processing the test wafers as if they were real. Well, I guess they are real, they just aren't normally included in the count. See?"

"No, I don't see."

"The *count*." She raised her voice as if that would make me understand. "Say we have a work order for a hundred wafers, okay?"

I nodded.

"We would have one hundred wafers for the lot and one additional wafer for the test. Right?"

"That sounds right."

"Well, there would be one hundred die per wafer for the lot wafers, which would be a total of ten thousand die. We usually get a yield of about ninety-two percent. That means after the wafers are scribed and the die tested, I usually receive about ninety-two hundred die to package."

"Yes."

"Well, now, with the new test procedure, there's one more wafer being processed, only instead of being destroyed in the ball bevel test, it should be coming through to the end of the process. That means about one hundred more die, minus the eight percent yield loss, so I should be getting ninety-two more die. Each lot should yield nine thousand two hundred and ninety-two die."

"What have you been getting?"

She handed me her pages of the log.

"I haven't gotten one that is over nine thousand two hundred. See here?" She pointed to a column marked *Die Received*. "We get 9190, 9199, 9198, but never more.

"See, the five-fifty-five-oh-eighties have a ninety-three percent yield," she continued as she flipped to the figures on the next page. "Then we have the five-fifty-five-oh-eighty-sevens. They're the same process, except the oh-eighty-sevens are a prototype pattern. They should gain some extra parts somewhere after materials test, but they don't. Both styles have the same kind of numbers."

"God, Shannon. I don't need this today."

"Sorry, boss." She started to take the papers back. I stopped her and picked them up.

"Check with Min. Maybe he's throwing out the test wafer anyway. You did the right thing telling me. Let me know what Min says."

"I just thought you should know. That particular die is worth about four hundred dollars when it reaches my area. If we can save thirty-seven K dollars every time we run a lot, we could pull ahead of the DRAM group in the quality improvement contest."

Sil-Trac has an aggressive improvement program. All workers in the company are on teams. Throughout the year, each team submits quality improvement ideas. Supervisors evaluate each idea, and if it's approved the team gets credit for the savings. At the end of the year, the groups give presentations of their results and the top teams get prizes. The top prize for overall improvement this year is a four-day cruise to Mexico. My team is in contention so far, but it's a very close race. Somehow, after last night, it didn't seem very important.

I decided to go talk to Karen Hatcher. My people needed the counselor, and I needed the cup of tea and understanding she could provide. I was about halfway to her office when I heard her call my name.

"Harley, I was just on my way to see you."

"I was coming to see you." I said. "Great minds think alike, huh?"

She wasn't smiling.

"I've got some bad news, Harley."

"I know, I was with Rebecca last night," I said. "It was really awful. I was coming to see if you could arrange a counselor."

"I'm sure I can set something up. But, Harley, I don't know anything about Rebecca."

"What's it about, then?" I was getting a bad feeling. Karen had on her game face. The one she wore when she was firing people.

"We need to go into a conference room," she said and led the way to a small, enclosed room. I knew this must be serious if we couldn't talk about it in her cube.

"Sit down, Harley," she said, indicating one of the chairs. "There's no easy way to say this, so I'm just going to tell you. There has been a pretty serious accusation against you for sexual harassment and discrimination. Now, before you say anything, I'm not saying I personally believe it."

"Karen, you know me. How can you take this seriously?"

She stared at the table.

"I said I *didn't* believe it. As a representative of this company, however, I'm obligated to investigate the charges. You know that. I'm sure you'll be exonerated."

"Jesus, Karen." I slammed my folder on the table. "Can you tell me what, exactly, I'm being accused of?"

"Yes, I can tell you that," she said. "You are being accused of having an unwanted sexual relationship with Mike Wyzcek. And, further, you are being accused of making discriminatory promotion decisions based on that relationship."

"That's ridiculous. It's beyond ridiculous." I could feel my blood pressure going up. "Can anyone just make up an unfounded story and have you take it seriously?"

"Of course not. Unfortunately, there has been some evidence supplied. I'm not saying it's conclusive, but it is enough to require an investigation."

"I can't deal with this right now." I got up and shoved my chair, banging it into the wall. Karen grabbed me by the arm.

"Harley, you know the law as well as I do. We always have to err on the side of the accuser. I'm sure when Mike comes in we can straighten this out."

I pulled my arm out of her clutch. "I guess you *haven't* heard the news."

"What news?"

"Mike's dead." I pushed past her and slammed the door on my way out.

CHAPTER SEVEN

IWENT BACK TO MY DESK and tried to organize my ISO 9000 plan. I couldn't concentrate. I kept thinking about what Karen had said. Scott and Jose were meeting with a vendor trying to peddle bunny suits in fashion colors. Being they were fellow supervisors, they were the only ones I could safely discuss this kind of problem with. It was too early for lunch, but I decided to go over to the Whale to have a Diet Coke and contemplate my options.

"Mary," I called over the partition, "I'm going across the street for an early lunch."

"Are you all right?" She stood up and looked at me over the partition. "You look terrible."

"I'm fine. I just need a little fresh air. I didn't sleep much last night."

"I heard about Mike from Min this morning," she said. "That's really too bad. I bet Rebecca is taking it hard."

"Yeah, she's pretty upset."

"Did you have to tell her?"

"No, actually, she told me. She was the one who found Mike's body."

"How awful! We should send her flowers. The company automatically sends flowers to the next of kin, but she wouldn't be included. Maybe we could take up a collection."

"Just send them, Mary. Call that florist in Hillsboro. I have an account there."

I absently went to the coatrack just outside my cube before I remembered I'd left my coat in the afterhours drop-off chute at my cleaners. Mary handed me her umbrella.

"You're going to need this," she said. "It's been raining off and on all morning."

I took the stairs at the side of the building — there was less chance of running into anyone there. Most of the nonproduction workers in the building belonged to a nearby health club. I never understood why they spent half their paychecks buying exercise clothes and club memberships so they could achieve perfect fitness and then fought over front-row spots in the parking lot and stood in line to wait for the elevator.

I safely escaped the building and made my way across the street to The Blue Whale.

"Geez, Skip, don't you ever go home?" I asked as I shook the rain off Mary's umbrella and hung it on the coatrack by the door.

"Rena is off havin' her kid," he replied. "I guess Andy can't find anyone to replace her. It's not so bad — it's not like my social calendar is overflowing with activity. Besides, this beats the hell out of daytime TV." He put a diet cola in front of me. "You want something to eat?"

"Are you serving lunch yet?" I wasn't hungry, but I hadn't eaten since sometime yesterday. My stomach couldn't take much more diet cola without a little food.

"Not yet, but I been experimenting with a new guacamole chicken burger. I got three of 'em back there. You can be my first taster."

"Sounds interesting."

"You want it or what?"

"Sure. I'd be happy to be your guinea pig."

Despite my reservations, Skip's creation was good. I ate it in silence; my stomach felt better with every bite.

"Well, what do you think?" He came back to my end of the bar.

"Very good. Should be very popular with the production crowd." He actually blushed. "Skip, I'm going to ask you something, and if you don't want to answer I'll understand."

"Ask away, boss lady. My life is an open book."

"This isn't that kind of question." I tied the paper straw wrapper into tiny knots. "I need to know if you've heard anyone talking about me lately."

"Geez, Harley." Skip ran his hand over his thin blond hair. He sorted out the half-dozen long strands and patted them back over the bare spot before he spoke again. "People talk about you all the time, you being the boss and all. Nothing new, though. Just the usual grumbling about overtime and that inspection you got coming up. Jake didn't like the last review you gave him. Don't seem like any of them ever like their reviews, though. Why do you want to know? Is someone giving you a hard time?"

"It's nothing I can talk about, but if you hear anything out of the ordinary, I'd like to hear about it."

"No problem, I'll keep my ear to the ground."

"I'd appreciate it if you'd keep this confidential."

"No bartender worth his bar rag would gossip. We got our code of ethics. Everyone knows our job is to listen."

The pride in his voice made me want to believe him — almost.

"How much do I owe you for the sandwich?" I asked as I got up.

"On the house. You were my official taste-tester."

"Thanks again, Skip."

As I reached for the door it opened and Ralph, the Implant maintenance man I'd seen Monday night, came in. His cloth jacket hung off his thin frame. He stopped me as I started to go out. We made small talk for a moment. He seems so lost since his divorce.

"By the way," he asked after we'd covered the basics, "what were you doing with Mike's uncle the other night? Is he doing another play?"

"What are you talking about?"

"Mike's Uncle Andrush. He's an amateur actor. I went to his last play — he was some kind of doctor. He's really good. It looked like he's playing some kind of gangster this time. He must be really broken up about what happened."

"Ralph, I have no idea what you're talking about. I've never met Mike's uncle."

"Sure you have. You were sitting with him. I know I had a few beers Monday, but I wasn't *that* drunk. He came in with his boys and sat right over there." He pointed at the table I had shared with the blackmailers. "He looked a little weird with that padded stomach and white hair, but I'd know him anywhere. I fixed his water heater last year."

"You're sure about this?"

"I'd bet my kids on it."

"What's his name?"

"Andrush Wyzcek."

"Oh, my God! That was Uncle Andrush?"

"Who did you think you were talking to?"

"I don't know. I mean, we never got around to names. I mean — Oh, never mind." I sank down onto the chair by the door.

"Harley, you don't look too good," Ralph said. "You want a glass of water or something?"

I was tired of people telling me how bad I looked, but at that moment, I *didn't* feel real great. "That would be nice, thanks."

Skip brought a glass of water as soon as he heard Ralph offer it. I took a few sips.

"You get some bad news or something?" he asked.

"No, no, I'm fine." I pushed the glass back into his hands and got up. "I need to get back to the plant."

I walked back to Sil-Trac and went up the stairs again. I could see Mary pacing in front of my cube as I approached. She has medium-brown hair done in one of those beauty salon styles. Either she invests heavily in shellac or it's a wig — I've never been quite sure. All I know is, the individual hairs never move. I ran a hand through my own tangled mass.

"Mary, what's up?" I asked when I got there.

"Oh, Harley, I'm so glad you're back."

"Speak to me, Mary."

"Well, you know how all the secretaries in this building have a meeting every two weeks?"

"Yeah, I guess." I didn't really remember, but it seemed important that I should.

"We talk sometimes." Mary's face reddened.

"I'm not surprised."

"No, I mean about other stuff. Not just procedures and practices."

"I've always suspected you secretaries of secretly running the company."

Mary's blush deepened. "We all know how difficult it is to be a woman in a man's business. So, well..."

"Mary, I am going to have a stroke here. Just spit it out. What did you hear?"

"Well, it would be a breech of ethics for Jansi to copy what she

45

sees on Karen's desk. She can't even repeat what she saw, so I didn't really *hear* anything. But I guessed what it was, and she couldn't control her reaction so she didn't break any rules. If you were to guess, I probably couldn't control my reactions, either."

"Mary, I can't imagine what you go through to convince each other you aren't leaking confidential information. But you are. If you still want to tell me I'm not going to stop you. The best I can do is promise to keep your name confidential."

Mary paused so long I thought she had changed her mind. "Okay, fine. You're going to need all the help you can get. Whatever is happening has to do with you and Mike at the company Christmas party. Did you spend the night with him?"

"Jesus, what kind of a question is that?"

"I've worked for you for a while, now, and I like to think we've become friends, of sorts."

"So, is this how you treat your friends? You believe any wild accusations against them?"

"Harley, what you do in your spare time is your own business. If you did sleep with Mike, I'll try to understand. I may not agree with the decision, but we both know more than one male manager who's slept with his employee and lived to tell about it at coffee break."

"I can't believe you think I slept with Mike."

"You still haven't answered my question. I said I'll support you, but I think I have a right to know."

"What? Just because you took it upon yourself to read a confidential file, you have a right to pry into my personal life? For your information, I did not sleep with Mike. I spent the night with him, but...it's not what you think. Is that all they have on me? What am I saying? There's nothing else to have."

"What else do they need? A supervisor sleeps with a person who reports to her. Don't you think that's more than enough?"

"Lower your voice and sit down." I pulled Mary into my cubicle and pushed her toward my guest chair. "Let's get one thing clear. I did not sleep with Mike or any other person who reports to me. I did spend the night in the same rented hotel room with him. He was drunk and sick, and I was afraid he might hurt himself so I stayed in the room with him until he stopped barfing and sobered up a little.

"That was the whole idea. The hotel gave a discount on rooms to encourage us not to drink then drive home after the Christmas party. I know I'm not the only supervisor who helped a person to his or her room."

"They have pictures."

CHAPTER EIGHT

"T HEY CAN'T HAVE PICTURES," I said. "There was nothing to have pictures of."

"You and him asleep on the bed...his shirt off...your red velvet skirt hiked up to there...Harley, no matter what really happened, I have to tell you it doesn't look good. Besides, you know better than anyone that the same rules don't apply to women. When that product engineer slept with his secretary at the party two years ago he just got a slap on the wrist. And she got promoted. That's why we decided to help you."

"I can't believe it. The guy was so sick he couldn't stand up. I helped him get his shirt off 'cause I knew how much Debbie paid for it. It was silk, he didn't want to ruin it. If he and Debbie hadn't gotten into a fight that night she would have been there instead of me."

Mary slumped in the chair like a spent balloon. "I'm sorry, Harley. I thought you should know what you're up against."

"Look, Mary, I appreciate this. I know you've taken a big risk telling me. I'll do everything I can to make sure no one ever finds out."

She got up and went back to her cubicle. I added a note to my to-do list to see Karen about the specific details of the accusation against me. I penciled in a footnote to call my attorney. He charged fifty dollars just to tell me to keep my dog on a leash. I could hardly wait to see what this might cost me.

I went into the clean room to check on the day's production. I could have called the lead ops from my desk and had them check the logs; but when you need time to think, the clean room is a good place to hide from the workday troubles that are the lifeblood of supervisors. People won't go inside unless you're paying them to do so.

When I emerged from the second air shower, I stepped into the middle of a rather vigorous discussion among Debbie Red, Shannon and Min. They were all in the central hallway. The air shower opened into the hall at one end, and all the functional areas on one side. The other side had intercoms and pass-through chambers to an outside hallway that allowed people to take materials out of the lab. The air pressure in the clean room hallway was positive, which prevented any dust from coming in when these little doors opened.

"Look, I don't care what Tommy says," said Debbie Red. The particle mask muffled her voice. "My count doesn't agree with his."

"We matched what Mike had in the log with what we had from *our* machine." Min said. "We don't know anything about how you track the wafers before they come to us. If you can't count, that's not my problem."

"My counts agree with Tommy's," Shannon added. She held her mask away from her mouth with her gloved hand. The masks have elastic bands that go around a person's head and hold them in place. If her hand slipped, it would slam onto her face. "I'm not sure our counts are right, but at least we match."

"I'm tired of fighting about it," Min said as he opened the door to his area. "When Tommy gets back from lunch you can take it up with him. If you want my advice, don't rock the boat. The ISO Nine-thousand people don't care what we really made last month. They just want us using a consistent procedure. We can figure out what's really happening after we get our certification."

"There's a great attitude for you," said Debbie Red as she went off to pout in the metalization room.

The hall intercom buzzed. Shannon answered and said it was Mary. I waited to see if she wanted me.

"Which Debbie do you want?" I heard her say. She turned to me. "Mary says the police are here and want to talk to Debbie Dayshift." Into the phone she said, "She went to Hieu's parents' for lunch. Hieu's mom brought her a jade Buddha from Viet Nam for her collection — she just got back yesterday. Debbie said she was going to pick it up during lunch."

She listened a minute to what I imagined were Mary's demands for her to produce Debbie D, and then she hung up. She asked me, "Have you seen Debbie Dayshift since lunch?"

The missing Debbie chose that moment to step out of the air shower. She couldn't have orchestrated a grander entrance.

"Did I hear someone called for me?"

"Mary called and said the police are in the lobby asking for you," Shannon reported. "I told her I thought you were still at lunch. Did you get the Buddha?"

"Yeah, and it's a real beaut, too."

Debbie had an extensive collection of Buddha images. Some of her early finds were cheap, poorly crafted items. During her reign at Sil-Trac, her collection had improved a lot. Debbie latched on to every new Asian who came to our area and bugged him about helping her add to her collection.

"Why couldn't they have called before I suited up?" she asked no one in particular. "I guess I better not keep them waiting."

She stepped back into the air shower — it wasn't necessary to have the particles removed from your suit on the way out. There was a bypass switch that allowed you to avoid the cycle if the door to the inside hall was opened before the door to the dressing room was.

Shannon turned to me and spoke in a whisper. "Don't you think someone should go with her?

"For what?" I asked. "They just want to ask her some questions."

Shannon made a face. "Yeah, but you know how Debbie likes to talk. She's liable to say anything as long as they keep listening."

"There isn't anything we can do about it. Besides, why do you think we would want to?" I asked.

"Rebecca, for one thing. I don't believe she murdered Mike, but Debbie might take this opportunity to pay her back for stealing him."

"Let's give the police a little credit." As the words came out of my mouth, I had visions of Detective Green and his zipper. "I'm sure they'll be able to see through Debbie's revenge plan if, in fact, she has one."

I wasn't sure at all, but I was trained to support authority figures. For that matter, I was one. Sometimes I wondered just when I had learned to spout the party line so easily.

Shannon turned and went back to her packaging area. For the next half-hour, I reviewed each area's output and compared it to the plan for the day. At least we were still on-target for output. I thanked God for small favors. Until we got some additional equipment, our capacity was accounted for down to the minute. We couldn't afford to let the schedule slip.

Only one person at a time could pass through the air shower. Lunch times were staggered so everyone didn't come and go at the same time. I had to wait a few minutes for one of these smaller groups to come in. The last person through was Debbie Dayshift. I was a little surprised to see her back so soon.

"How did it go out there?" I asked.

"Okay, I guess. I told them I couldn't spend too much time away from the area. They want me to come downtown after work."

"What kind of things did they ask you?" I wasn't sure if I should be asking her this but being falsely accused of things gives you a sort of cavalier attitude towards the everyday worries of your life. It's quite liberating, actually.

"It was kind of weird. They mostly asked whether Mike had any affiliations with any other companies. They asked a lot of questions about MiCorp."

"What kind of questions?"

"I don't know. Did Mike ever apply for a job at MiCorp? Did Mike do any moonlighting? Was Mike happy at Sil-Trac? Did he have any friends who worked at MiCorp? I just answered what I could. And I asked why they were asking about MiCorp." Her face flushed, and she looked down. I wondered what she was hiding.

"What did they say?

"They said, 'You just let us do the asking here, young lady.'"

"Sounds like the detectives I spoke to last night." I was having a hard time with the idea Mike was into corporate espionage. After working with people for a while you get a sense of their boundaries. Sometimes I was disappointed to find out what people had done but not surprised. If Mike were a spy I'd be stunned.

"By the way," she said, "they want you to come out and talk to them."

CHAPTER NINE

DETECTIVES GREEN AND HARPER were waiting in a conference room off the lobby. These rooms are reserved for outsiders' use. The detectives sat in a deep, low couch covered in soft dark-brown leather. The only table in the room was a chrome-and-glass number that echoed the decor in the lobby. It was quite unlike the beige steel table and straight-backed chairs in the working conference rooms.

I entered and had to wait for Detective Green to wrestle his bulk out of the sofa and stand so we could shake hands. Detective Harper had figured out the sofa trick. If you balanced on the front edge it couldn't grab you. She rose in one graceful motion and extended her hand. Her grasp was firm. I bet she had good manual dexterity.

"What can I do for you?" I asked when the greetings were over.

"We'd like to ask you a few questions about Mike," Harper answered.

I was relieved Green had on a baggy sweater that covered the waist area of his pants, concealing the top area of his zipper. It also covered the bottom of his tie, so I couldn't see if it reached his belt or not. All things considered, it was good camouflage.

"What can you tell us about Mike's involvement with MiCorp?" Green asked.

"Nothing, really," I said. "I have no knowledge that he had *any* relationship with them. Why do you think he did?"

"Did Mike have any access to classified information?" Harper asked.

"Well..." I stalled for a moment, trying to think of a way to explain our situation in simple terms. "Technically, everything we do at Sil-Trac is classified. Everyone who works here is required to sign a nondisclosure statement. Upper-level managers and technical people sign noncompete agreements, too. All that means is everyone promises not to talk about Sil-Trac products and processes. In addition, the high-level people agree not to work for our direct competitors for one year after their termination date from Sil-Trac.

"In reality, the people in the clean room don't really know anything useful. Everyone in this business has similar processes. Sometimes a company invents a new way of using a material or a new sequence of putting materials together, but anything like that becomes patented before we see it in production. Anyone who wants to buy the chip can easily analyze anything we put in the product. Everyone does it. I just can't imagine what one of my people could know that would be of enough value for anyone to risk their job. If we were the research and development group, it would be different."

"Does anyone in your group have any access to the research and development area?" Harper asked.

"No, they aren't even in this building," I answered. "They have a lab in a building that houses several different research groups. My people toured the place once, but that's all."

"You're sure Mike never mentioned his relationship to MiCorp?" Detective Green asked.

"What are you trying to get at?" I demanded. I could feel my voice rising despite my efforts to stay calm. "I keep telling you to my knowledge Mike did not *have* a relationship of any sort with MiCorp."

"Look," said Detective Harper, "we found part of a pay stub at Mike's apartment. It appears to be from MiCorp. It doesn't have a name on it, but it has a note stuck to it. It says 'See Harley about this.'"

"I can't believe it," I said. "Can I see it?"

"The lab has it." Harper replied. "I can get a copy to show you, but I'm not sure what good it would do. It doesn't have the name on it, and the end with the employee number is torn off."

"Do you mind if I make a quick phone call?" I asked.

"You calling a lawyer?" Green asked.

"Hardly."

I went to the lamp table beside the sofa and got out a phone book from the small drawer. I looked up the number for MiCorp and used the phone in the conference room to make the call.

"Can I speak to the Human Resource Department?" I asked. "I need to verify employment for an applicant who used you for a reference." I waited while they transferred me to the records department. "The name is Mike Wyzcek...Thank you, I'll hold."

I turned to look at Detective Green while I was waiting. This delay clearly annoyed him.

"Yes, thank you...You're sure?...How far back do your records go?...Okay, thanks." I hung up the phone and turned back to Detective Harper. "According to MiCorp, they have no record of a Mike Wyzcek ever working there."

"I don't know what you think that proves," Green said as he struggled to stand up again. "He obviously would use fake ID. He could be working under any name."

"Did you find any fake ID?" I asked. "Being an alien, he would have to have at least two pieces to get an I-nine. Everyone has to fill out an I-nine or they can't work. Plus, he would have to have a green card in the other name. Did you find any of that?"

"I don't imagine he would just leave that kind of stuff laying around, do you?"

"I don't think Mike had that level of sophistication."

"You just don't want to believe it," he said. "Now, I'll ask again. Are you sure he never talked to you about MiCorp or asked you anything about working there?"

"You can ask me as many times as you want, but he and I never discussed the subject."

"Don't think I didn't notice how easily you lied to that other company just now on the phone," Green said.

"What about that inspection you have coming up?" Detective Harper asked.

I was amazed at how cool and collected she remained. Her suit wasn't wrinkled even though she had driven here in a car and been hanging around the conference room for over an hour. Even her lipstick looked fresh.

I fingered the tube in my pocket. My own lipstick usually turned bright orange about thirty seconds after I applied it. It glowed on my lips for half an hour then disappeared completely. I've tried all the tricks they tell you in magazines. I had the tubes of green and yellow primer in my bathroom at home to prove it. Nothing helped. I was beginning to think it was a genetic thing.

"Could MiCorp have an interest in having you fail?"

"I don't think so," I said. "Maybe a year from now, when certification means something to our customers. Right now, everyone is just trying to pass his or her initial inspection. I don't think anyone knows yet what the impact of the certification will really be on our business."

"I think we're done for now," Detective Harper said. She stood up in one smooth movement. "We may have more questions for you later. I trust you will remain available."

"I wouldn't have it any other way," I said. "If you're done, I'll see you out."

They seemed reluctant to leave, but I guess they couldn't think of a good reason to stay. I walked them to the lobby and watched them sign out on the guest register and turn in their visitors' badges.

Detective Green stopped at the display case. "This the stuff you make here?"

"Yeah, most of it is made here."

"You know how it all works?"

"Not really," I said. "I just know how to make it."

He seemed to take some kind of satisfaction from my reply. He hustled over to the door Detective Harper held open for him, and they left. I went back upstairs to the clean room. Sometimes my workers came up with their best insights right after their most brutal arguments. I wanted to see if today's discussion about count had yielded anything.

After I went through the first air shower and took my bunny suit off the rack, Tommy came in from the clean room.

"How's it goin', boss?"

"Frankly, Tommy, I've had better days. Did you guys figure out anything about the logs?"

"We're pretty much deadlocked. Shannon and I agree, and Debbie D almost agrees with the guys in metals. But there's still a gap between them and us. Can't we just write it off and start over?"

"Not if you want me for a boss. Tommy, Mr. Nakata gets upset if he has to write off five or six parts. You're talking about hundreds. My head could end up on the chopping block over this."

"Geez, Harley, I had no idea they tracked it so close. Our counts have always been off."

"The problems tended to offset themselves, though. In the end, the overall count balanced, even if the lot numbers were off. Now we're talking about a large number, and it's all going one way."

"Maybe you didn't get Mike's latest figures." Tommy said. "Where'd ya get the ones you gave us? Did he do those before he left for the weekend?"

"He left them for me after he got back." I said, stretching the truth just a little. "I'm sure these are the latest he did."

"Is there any chance he was tryin' to do something funny with the books?" Tommy asked.

"What do you mean? Have you heard something?"

"No, it just seems like he was havin' a hard time doin' something that should have been simple. Forget it. Do you know anything about funeral arrangements?" he asked. "People are askin' about it. I was thinkin' maybe I could take up a collection. His uncle doesn't seem to have much money."

The memory of Mike lying lifeless on the ambulance gurney flashed into my mind.

"You don't look too good, boss. Maybe you should sit down here for a minute."

I sat down on the lacquered pine bench. "I'll be okay. It's just that I was there right after Rebecca found him. I can't get the image of him lying dead out of my mind."

"Sorry I brought it up."

"No, Tommy, it's okay." I put my hand on his arm. "I think it would be really nice if you guys took up a collection. Debbie Red is working on a scheme to bring Mike's mom here for the funeral. She was going to talk to Rebecca about calling her. Maybe you could coordinate with her."

Tommy went out, and I got up and resumed the process of getting dressed.

Sometimes my people were hard to understand. Debbie Red was the one making up vicious rumors about Mike, and yet she was the one leading the efforts to get Mike's mom to Portland for his funeral. It hurt my head just thinking about it. Or maybe too much had happened these last few days. I promised myself a nice big bowl of hot pasta with fresh vegetables, olive oil and Parmesan. It was my favorite meal, and I counted on Mrs. Johnson to have it on the menu at least once a week. I could almost smell the ripe avocado I knew was sitting in my fruit bowl on the counter in the kitchen.

I had just gotten into Debbie Dayshift's room in the lab when the phone rang. The operator said there was a crazy woman on the line who insisted on talking to me. Ordinarily, the receptionist would just take a message, but this caller had insisted it was an emergency.

When the call was connected, I found a hysterical Neva Dean Willet at the other end.

"Hello? Harley, is that you? It's Neva Dean."

"What's wrong, Mrs. Willet?"

"It's Rebecca, and it's my entire fault." I heard a muffled cry, as if she had her hand over the phone so I wouldn't hear.

"Slow down and tell me exactly what happened."

"I saw Mike's apartment door was open. I thought maybe the police hadn't latched it last night. I went over to close it, and I could see his apartment had been destroyed."

"What do you mean destroyed? And how does Rebecca fit in?"

"I'm coming to that," she scolded. "The sofa was ripped, and the lamp was on the floor. I heard a noise coming from the bedroom, and I thought maybe whoever wrecked the place was still in there. I ran back to my apartment and dialed nine-one-one. The police came. Not those detectives. These young men were in uniforms and thin. They came in to look, and when they checked in the bedroom, they found Rebecca. I think you should come right away."

I felt trapped in *Groundhog Day*. You know, the movie where the person is doomed to keep reliving the same day over and over again until he gets it right?

CHAPTER TEN

MADE THE TRIP TO NEVA Dean's apartment in record time. There were two police cars out in front of Mike's place. I was surprised at the absence of an ambulance. But then again, there was no need to hurry in a situation like this. Neva Dean came out as soon as my car stopped. Her black Lycra workout pants and hip-length teal sweatshirt made her look younger.

"I'm so glad you're here," she said as she guided me in the direction of Mike's place. "Let's go over."

"Mrs. Willet, I'm not sure I'm ready for this. Couldn't we talk a few minutes first? Maybe wait for the ambulance."

"What are you talking about?" she said, raising her voice. "Rebecca doesn't need an ambulance. She needs an attorney."

"An attorney?" I felt my jaw drop. "I thought you said they found her. I thought you meant like Mike."

"They did find her. She was sitting on the end of Mike's bed. Or what's left of it. She was hugging that religious picture, kind of rocking back and forth and crying."

"Is she still in there?"

"I haven't seen anyone come out."

We closed the distance to the door. I knocked on the jamb. The officer who came to the door had blond hair and bad skin. He had been here with Mike's body. He recognized me with a look that could only be relief.

"Boy, am I glad to see you," he said. "We can't get Miss Valenta to stop crying long enough to read her her Miranda rights."

"What's she accused of?"

"At the very least, destroying a crime scene," he said. "But more than likely she'll be charged with the murder of Mr. Wyzcek. Most homicides end up being done by the victim's loved ones."

"That's ridiculous. Rebecca didn't kill anyone."

"Yeah, that's what they all say."

I followed him into the bedroom. It bore no resemblance to the room I'd seen yesterday. Drawers were hanging out of the dresser; the curtains were torn. The sight of me renewed the energy of Rebecca's crying. She looked just like Sonny did the time I tried to get him to sleep in a doghouse outside. Except her eyelashes were wetter.

"Rebecca, what is going on here?"

She looked at the police officer then back at me. "I can't say."

"Could you give us a moment alone?" I asked the officer.

"I'm sorry, lady, but we can't leave you alone with a murder suspect. It wouldn't be safe."

"Fine." I crouched down in front of Rebecca and looked straight into her eyes. "Tell me what is going on here, Rebecca. They think you killed Mike and then came back to destroy the evidence. You didn't do that, did you?"

She shook her head back and forth silently.

"Did you tear this place up for some reason?" I asked. She shook her head again. "Then you need to tell these policemen what happened. Why are you here?"

"I came to find..." She held up the picture she was clutching.

"Well, see? That makes sense. Let's just tell these men."

It took a little more coaxing, but eventually I got Rebecca to explain what happened. She claimed she came back to get Mike's picture of the Black Madonna of Czestochowa. She found the door open and the place trashed.

"See," I said to the blond guy. "She just came here to get the picture. Can I take her home now?"

"Geez, lady, you can't be that naive. She's got to come to the station with us. The detectives want to talk to her. I paged them, and Harper said bring her to the station."

The other officer grabbed the edge of the picture and tried to remove it from Rebecca's grasp. It reminded me of a cartoon. He pulled, and Rebecca's arms would extend then snap back to her chest, pulling the picture and the officer with it. They went back and forth.

"Let go!" he demanded. Rebecca said nothing. If anything, her grip tightened.

"Could she possibly take the picture with her?" I asked. "The Black Madonna is an important religious icon to the Polish Catholics. This one is just a reproduction. Rebecca brought it from Poland for Mike — he talked about it at work. Maybe she just loaned it to him. It isn't evidence, is it?"

Rebecca stopped crying and looked at the officer.

"Well, I suppose it really isn't in the immediate crime scene," the blond officer admitted.

"Okay, Rebecca, you can have the picture or icon or whatever it is. Listen, go down to the police station. I'll get a lawyer and meet you down there."

She hadn't taken her eyes off me. She pressed the picture of the Madonna into my hands.

"Don't give to no one," she said and turned to the officers with her wrists up and together.

"You don't need to handcuff her, do you?" I asked.

"No, I don't think that will be necessary," said the blond.

The police drove off with Rebecca. I asked to use Neva Dean's phone, and she led the way back to her apartment. I made a quick call to my attorney. He assured me he would line up an attorney from legal aid and a translator to meet Rebecca at the police station.

Neva Dean's apartment smelled better this time. She must have finished cooking the sweat socks.

"I'm sure Rebecca didn't kill Mike," she said. "Her angels just don't indicate she's capable of such a violent act."

She set a steaming cup of tea in front of me. I could not quite identify the smell — some kind of flower, maybe. I took a drink and hoped Neva Dean wasn't a zealot who believed in psychoactive drugs.

"It kind of amazes me that Rebecca would come back to Mike's just to get that picture," I said. "It's clearly marked as a crime scene."

"Maybe she just didn't understand."

"Please, Neva Dean. Rebecca may not have good language skills, but she's a bright girl. I'm sure she knew the risk she was taking. I just don't understand why." I put the picture up on Neva Dean's kitchen table. "This picture is a cheap reproduction. Rebecca brought it from Poland because you can't get them here. As I understand it, they're a dime a dozen in Poland. Ninety percent of the Polish population is Roman Catholic.

"This Black Madonna is a major religious icon there. According to Mike, the original is in a fourteenth-century monastery seventy miles from Krakow. He told me people go on pilgrimages to view it. I guess it's like Mecca is to Muslims. Rebecca probably has two or three of these at home."

"Well, maybe it isn't the picture that has value. Maybe the frame is a family heirloom or something."

"Neva Dean, you are brilliant. Look at how thick this frame is. Do you have a screwdriver or something?"

She dug through a drawer in the kitchen and handed me an antique silver butter knife. I pried gently at the staples holding the cardboard backing to the frame. I was trying not to scratch the knife.

"Give me that, honey. We're going to be here all day if you keep on that way."

Neva Dean grabbed the frame and knife and pried the staples off one after the other. When she got them all loose, I lifted the backing off, took the picture out of the frame, and then separated the layers of matting and backing.

"Oh, my God! Look at that," Neva Dean exclaimed.

Between the copy of Our Lady of Czestochowa and the backing material was a finely rendered image in oil paint on canvas. The paint had cracks in places and aged yellow edges. It was a portrait of a man in religious garb.

"Who or what is it?"

"I have no idea, Neva Dean."

"Could be it's a religious icon," she said. "An old one, too, by the look of it. They have something like this at my church. This looks a lot older, though. This fellow must be why Rebecca was willing to risk everything."

"This is amazing." I ran my hand over its surface. "It looks like it's centuries old."

"Why do you suppose it's hidden?" she asked.

"I don't know, but I intend to find out."

I took the icon and headed for my car, but Neva Dean ran after me waving a bag.

"Harley, I almost forgot," she said. "Mike gave me this smoked fish before he left last weekend. He said Lech didn't like it. He says his Uncle Andrush made it. I guess he forgot I told him about Fluffy's gum disease. I know I told him how I brush Fluffy's teeth every day. He thought it was so funny. Well, at any rate, Fluffy doesn't have enough teeth to chew a marshmallow. You have a cat, don't you?"

I didn't remember having mentioned Cher, but I took the fish and put it in the trunk with Rebecca's picture or icon or whatever it was.

As I drove from Neva Dean's to the police station, I tried to review what I knew so far about Mike's death. First, Mike's uncle tried to scam me out of a few thousand dollars. Either he was holding his own nephew hostage or Mike was a willing accomplice. It made me sad to think Mike would do that to me, but the fact was he had been in town but avoiding work at a very critical time.

Second, there was this ransacking of Mike's apartment. Someone was looking for something, but what?

The last and most troubling thing was Rebecca. On the surface, she seemed like the innocent victim of a cruel act. But what was she doing at Mike's today? And, more important, what was a poor immigrant girl doing with what appeared to be a priceless religious artifact? It seemed like everything I had learned today was a direct contradiction of what I knew to be true yesterday.

CHAPTER ELEVEN

ARRIVED AT THE POLICE station with no more answers than I had when I left Neva Dean's.

Central Precinct is located on the west side of the Willamette River, in the downtown area of Portland. They share a building with the jail. Police have the first floor and floors eleven through fifteen. The detective division is on the thirteenth floor. Bet that makes the accused feel lucky.

I crossed the lobby to the information window. I was informed the detectives were expecting me. The officer at the desk pulled out a special nametag and told me to put it on my lapel. The label had a time-release strip that would get darker as time passed. If I stayed more than an hour, my badge would read expired where my name used to be. I didn't plan on finding out what they did to you if that happened.

I ran into Rebecca's father at the public elevator.

"What has happened to Rebecca?" he asked.

"The police detectives just want to ask her a few questions," I said and hoped I was telling the truth. "Do you know what she was doing at Mike's apartment today?"

"She say she is leaving something at Mike's house," he said. "She was getting her possession. It makes no sense. Is this so terrible?"

"No, she should be fine. Someone ransacked Mike's place before Rebecca got there."

He looked at me with a blank stare. I tried again.

"Some person cut holes in Mike's chair and bed." I made gestures like ripping with a knife.

"Ah, someone is looking for something." He smiled briefly.

"The police think maybe Rebecca," I said in the stilted English we sometimes used at work.

"Paugh!" He made a dismissive gesture and stomped off the elevator.

I followed him down the short hall into the waiting area and up to the desk. I was disappointed by how modern the place looked. I guess I was expecting the dark wood and high ceilings you always see on TV.

"I come for my daughter," he announced. As he was giving her name, a door opened and Detective Green came out, followed by Rebecca. Detective Harper emerged last, closing the door behind her.

"That will be all for now," Harper said. "Just don't leave town. We may have more questions after we check your alibi."

Rebecca looked at me.

"Just go home," I said. "They want to be sure you told them the truth." I could see her father tense up. "Relax, Mr. Valenta. It's their job."

I took him by the arm and guided him toward the door. When he and Rebecca were gone, I turned back to the two detectives.

"You don't really believe Rebecca is behind all this, do you?" I asked.

"Well, stranger things have happened," Green said. His shirt stretched tight across his belly; his tie fell a good four inches above his belt buckle. He wore a real belt — I gave him points for not wearing those polyester pants with the expanding waist section.

"I'll be surprised if Rebecca is involved," Detective Harper said in her cool voice. "But it would appear she showed up right after whoever tore up the place. We thought she might have seen or heard something."

"Do you have any idea who did it?"

"Oh, you'll be the first one we call when we learn something," Detective Green said.

"I'm sure you understand we can't discuss the case with anyone," Detective Harper added.

I thanked Harper and ignored Green. I glanced at my watch as I left the police station. It was after four-thirty. I decided to call it a day. Mrs. Johnson had made up some posters about Sonny, and if I went straight home, I could hang up a few in the neighborhood before it got too dark.

I was halfway there when I remembered my coat. I swung my car into the turn lane and went back to the cleaners. My coat looked a lot better.

It wasn't raining when I turned into my driveway, so I decided to put the car in the garage and walk around the neighborhood with the posters. My garage is set back from the house, the front even with the edge of the back porch. It was a common arrangement back in the forties. I pulled off a flake of paint as I walked by. It needed a new coat. I was saving that little job until Noah got out of school for the summer.

Sam never participated in domestic chores inside or outside the house. He was always too busy with "bigger issues." I'm determined Noah won't grow up as self-absorbed as his father is.

The screen door to the porch was open, flat against the wall. The spring was broken, so if you didn't push it all the way shut, it wouldn't latch. The first breeze would fling it open. I made a mental note to ask Mrs. Johnson if she had made any progress in getting her husband to fix it. I pulled it shut as I went into the porch. She was usually careful to close it until it caught in the latch.

I forgot the broken latch when I saw the back door was ajar. You couldn't arm the security system unless you closed all the doors. Mrs. J might miss the latch of the screen door, but she would never leave without setting the alarm. I pushed the door open.

"Mrs. Johnson?" I called. The kitchen was dark. I flipped the light switch by the door. Nothing happened. "Mrs. Johnson?"

I thought I heard a muffled thump. My eyes adjusted to the diminished light. I stepped into the kitchen and froze.

It looked like a tornado had touched down. Boxes of cereal had been dumped on the floor and mixed with broken crockery from my dishes. Even the refrigerator had been emptied onto the floor. The fading daylight gave the whole scene a nightmare quality.

A definite thump jerked me out of my reverie. This one was much louder than the first, and it seemed to be coming from the living room. I probably should have backed on out of the kitchen and called 911 from the neighbor's place, but this was my house, and I wasn't ready to abandon it. I walked toward the living room.

The drapes were drawn. I could barely make out the source of the thumps.

Mrs. Johnson sat in a dining room chair. Her hands and feet were bound to it with duct tape, and my sixty-five-dollar Gloria Vanderbilt scarf was jammed into her mouth. Her eyes bulged as she stared at me and made muffled noises.

"Mrs. Johnson!" I cried. "What happened?" I quickly removed the gag from her mouth. She just as quickly began screaming. "What happened?" I asked again.

"It was so awful!" she gasped. "Oooohh, my God."

"Are you hurt?" I asked, looking her over.

"She hit me in the head," she cried. "I was at the counter chopping lettuce for your salad. I heard a noise, and I turned from the counter to see what it was and she hit me. Right here." Mrs. Johnson pointed at her left temple. A good-sized egg nested there. A thin stream of blood ran from the lump, following the wrinkle lines down the side of her face to her collar.

"I'm going to call nine-one-one," I said. "I think maybe you should be looked at by paramedics, maybe even spend some time at the hospital."

"Oh, do you think so?" she asked, perking up a little at the prospect of an ambulance ride.

I called 911 and reported the break-in, and then I called Detective Harper. By the time the ambulance arrived, I was putting a pressure bandage on Mrs. Johnson's cut. One of the benefits of being a supervisor is that you have to be recertified in first aid every year. Unfortunately, as careless as people are, you get many chances to practice your skills.

A patrol car followed the ambulance.

"You get around, don't you, lady?" said the blond officer I'd met twice at Mike's house as he walked into my living room without knocking. "You the one who called in the complaint?"

"Yes," I said. "This is my house."

"Geez, what a mess," he said. He flashed his light over the wreckage that was once my home.

"Thanks for the synopsis."

"You got any idea who did this?" he asked. "Any enemies?"

"No and maybe," I answered. "I don't have a clue who might have done this, but on the other hand, I am a manager. There's always the possibility of a disgruntled employee."

Detective Harper came through the door at that moment. "Do

you think a disgruntled employee was at Mike's house, too?" she asked.

"Well, at least we know it wasn't Rebecca," I said. "Mrs. Johnson said the woman came around four o'clock. Rebecca was in your custody at that point."

Harper and I walked around what was left of my house. I stopped in the stairwell where the breaker box was located and flipped the switches. The lights came back on. I'm not sure why they bothered to make it dark, since Mrs. Johnson was in no condition to recognize anyone.

All the rooms had been trashed, but so far, I couldn't see that anything of value was missing. I have a couple of pieces of original art that are worth a few dimes, but they were untouched. I keep my everyday jewelry in one of those wooden puzzle boxes. You have to move a series of wood slides in a particular sequence to get into it. I doubted the thief had recognized it as a jewelry box. The medicine cabinet in the bathroom had been dumped, and the lid was off the toilet tank. Whoever had done it had been thorough.

My ex-husband had been paranoid about a lot of things. His legacy to me, besides Noah, was a concealed wall safe. It's located behind the breaker box in the stairwell. His theory was that most people were afraid of electricity. My burglar may have been thorough, but he or she had not been sophisticated enough to find the safe. There was a little green light on the inside face of the breaker box that indicated the safe had not been disturbed.

I decided Harper and company didn't need to know about this little item just yet. I'm not convinced my ex-husband isn't the two-bit hustler he appears to be on the surface. I'm certainly not prepared to defend some of his more bizarre actions to the police.

"Did she see the person who did it?" Harper asked, waving a hand toward Mrs. J. A muscular young paramedic with shoulder-length brown hair ministered to her. She announced she couldn't answer any questions until he was done.

"She told me she just caught a glimpse before she was hit, but the person had a ski mask on. She's assuming it was a woman because the person was smaller than she is."

Mrs. Johnson is of hearty farm stock and stands almost six feet tall. I couldn't begin to guess how much she weighs, but I'm pretty sure she's heavier than most of the men I know. I didn't think it was necessary to pass that observation on to Detective Harper.

"Do you have somewhere else you can stay tonight?" Harper asked.

"I could probably stay with a friend, but do you really think that's necessary? I have a good security system. You guys monitor it. Mrs. Johnson doesn't like to put it on during the day when she's going in and out a lot, but it's really a top-of-the-line system."

I sounded like Noah when he was trying to talk me into one of his schemes.

"It's up to you, but if this person didn't find what they were looking for and they think it's here, they will be back."

"If I don't stay tonight, when will I? Almost every house on my street has been robbed in the last couple of years. You guys don't even come anymore — we just fill out a form. My dog is missing, and I need to be here in case he shows up."

"We can't stop you, but my gut says this is not your average house burglary," Harper said. I wondered if intuition still worked when the cop in question had such a thin midsection.

"I need to get this mess cleaned up. I don't think I could sleep somewhere else, knowing what this looks like."

"Set your alarm as soon as we leave. And don't hesitate to call if you see or hear anything. I'll have the patrol car in this area drive by a few times during the night." Detective Harper took one last look around and left.

The paramedics strapped Mrs. Johnson to their gurney and wheeled her to the ambulance. She was positively glowing with all the attention. This trip to the hospital would be the highlight of her year.

Detective Harper had the criminalists come and videotape the mess. They promised to give me a copy for my insurance man. They also dusted for fingerprints and shoe prints. I gathered from listening to them they didn't usually work robberies. Harper wanted them to take samples because she believed this was related to Mike's murder. Living in Northeast Portland made me more skeptical. Most crime in the city took place within a five-mile radius of my humble abode.

It took about two hours for them to complete their tasks. I had time to call my insurance agent and a locksmith to repair the back door. The locksmith came almost immediately. When everyone was gone, I set the alarm and walked through the wreckage, trying to decide where to begin.

My insurance agent had advised me to make a list of damaged items as I cleaned up. I picked up a few shards of my dinnerware in the kitchen and then wandered into the living room. The vandal had spared the ceramic statues that sat on small tables here and there. They were Buddhist figures my ex-husband had brought from Tibet several years ago. They would have been hard to replace. Whoever had been in my house had carefully set the statues on a sofa cushion and put that on the hearth.

They weren't as careful with the set of oil paintings my friend Clifford had done. The glass that covered the ocean scene was shattered. It looked like the canvas was okay, though.

After stacking the books back into the case that ran the length of my entry hall, I drifted into Noah's room. They had spared nothing. It had been difficult looking at my own stuff torn to shreds, but the sight of Noah's stuffed monkey Banana with its head ripped off, stuffing hanging out of his limp torso, was more than I could deal with. I cradled his torn body in my arms, sat on Noah's bed and bawled. I rocked Banana and cried until I couldn't cry anymore.

When I was able, I gathered the bits of stuffing that had fallen out of the monkey and took him upstairs to the attic room that served as my office, library, sewing and all-purpose junk room. The intruder must have been getting tired of wrecking stuff. Or maybe something interrupted her. A few baskets were on their sides with their contents spilled on the floor, but this room was otherwise untouched.

I was able to find a needle and thread. I attached Banana's head without too much trouble and somehow felt better for the effort.

I called the hospital to check on Mrs. Johnson. She was sleeping, but I was able to talk to Henry. He said she was feeling better, but the doctor wanted to keep her overnight for observation. He said she wasn't able to remember any more details about who hit her. I expressed my apologies, and he assured me it wasn't my fault. I knew it was, though. I just wished I knew why.

My neighbor Sarah came over with a plate of sandwiches at about ten o'clock. She had seen my lights on and figured I might need a friend. She stayed until midnight. The house looked substantially better when she left. I took Noah's pillow and blanket and slept on the futon in the attic room with Banana. I did want to be at home, but it was creepy in my bedroom with the curtains hanging in shreds.

CHAPTER TWELVE

I DROVE TO WORK THURSDAY morning feeling as if I hadn't slept. The Grande cup of coffee I bought at Starbucks seemed like a good idea until the bus in front of me hit its brakes. I dropped my coat off at the cleaners.

"Don't ask," I said to the woman behind the counter.

I finished my round of morning meetings and returned to my desk. Before I could sit down, Mary came around the divider waving a message slip.

"Harley, you need to go see Karen Hatcher. She said to come as soon as you got out of your meeting."

"Tell her I'm on my way." I hoped this wasn't more bad news. I wasn't sure I could handle anything else.

I approached Karen's cube, not sure if I was going to the gallows. I could smell peppermint in the air. That usually meant someone had a cold.

"Harley, come in, sit down." She guided me to the guest chair and handed me a cup of tea. "Here, I made this for you."

"I don't understand. Am I going to be sick?"

"I hope not. I just thought, after the last few days you've had, you could use a little strength."

"I'm a little confused. I thought you called me here to tell me I'm going on a leave of absence while you investigate."

"I hope I'm not that unreasonable. You know the law as well as I do — I have to start investigating within twenty-four hours. It doesn't say you can't be here. Putting you off work is a company decision. We base that action on the strength of the initial

71

evidence."

"You sounded like you had a pretty strong case yesterday."

"If you'll remember, I also said I believed you'd be exonerated. Now, I've got good news and bad news. Which do you want first?" She unlocked her file cabinet and pulled out a red manila folder. At Sil-Trac, priority items were always in red folders.

"Definitely the good first."

"This is the complaint that was turned in." She handed me a typed sheet. "Look at the date stamp. We always stamp the date and time on mail as we receive it. According to this..."

"Mike was dead when he turned this in," I finished.

"It looks that way."

"If Mike didn't turn this in, then who did?" I asked.

"The only signature on this is Mike's. I checked his insurance forms. It is either his signature or a very good forgery. It appears to have been hand-delivered. I asked the mail person. It definitely came from inside."

"Why would someone want to do this to me?"

"There are always the usual reasons — lack of money at review time, someone you passed over for a promotion. Maybe it's just someone who has a problem with authority figures. Has anyone seemed unhappier than usual?"

"I can't think of anyone. I thought everyone in my group was feeling pretty good."

"Well, don't rule out people from other groups. Are you ready for the rest?"

"Oh, God, this isn't the day for this." I set my cup down and grabbed the edges of my chair to brace myself.

"Has something happened I don't know about?" Karen asked.

I filled her in on my previous night's activities.

"I'm really sorry, Harley. I wish I didn't have to add to your troubles."

"Let's get it over with."

"There's been a second complaint. This one is anonymous."

I leaned my head back and shut my eyes. "I can't believe this is happening. What does this one say?"

"Uh, let me see here. Fondling, groping, touching. Unwanted advances, too. They pretty well cover every possible option."

"This is too much!" I stood up to leave.

"Wait, sit down. I agree. The scenario described in this is a little improbable."

I sat back down slowly. "What're you talking about?"

"Well, this would have taken place in the clean room. It says the person was trying to do their job. You cornered them in the stockroom. When are you ever in the clean room with only one person?"

"Hardly ever, but it does happen occasionally."

"What about the stockroom?"

"You're right. There's a person in the cage during the hours the assemblers are here. Unless it was the stockroom person who filed the complaint."

The stockrooms in the production area are sections of the floor cordoned off with rubber-coated chainlink fence. They're locked unless an attendant was present. The Sil-Trac processes use precious metals that are both valuable and portable. We also keep clean room paper supplies under lock and key — people have a tendency to forget that the special lint-free towels we use in the clean room cost a dollar apiece or more. I don't want to be one of those managers who makes people beg for every pencil, but before I locked them up, I'd found people sopping up coffee spills in the breakroom with the lint-free wipes.

"It's not an airtight alibi, but then again, an anonymous letter is less of a threat. We would need a specific name and incident to take any further action. At this point, all we can do is wait."

"Fine, you wait." I stood up again. "Meanwhile, I'm going after some answers."

"Harley, don't do anything foolish. We are handling this."

"Great. Meanwhile, what am I supposed to do? Twist in the wind while who-knows-who takes potshots at me? I'll see you later."

"Harley?"

I walked off, ending the discussion.

CHAPTER THIRTEEN

I DECIDED IT WAS TIME for me to pay a visit to Uncle Andrush. I didn't know what kind of a scam he was running, but I intended to find out.

Before I reached the clean room exit, a tall, bunny-suited figure stopped me.

"Harley," a familiar voice called out. "Do you have a minute? I'd like to show you something."

The voice belonged to Hieu, Mike's second-in-command. I guess that made him leader of the group now. Hieu's family had come to America in a leaky boat when he was about ten years old. He must have benefited from the change in nutrition or something. His family members were the diminutive size many Southeast Asians are; they run one of the more successful Chinese restaurants in the area. Hieu towered over them at almost six feet tall.

"Sure, Hieu. What have you got?"

"Well, I took a copy of each area's log book. I've been looking at each one and comparing them to each other. You know, trying to see if I can figure out a pattern or something."

"Have you found something?" I asked as I looked at the paper he was holding out. It looked like some kind of chart.

"I *think* I've found something," he said. "I'm not sure what it means, but sometimes the amount of error is consistent if you look at it as a weekly quantity."

"What do you mean?"

"Well, look at this day." He pointed at a column on the paper. "There were three lots through the areas. Each count is off by a different amount as it goes from area to area, right?"

"Yeah, so?"

"If you add up all the lots for the week and look at the total number they're off at the end, it's almost the same number every week."

"Bottom-line it for me, Hieu," I said. "What does it mean?"

"I don't know yet, but I will. It's too consistent an error." He snapped his notebook shut. "This is going to sound weird, but I feel like I *need* to figure this out. You know, for Mike."

I put my gloved hand on his arm. Harassment suit be damned! "I don't think it's weird. I think it's a very nice gesture. I'm sure Mike would be pleased."

Hieu ducked his head and blushed. At least, the three centimeters of skin I could see of his face appeared to be blushing.

"Keep up the good work, Hieu. And tell me as soon as you figure something."

I went back to my desk to check for messages. I decided on a stop at the pop machine for diet cola. You know, to fortify my nerves. I had just started down the padded cubicle aisle when I heard my name come floating over a divider.

"You're kidding. I can't believe Harley's been groping her guys," an unidentifiable voice said.

"I didn't think she even *liked* guys," was the reply.

"Who said she was groping guys?" the first voice said.

I hurried past, walking right by the pop machine without stopping. I needed to get out of the building before I did something I would regret.

As a supervisor in a factory, you know you're the butt of a lot of jokes and the topic of a lot of nasty comments. The knowledge doesn't offer much protection when it is rubbed in your face. I felt like quitting. There wasn't enough money in the universe to make it worth this kind of abuse. I knew this feeling would pass. I just needed to get away from Sil-Trac for a while.

A trip to see Mike's Uncle Andrush was just what I needed. I had a feeling I'd solve my problems when I figured out what happened to Mike.

Uncle Andrush lived in a working-class neighborhood in southeast Portland. Well-kept gardens alternated with weed-infested dirt patches. It reminded me of my own neighborhood. I glanced at the paper Mary had given me with the address. The pink house I was looking at had to be the one. I realized I'd been expecting something much more sinister. This looked like a doll's cottage.

The door opened on my second knock.

"I'm looking for Andrush Wyzcek," I said.

"I am he," the man replied.

The room behind him was cozy. The rugs were hand-braided wool. There were plastic religious items scattered about on tables and shelves. A faint smell of cabbage floated in the air. The neatly patched spots on the sofa arm would have been invisible if the morning sun hadn't been shining just right. A hand-crocheted lace piece was draped across an expensive Japanese radio/CD player on a shelf made from concrete blocks and boards.

"I'm sorry, I'm looking for a different Andrush Wyzcek. My Andrush is older, middle sixties maybe."

This guy was muscular and looked to be in his forties. His shirt was a little snug in the shoulders, like all those muscles just couldn't wait to get out.

"Do you have an uncle or father with the same name?"

"I am the only Andrush Wyzcek in Portland. What do you want with me?"

"I'm looking for Mike Wyzcek's Uncle Andrush. Do you expect me to believe that's you?"

"I don't care what you believe, miss." He spoke only slightly accented English.

"No, I suppose you don't. Are you Mike's uncle?"

"I was when he was alive." He looked down. "Now, I ask again. What do you want from me?"

"I'd like to ask you about Monday night. At The Blue Whale."

"I don't know what you are talking about. What is this Blue Whale?"

"Don't be cute," I said. "I have an eyewitness who places you at the Whale Monday night. He said you're an actor. I just didn't realize how good you were."

"I think you better go now," he said. He grabbed my arm and pushed me toward the door.

I wedged my sensible shoe against the doorframe. "Look, I'm not going anywhere until you tell me what's going on," I said. "You can either tell me or tell the police."

It was an empty threat, but I could see the muscle in his jaw tighten. I felt kind of bad. A lot of the people at Sil-Trac came from countries where the police were more dangerous than the criminals. The feeling passed.

"Why can't you leave us alone?" a new voice asked from an interior doorway.

I looked beyond Uncle Andrush and saw one of the young men from Monday night's little drama. He was dressed in baggy stonewashed jeans and an earthtone T-shirt. A backward baseball cap covered his hair. So much for the Euro-peasant look.

"Mike's dead. What difference does it make now?" He came into the room. His face was flushed and his eyes were rimmed in red. He had done some serious crying sometime in the recent past.

"It makes a lot of difference if you killed him," I said.

The kid charged toward me, and after only a slight hesitation, Andrush let go of me and grabbed the boy.

"You seem to be sincerely upset about Mike," I said to the boy. "And I really do feel sympathy for your pain. I cared a lot about Mike. But the night before he died, you were telling me to bring unmarked bills to a phone booth. I think I deserve an explanation."

"I don't know what you are talking about," said Andrush again. "I must ask you to leave."

If he chose to stonewall me I was going to be out of luck. I stood there running possible scenarios through my head. Before I could come up with a workable plan, the young man spoke again.

"Give it up, Dad. She's going to call the police."

"Shut up, you idiot," Andrush said.

"You said your plan wouldn't hurt anyone. You said Mike would never even know. Now he's dead." The boy stormed out of the room.

"What do you want?" Andrush demanded again. "Mike is dead. I took nothing from you. No crime was committed."

"What do you mean, 'no crime?'" I asked. "You tried to collect ransom from me. Mike's dead. Rebecca is in jail. My house is trashed. Do I need to go on?"

Andrush sat down on the arm of an overstuffed chair. "Rebecca is in jail?"

It was only a slight exaggeration. Rebecca's legal aid attorney had gotten her released to the custody of her parents. They didn't have enough evidence to charge her with anything. Yet.

Andrush's tanned face went pale.

"I can see that's news to you," I said. "What were you looking for at my place? I can't imagine what I have that you'd want. Surely, you don't think I keep cash at home."

"I don't know what you are talking about," he repeated for the third time.

"Yeah, right. Just like you didn't know about the kidnapping."

"I know nothing about your home," he said. "I may have staged a small deceit, but I would never hurt Rebecca. The child is like a daughter to me. I always thought she would be Mike's wife someday."

I wondered if he'd ever met Debbie Dayshift.

"Where is Rebecca? What jail is she in?"

"Look, her parents are handling things."

"What do they know of these things? They are simple peasants."

I was having trouble imagining by what measure the two yuppies I had met at Rebecca's house could be considered peasants. Somehow, this didn't seem like the right moment to debate it.

"Where is she?" he demanded again, stepping closer to me. I could smell his cologne, one of those designer fragrances found on cards in the middle of magazines. "Why is she in jail?"

"You tell me about the small deceit, and if I believe you, I'll tell you about Rebecca. Agree?"

"It would seem I have no choice. First, you must agree not to tell the police."

"First, tell me the story. I'll decide after I hear it."

He was silent for over a minute. Finally, he shrugged and began his tale.

"It is a very simple story. I am a humble workingman. I have seven children to feed and one more on the way. My sister, Mike's mother, is living still in Poland. Conditions are terrible there. She has no food and no money for medicine."

"Wait a minute," I said. "Mike told me he asked his mother to come to Portland, but she wouldn't leave Poland."

"Yes, I know," he said. "She just didn't want the boy to feel bad. He only had enough money for one ticket. My sister takes care of our mother and our mother's sister. She could not leave the two old women alone in such a terrible situation. And I try to save a little, but with the children..." He shrugged. "...there is never extra."

Rebecca had told me Andrush was in America several years before Mike came. That meant at least three of Andrush's children had been born after he immigrated to America. I never could understand why so many immigrants came here to escape communist governments and then had endless children, which caused them to become hopelessly dependent on a welfare system that was not a lot different from the one they escaped. At least communists knew they were on the plan for life from the beginning.

"Go on," I urged him.

"The old ladies are becoming...how do you say...?" He waved his hand in the air, as if the word were floating out there waiting to be grabbed. "Frail, they are becoming frail. They must come to America while they can still survive the rigors of such a trip."

"So, you and Mike decided I would finance it?"

"No, not Mike," he said, "I planned our little charade. I sent Mike to his Aunt Sophie's house. She was to keep him busy until Thursday." A grin flickered across his face. "What can I say? He didn't cooperate."

"So, you were going to let me think Mike was kidnapped and then, when you collected the ransom, he would just come back to work like nothing happened?"

He ducked his head then looked up through the curly hair that lay across his forehead.

"I can see you are a bright girl." He was turning up the charm, but I wasn't falling for it. When you're the person who hands out the money at review time, you have a lot of experience with this kind of charm.

"The police wouldn't stop investigating just because Mike was back. For that matter, they wouldn't have let me give you the money."

"I think you exaggerate your importance, miss. My neighbor Henry was robbed. The thief took two thousand dollars' worth of tools. No police even came. They just send a form to fill out. I think you would just fill out a form, your insurance would pay you for the loss, minus some small portion, and everyone would be happy."

"Geez, you need to watch more movies of the week. Kidnapping is a whole different thing from simple theft. We would have had the FBI here and everything. I think it might be a federal offense."

"Really!" His eyes widened, and he raised his left eyebrow.

"Besides all that, I'm pretty sure my homeowners insurance doesn't cover ransom."

"Perhaps you need to consider a new policy. I have a friend who could arrange it."

"I'll just bet you do."

"I believe it is your turn. Why is Rebecca in jail?"

"Not so fast, buddy. When did Mike come home from his aunt's?"

"Oh, phew." He gestured with his hand in the air. "You expect me to remember trifles?"

I stared at him without speaking.

"Let me see," he said. "When I came home from church, there was a message on the phone machine from Sophie that Mike was coming."

"You mean Sophie was in on this, too?" I asked. Was there no end to his conspiracy? "Did she know she could be put in jail as an accomplice?"

"I think you exaggerate. No, Sophie did not know why I wanted Mike to stay with her. I told her I was making a surprise for him. It was the truth — if his mother comes, he would be very surprised."

"Why did he come back?" I had to ask.

"He said he had to work. He had some papers at his apartment he was working on. I finally had to tell him the truth. He was angry, but I told him he could not go to his work until Thursday. So, what could he do? He said he would work at home. He promised he would keep out of sight. He left his car here and walked home after dark on Sunday night. That was the last time I saw him."

Tears welled up in the man's eyes, and I could almost believe they were real. I hoped he would forget about Rebecca. I wasn't that lucky.

"Now, tell me about Rebecca," he said.

I hesitated a moment then decided I had nothing to lose if I told him some of the truth, anyway.

"Mike's place was broken into and torn up. I assume you and your boys went there to destroy some evidence you left of your kidnap plan."

"I'm wounded you would think such a thing," he interrupted, putting his clasped hands over his heart for dramatic effect.

I ignored him and continued. "Rebecca went there right after the break-in to get something she left with Mike. The police concluded she had done the breaking in. They took her to the station for questioning and then released her to her parents' custody."

"Then she is not arrested," he said and sat back on the arm of the upholstered chair. His look made me blush. It was somewhere between anger and disappointment. With seven kids to practice on, he had honed his glare to perfection.

"Not yet. But they could still take her in after they finish checking Mike's place." I tried unsuccessfully to keep a defensive tone out of my voice.

"Why did she go to that place?"

"She was getting some picture." I decided that was all Andrush needed to know. Rebecca was willing to risk everything to get that particular picture, and I wanted to find out why before I told him anything else.

"What picture was so important?"

"I don't know," I lied. "Maybe it was a picture of her." That seemed to shut him up. "The people at work are taking up a collection to bring Mike's mother here for his memorial service. I understand you are making the funeral arrangements."

"That would be a lovely thing if my sister could come here."

My distraction worked. Andrush's demeanor sharpened at the mention of bringing his sister.

"I told you, I have no money. The church is helping to give Mike a simple burial in at the church cemetery. Do you think they will bring my sister here?"

"I think it is a good possibility. Everyone is donating, and the company said they would match what the workers contributed. Besides that, Mike's company insurance policy will probably cover his burial costs. Why don't you see if the church will donate their money toward the ticket?"

"I know I ask much." Andrush was giving me a look I could only describe as coy. "Do you think the people might bring my mother here, too?"

He was right— it was a lot to ask. "You'd have to talk to the church about that."

I left Andrush and walked back to my car. His story was simple enough on the surface, but something wasn't right. His description of Mike's mother's situation didn't seem to match the image I'd gotten from Mike. Then again, I guess we all tend to see our mothers as strong, infallible women. I can remember my own mother driving through a raging snowstorm to get glitter for my sister's hair before a church Christmas pageant. Now, she worries if we get three flakes.

It wasn't lunchtime yet, but I was feeling the pull of comfort food. My favorite Vietnamese restaurant is a small place on the corner of 31st and Hawthorne. It's run by a woman just a few years older than I am and is located in an old house. You eat in what was once the front room. She cooks in a kitchen only slightly modified from its original form. The tables are covered with tablecloths and topped with glass. Diners slip their business cards under the glass. Businesses that could never co-exist in real life end up with their cards in close proximity on the tables.

So, Aldina's Belly Dance is next to Henry Bone, Obstetrician, and across from the Tummy Toners and Navel Needles. They pretty well have a corner on the female midriff. I don't think I'm a snob, but I always find my own card in the crowd. One time I found it touching the Junior Republicans. I try to keep it between the Woman's Wand Cooperative and Sheila Belden, Stock Advisor.

The open sign wasn't on the door yet, but I could see someone in the kitchen. Lan Nguyen looked up from the vegetables she was chopping and motioned to me to come in. I tried the door and found it unlocked.

"You want some soup? I got good soup today. I think you like some soup." She came out carrying a steaming bowl and set it in front of me.

"Yeah," I sighed, "soup would be good."

"I got big headache today," she said. "Inspectors coming. Inspector, I think he don't like womens. Maybe he don't like Vietnamese. Every time he look so hard, try to find something problem."

"It's not you, Lan. It's their job to find something. They're like that with everyone."

"It not fair. I have good kitchen. Clean kitchen. It not fair."

"Yeah, Lan, I know. Lots of things aren't fair."

The soup was a spicy tofu vegetable creation. It was one of those sinus-clearing dishes that take a while to eat because you have to keep blowing your nose.

When I finished, I paid my bill and tried again to reassure Lan that the health department didn't have a vendetta against her. I'm not sure she bought it. Then again, I'm not sure I bought it, either.

CHAPTER FOURTEEN

DECIDED TO STOP BY Rebecca's house while I was on the east side of town. If Mike's mother was going to come, we needed to get things moving right away.

I parked in front of the house and walked up the sidewalk. I hadn't noticed what the house looked like when I'd brought Rebecca home, but now I could see that four dormers topped the basic box shape, one in each compass direction. Judging by the multicolored roofing, at least two of the dormers were recent additions.

Rebecca's family had only been here a few months, but someone before them had planted bulbs all along the sidewalk. You could see the green tips just beginning to push through the soil — in another month, the yard would be a riot of color. Now, it was brown, with just this hint of what was to come.

Rebecca's mother had taken a few days off to stay with her daughter. I could see them sitting on a sofa in the front room. Rebecca opened the door before I had time to knock.

"Miss Harley," she said, "something is wrong?"

"No, nothing like that. May I come in?"

"I'm sorry." She stepped aside.

"I wanted to ask if you've talked to Mike's mother," I said. "I was in the neighborhood, so I thought I'd stop by and see how you're doing."

"I call Ruta last night," Rebecca's mother said. "She is planning to come on Saturday. She told me she much appreciate Mike's friends and his company to bring her to America. Can you come to Andrush house on Saturday? Six p.m.? We will have a small...party. Something to celebrate Mike. Can you tell his friends? Ruta want to say thank you."

"I'm glad we could help," I said. "I wish she were coming under happier circumstances."

"Andrush was plan to bring Ruta, Ruta's mother and Ruta's aunt Ana. He said he was getting some money. They come soon. They already have passport and visa."

"Did he happen to say where this money was going to come from?" I couldn't resist asking.

"She don't know, but who ever know what Andrush do? He has good heart, he's just not..." She looked up and then spoke to Rebecca in Polish.

"Practical," Rebecca said. "He never has regular job. He does acting and work a little here and a little there."

"He's — how do you say?— dreamer," Rebecca's mother finished.

"Did he work in Poland?" I asked.

"He was same in Poland," Rebecca's mom said. "I think it need more than change country to change Andrush."

"If I can do anything to help with Mike's mother's visit, just let me know," I said. I put my hand on the doorknob and started to open the door, then stopped. "By the way, Rebecca, can we talk about the pic— "

Before I could finish, Rebecca pushed me out the partially opened door and shut it behind us.

"That answers one question," I said. "I guess your mother doesn't know about the picture."

"Please, she must not find out. No one can know."

"You better tell me what's going on. That picture is obviously old. Who does it belong to?"

"It is Mike's. His mother give to him."

"Why the big secret? Unless Mike specifically wrote a will leaving it to someone else, all his property will go to his next of kin. Probably his mother."

"You don't tell anyone this. Mike's mother is coming. Few days and you can give to her. Until then, you just keep. Okay?"

"Rebecca, what is going on?"

"Don't tell no one."

I knew Rebecca well enough to know our discussion was over for now. Her mother opened the door and looked at me.

"If I can do anything, let me know," I said again.

Rebecca just watched me as I turned and left.

I was scheduled to go to a luncheon seminar at the Red Lion Hotel downtown. I needed to get back to Sil-Trac and check on the count problem, but the seminar topic was ISO 9000. Supervisors from all the high-tech firms in the area would attend. I couldn't pass up a chance to commiserate with others in my same boat. Besides, I might be able to pick up some useful info about the inspection.

I parked in the hotel lot and went into the lobby. I still had a few minutes, so I found a payphone and called Mary.

"Harley, I'm so glad you called," she said. "You're not going to believe what I just heard!"

"Why don't you tell me, then?"

"It's just so amazing, after what we've been through."

"Mary!" I could feel my blood pressure rising.

"Okay, okay," she said. "This is just a rumor, mind you. Jansi's usually reliable, though." I wondered if Karen knew the extent to which her secretary broadcast HR news. "Jansi says that a bomb threat was called in for Friday. Right when the inspectors are supposed to be here."

"Is this for real?"

"Jansi says she was right next to Karen when she got the call from security. And she says she sent email telling everyone to cancel any visits by outsiders scheduled for Friday."

"That does sound pretty reliable. Thanks for the heads-up, Mary."

As I continued on to the banquet room, Mary's news began to sink in. As a rule, I don't like bomb threats. I usually end up on the team having to hunt for them. The theory is that the supervisors are the ones who know if something looks out of place. In this case, it was a relief. Assuming it would take at least a week to reschedule the ISO 9000 inspectors, I would have a few more days to try to solve my count problem.

I also began to wonder if one of my people had called in the threat.

The seating at these seminars is pre-arranged, so I had to wander around and look for my name on a placecard. The vendor group that sponsors this series works with all of us in the electronics business. I guess they like to dilute us by seating each person from the same company at a different table. It worked. It was inhibiting to ask questions of the speaker when you were sitting at a table of virtual strangers. Especially when you didn't want the strangers to know too much about your own operations.

I found my place next to a large woman in a purple polyester suit.

"Have we met before?" she asked as I approached. "You look very familiar."

"I don't think so. We've probably seen each other at these things."

"That must be it," she said. "I just have this image of you in camping gear, though."

It was unlikely. Camping had been Sam's thing. He liked the challenge of man against nature. When we camped, we took next to nothing. I don't have anything against nature, but eating bugs and twigs isn't my idea of fun.

Sam was always a man possessed on these little sojourns. Our hikes were like a death march. Our trips usually ended with Noah and I holed up in the car, not speaking to Sam until sometime past the nearest McDonalds. The closest Noah and I had come to roughing it since Sam left was a dude-and-breakfast place we liked near Mount Adams. The rough part was walking outside from the lodge house to the hot tub.

"I buy birdseed at the Audubon House on Cornell road. Maybe you saw me there."

"I'm sure that's it," she said. She didn't sound convinced.

"That's a lovely charm on your necklace," I said. "It's unusual."

She had a series of necklaces of varying lengths around her ample neck. The two silver chains had beads. A leather thong had a rose quartz crystal held in a pewter eagle talon attached to it. The one I was interested in had a small gold Buddha charm.

"A new little gal on our night shift gave it to me," the woman said. "She collects all kinds of Buddhas. She said this one was a good luck Buddha. I guess she figured with ISO nine thousand coming up I'd need it."

I got a sinking feeling in my stomach. I had the twin to the necklace in my jewelry box at home. It had been a Christmas gift from Debbie Dayshift.

"My name is Harley. What's yours?"

"Betty," she said. "Betty Lou McFee. I'm a production supervisor at MiCorp."

She pulled a business card smoothly from her pocket with her left hand and extended her right. I had picked up my water glass in my right hand while we were talking. I fumbled between setting my glass down, reaching for my own business card and clasping her hand. Maybe people practice these moves at home. That's probably where I was going wrong. No home practice.

When I finally untangled myself, she took my card and we sat down. I was glad I had stopped at Lan's for my mid-morning soup. About three years ago, I made a New Year's resolution not to eat the food at these events unless it was really good. Noah finally got through to me that no children in China were going to be affected by my dinner habits, no matter what Grandma said.

"Betty Lou," I said after the speaker had finished her presentation, "one of my guys dates a woman who collects Buddhas. Maybe it's the same person. What does this lady look like?"

"Oh, this couldn't be the same person. Debbie's boyfriend left her a couple of months ago for a younger woman."

"I'm sure you're right," I lied.

I drove back to Sil-Trac after the seminar. The speaker had raised a lot of issues that were going to worry people at Sil-Trac. ISO 9000 requires a lot of documentation that assembly operators have to read and understand. At least half of the operators at most factories are immigrants. Between the Zero Population Growth movement of the 70s and the move of women into the work place in the 80s, women in America have delayed child-bearing until they're in their thirties, forties and now even fifties. What this means to industry is a gap in the supply of eighteeen-year-olds flowing into the workplace.

Labor watchers say this condition will continue until at least the turn of the century. If we didn't have the immigrant population filling the gap, there could be no growth in the economy. Most of the high-tech companies I was driving past in the Sunset Corridor wouldn't exist. Or they would be located in Third World countries.

Companies are having a hard time figuring out how to train such a culturally diverse population in the basic skills needed for world-class manufacturing. I have the full gamut in my group. I have Tran, who has a master's degree in math but lacks English language skills, and Jorge, who speaks English correctly but can't read in either his native Spanish or English. I also had people with every possible combination in between.

As I pulled into the Sil-Trac parking lot, I realized I probably wouldn't have to worry about it, given the way my career was going.

The raindrops on the smoke-colored one-way windows were blazing in the sun as I walked in through the front lobby. The Willamette Valley is amazing in its ability to change its look right before your eyes. When I left home that morning it had been so foggy you couldn't see the bums on the sidewalks of West Burnside. Later, it had rained. Now, the sun was out and the sky was clearing.

Karen's office was near the front of the building. I went there first. I needed to get official notification of the bomb threat and see what the official response was going to be. Sometimes, when a time is given, we can get at least half a day's work done.

I could smell a fruity tea brewing. I couldn't quite place the flavor.

"Oh, Harley," Karen said, "I'm glad you're back. We have another situation you need to know about." I love the euphemisms Human Resources people speak in. "There's been another bomb threat. Would you like a cup of tea? It's raspberry."

"Oh, no. What about the ISO nine thousand inspectors?"

"You need to brush up your acting skills, Harley."

"Okay, so I know we got a threat, but that's all I know. Can I have the details with my tea?

"I'm sure you know the inspectors were rescheduled. We were lucky. They had a cancellation for next Wednesday."

"Yeah, some luck," I said. "Do we get to work at all tomorrow?"

"I'm afraid we can't risk that kind of liability."

"Do you really think it was someone on the outside?" I asked.

"We can only assume each bomb threat could be real and follow the policy."

"So, what does that mean?"

"We're declaring a bomb holiday," she said. "We'll close after swing shift tonight."

"You mean no graveyard? Isn't that a little extreme?"

"Come on, Harley. You know I don't make those kinds of decisions. I'm sure Mr. Nakata informed everyone concerned what the impact of shutting down production would be."

"Sorry, you're right. I guess it's no secret we're running at maximum capacity right now. I'd better go inform the troops."

"Just make sure you tell everyone personally. Give me a list of anyone you can't talk to from dayshift. Anyone who is absent or away from the plant for any reason, too, and we'll call them when we call the night people."

I put my empty cup down, thanked Karen and went to my desk. There was a phone message from Neva Dean on my desk. I wedged it into the pocket of my skirt. I'd call her after I checked in with my people and officially gave them the news about tomorrow.

When I went into the clean room hallway I could see Tommy, Hieu, Debbie Dayshift and Shannon gathered around one of the workbenches in the test room. Tommy glanced my way and, when he saw me, came out into the hall.

"God, Harley," he said, "this is getting discouraging. I'm starting to think ISO nine thousand wasn't meant for us."

"I take it you heard about the bomb threat?"

"We all did. That's old news. We got new problems."

"Do I need to sit down for this?"

"No, it's not that bad. It's Hieu's notes. Before he went to break, he said he'd just about figured out the count problem. He just needed to get a few numbers from production planning. When he came back from break with the numbers, one of the squirt bottles of acetone had leaked all over his notes."

"Did it wipe them out?" I asked. Acetone is a solvent used in the IC manufacturing process. It's a close kin of nail polish remover.

"Pretty much," Tommy said. "We can reconstruct it all from the logs, if we can get them from everyone. Then Hieu can go through and do all the corrections again. If he can remember what they were." Tommy didn't look convinced. "We can all help him."

Hieu had been working day and night for three days. We would have a real challenge trying to duplicate all that work. Especially now, with Friday being shut down because of the bomb.

"Get as much of the data together as you can. Have Mary make two copies. Put one on my desk and send the other home with Hieu. See if he thinks anyone can be of any help to him. Tell Hieu I'll give him comp time if he works on it at home tomorrow."

"Gotcha, boss," he said. He made an about-face and went back into the test room.

CHIP AND DIE

The lead operators had returned to their respective work areas, and I officially notified everyone about the unexpected holiday. When I got to the photolithography room, I found Debbie Dayshift checking squirt bottles and throwing out worn-looking ones. A bag of new, unmarked bottles was on the workbench, along with OSHA chemical labels and marking pens.

"Don't you think this is kind of locking the barn after the horse is gone?" I asked.

"Well, it wasn't a bottle from my room. I checked the label. Mine all say photolithography all over them. I just thought it was a good lesson for all of us. I've thrown out all the questionable ones."

"Whatever," I said. "Leave a big note for the swing people reminding them they need to shut everything down, since the graveyard people won't be coming in."

Sil-Trac is one of the few companies in the area that runs three eight-hour shifts. Many of the neighboring factories have four or five groups of people who work twelve-hour shifts in some rotating fashion. Personally, I like our system. We have to work to stay efficient, given the relatively short periods of actual work time we have after you subtract all the time it takes to get suited up.

But everyone knows when he or she is supposed to be there. With the twelve-hour days, you either have to pay people for a thirty-six-hour work shift or do some rotation of three-day weeks and four-day weeks. Most people opt for the latter. Sil-Trac experimented with twelve-hour shifts before I came to work there. Jose said people had trouble remembering which week it was. He would end up being short people on the Saturday night half. Or two groups would come in on Thursday. I guess it was a real mess.

"I already wrote it in big letters in the shift leaders log book," Debbie said. "I'll tell Allan in person when he comes in, too."

At Sil-Trac, the swing shift and graveyard shifts are smaller than the day group. As a result, we have only two lead people each shift. Allan has all the in-lab people, and Gail all the packaging operators and test technicians for swing shift.

I checked with the lead people one more time to be sure everything was prepared for our unexpected holiday. They assured me they had reset the timers that automatically power equipment up and down, and they promised to communicate well with the swing people.

As I went out through the air shower, I finally started thinking about how I was going to spend the extra day off. Every supervisor has a stack of paperwork. I was no exception. I had upcoming performance appraisals to do for my people as well as notes to type up from the productivity improvement team I'm on with Jose, Scott and two other supervisors. It would probably make me feel good to catch up with some of these things.

That thought only lasted a moment. What I really wanted to do was see Noah. He didn't like being sent off to military school. He doesn't have a problem with the school itself; he just didn't like the idea he'd been sent. I don't blame him. I didn't like the idea, either.

The school was pretty flexible about visitation. A lot of the boys had prominent parents who could only see their children when there was a break in their schedule. They also had a policy that allowed boys to be jerked out of school at a moment's notice no matter what was happening in the classroom. You couldn't accuse them of having their priorities mixed up. They knew who paid the bills.

I try not to contradict what Sam says or does with Noah. After all, Sam is going to be Noah's father forever, and Noah is going to have to come to terms with that. On the other hand, I don't like to see Noah suffer from Sam's weirdness. I had the option of ending my forever with Sam, and I did. Noah doesn't have that option.

Before I could talk myself out of it, I went to my desk, called my travel agent and booked Noah on an evening flight out of San Francisco. I called the school and told them the flight and time. They said it was no problem. But then, I knew it wouldn't be. A three-day weekend was just what Noah and I needed. I'd rent some of those movies he liked, the ones with spaceships and big fuzzy animals that could fly them.

I had just hung up the phone when Jose stood up and leaned over the partition between our cubicles.

"Where ya been?" he asked. "I got back a while ago, but you were nowhere to be found."

"I went to that ISO nine thousand lunch. Since then I've been in telling my people about the bomb holiday. Why? What's up?"

"The marketing guys just got in from New Jersey. The hot news is that they promised RadNet ISO nine thousand."

"You've got to be kidding!"

"You heard me. If we don't pass, they pull their three-million-a-year order."

"Great," I said. "Do they know where we are on it?"

"They don't care. They just said they had complete faith that we would not want to be the ones to blow a contract that big." Jose sat back down. There wasn't anything else to say.

I sat down and leaned back in my chair. A crinkle of paper reminded me of Neva Dean's note in my pocket. It took a little maneuvering, but I got it out in one piece. Elves must design women's business attire. Or someone with really small hands. Most of the pockets on my skirts could hold a single breath mint, at most. My mother said they were for decorative purposes.

I called Neva Dean and arranged to come by her house on the way home.

"You're gonna think I'm goin' crazy," she had said.

"No," I'd assured her, all the while thinking *There's no "gonna" about it.*

I finished some paperwork at my desk. Supervisors spend a third of their time working and the other two-thirds documenting what they did in the first third. I grabbed a stack of phone messages and a folder from Karen. She might believe I hadn't harassed anyone, but she still had to complete her investigation. She wanted me to reconstruct my actions and come up with people to verify my whereabouts on several otherwise ordinary days. If I'd known I was going to be falsely accused, I would have kept a journal. I'm not sure anyone could look back two or three months, pick a day and reconstruct everything that happened.

I was going to have to try, though. I planned to look at the various logs from the clean room. I was hoping I could tie Karen's dates to events in the lab. I always remember when we have a new reject type or equipment failures. It was a stretch, but what could it hurt?

I checked the clean room one more time. The swing shift people were busy at the machines. Through the window, I could see Tommy hunched over the logbooks with Hieu. If my leads pulled this off I would have to lobby with management to override the normal three-percent yearly increase.

I wonder sometimes if the people who make the budgets ever stop to figure out the actual numbers we end up offering people. Three percent does sound like something, but $7.39 in take-home per week fails to impress the people on the receiving end.

It wasn't until I was in my car and on the road to Neva Dean's that I realized what I'd set up for this weekend. It hit me like a wet mop. I pulled my car over to the curb and pounded my fist on the steering wheel. I noticed a man, bent over at the waist looking in my window.

"You all right, lady?" he asked.

"I'm fine," I said and pulled away from the curb.

How could I have forgotten about Sonny? Noah loved Sonny more than anything on earth. How could I be so insensitive? Noah was having enough trouble accepting all the changes in his life. Now, I was bringing him home so he could see firsthand that his best friend was missing. I knew I wasn't going to get many votes for mother of the year, but this was low even for me.

Neva Dean opened the door on my tearstained face before I had time to knock.

"Come on in here, honey, and tell Neva Dean what's wrong."

A half-hour later, after downing a cup of tea that smelled vaguely of farm animals, I had to admit I did feel a little better. Neva Dean shared tales of her children and reassured me. If this were the worst mistake I made with Noah, I'd be in good shape.

"I've been so upset about Noah," I said. "I haven't even asked you why you wanted to see me."

"Well, your Noah is much more important than the imaginings of an old fool like me."

"I don't believe that," I said. "You may be a lot of things, Neva Dean Willett, but I'll never believe you're a fool."

"You just wait till you hear what I have to say."

I looked at her. She was dressed in lavender from head to toe. She had on polyester pull-on pants and a short-sleeved print shirt. Her sweater was that pattern that used to come on the yarn packages. It said you could make this sweater with just two skeins of yarn. My mother and all her friends had made them one winter. On Neva Dean, the effect was right out of central casting. She looked frail, vulnerable and very different from yesterday's spandex and Nikes.

Her swollen fingers were absently twisting her handkerchief into knots. "Someone is watching me."

"Do you know who?" I asked.

"Well, here's where it's going to sound crazy. It isn't just one person. It's a group of people. Or at least more than one."

"Are you sure?" I asked her. I could see from her face that it was the wrong thing to say. "Come on, Neva Dean, I'm not saying I don't believe you. I just need to hear more. Maybe we should call the police."

"I called Detective Green this morning."

"What did he say?"

"He said there was no law against lookin' at a body. He asked if I was threatened in any way. I said my peace of mind was surely threatened. He said the stalking law was written for a single person threatening or harassing another person. He said it don't cover groups. He said to call him if anything changed."

"Somehow, that doesn't surprise me," I said. "So, what, exactly, is happening?"

"It's hard to say directly. I just feel I'm being watched."

CHAPTER FIFTEEN

NEVA DEAN HELD UP HER hand to silence the protest that was forming on my lips.

"I've lived on this street for twenty-five years. I know who belongs and who don't belong. It's a quiet street. Oh, we get the occasional gardener or tree doctor, you know, when the tree limbs start rubbing on the wires and such. And we get deliverymen from time to time. But you get to recognize those people. They have regulars. And they don't come all in the same week." Her blue eyes flashed with defiance. "There has been someone on my end of the block doin' something ever since Tuesday, and it isn't right."

"Maybe it's just a coincidence someone has been here when you've been home."

"Honey, where do you think I would go? I've been home since the day before Mike passed on."

"You mean you haven't even been to the store or anything?"

"I go shopping on Sunday afternoons. Danny Junior comes on over and takes me. He thinks I can't carry the bags myself. And my yoga teacher is off having a baby so she gave me a workout videotape. I'm telling you, there has been someone across the street the whole time. Like, there have been gardeners raking and poking outside those apartments across the street. I've known Henry Cooper for years. He's too cheap to hire out his gardening. He makes his grandsons come do the yardwork.

"And when the gardeners aren't here, someone is climbing the power pole or messin' with the water meter or delivering something. Any one of them alone wouldn't be a problem. It's the entirety of it that has me bothered."

She spread her hands wide.

"Have you tried to talk to any of them? You know, ask them what they're doing?"

"That's another odd thing. When I go out, they kinda drift away, like a stray dog. Staying just out of comfortable talking range."

"Is there anyone out there now?"

"There was a man cleaning out the storm drains. He was bagging the leaves right there on the corner." Neva Dean pointed out the window toward the corner. There were bags of refuse, but no one was visible. "I just can't imagine why anyone would want to watch me."

"Do you have deadbolt locks on your doors?"

"Yes, Danny Junior has checked all my locks, and I have one of those instant call units by my bed. All I have to do is press a button. It has a button on a neck chain, just in case I fall and can't get up. I don't use that piece. I don't think I'm doin' that poorly yet."

"It might not be a bad idea to wear it for a while. I don't know what else to tell you. If they aren't coming on your property, and they aren't threatening you, I don't know what anyone can do. If they come here, call on your buzzer immediately. Let me know if they do anything else."

"I'll call you right away if anything changes." She shivered. "It just makes my hair curl to think they're out there watchin'."

I gave her my home phone number and assured her she could call any time.

"By the way," I added, "would you like to come to the memorial gathering at Mike's uncle's house on Saturday? His mother and possibly his grandmother and great-aunt are coming in from Poland. The funeral service will be on Sunday afternoon. They want to have something more personal so the Polish group can get a feeling for the people who surrounded Mike.

"The funeral will be at St. Stanislaus. I'm guessing it will be pretty formal, and all in Polish. Rebecca left a message at work inviting us both to that, too. I could pick you up here at about six o'clock on Saturday."

"I think that would be nice, honey. You sure you don't mind

comin' over here to get me?"

"It's no problem at all. Andrush lives a couple of blocks from here."

"Then I'd be pleased to come with you. I can bake some apple cake for his family."

"That would be nice. I'll see you here at six. And remember, call me if anything changes." I left and went to my car, wishing Neva Dean had a roommate or that her only neighbor under the age of seventy hadn't just been murdered.

The drive home was uneventful right up until I turned onto my street. A maroon car was parked in my driveway. As I got closer, I could see was an unmarked police car — those bars in the backseat windows give it away every time. As I pulled in beside it, Detective Green got out of the driver's-side door.

"Miss Spring," he said, "you pulling long hours at the factory?"

"I'm not sure that's any of your business."

"Now, don't go getting your feathers ruffled. I just need to ask you a few questions. Can I come in?"

"Where's Detective Harper?" I looked in his car to see if Harper was hiding inside, changing her pantyhose or something. I didn't see any sign of her.

"She should be along any minute. We were supposed to meet here."

"I hope you'll understand if we just wait out here for her."

His expression said he minded a lot, but he didn't argue.

"We wouldn't be alone, you know. There's some old guy in your house. He came crawling up from around the corner about fifteen minutes ago. He was pulling a wagon with a box in it. He let himself in, so I assume he knows you."

My back had been to the house. I turned and looked at the kitchen window. I could see Mr. Johnson working at the sink.

"All right, you win."

I opened the back door, and we were immersed in the smell of carrots and onions simmering in a beef burgundy sauce. The scent of fresh-baked biscuits floated over the top.

"Mr. Johnson, I'm surprised," I said. "I thought Mrs. Johnson was supposed to stay in bed for a few days."

"She is," he said. "I'm taking good care of her." His face flushed with pride. "I cooked some dinner for her. I was a cook in the merchant marine, you know. By the time I got done chopping and mixing I had enough for a small army. I was thinking maybe you could use some stew."

A buzzer went off. Mr. Johnson grabbed a mitt shaped like a pig and pulled a tray of biscuits from the oven.

"Boy, those smell really good," Detective Green said.

"Sit down, there's plenty." Mr. Johnson pulled out one of the chairs at the small table in my kitchen. "Okay, Miss Harley?" he added when I didn't join in extending the invitation.

They both looked at me. What could I say?

"Detective Green, would you care to join me for dinner?"

He sat then took a cloth napkin from the basket on the table and spread it on his lap. Mr. Johnson brought over a big bowl of the steaming stew and a basket of biscuits. I headed toward the hallway out of the kitchen.

"Hey, you aren't going to make me eat alone, are you?" Green asked between bites.

"No, I'm just going to get another chair. You did say Detective Harper was joining us, didn't you."

I went upstairs to get a folding chair. When I came back down Green and Mr. Johnson were chatting like long-lost schoolmates. Mr. J stood as I came into the room.

"I better get back to check on Mother. She was just worried about you since she knew you didn't have any food left." He took the pig off his left hand and grabbed his coat from the rack by the back door.

"Tell Mrs. J I hope she feels better."

"I'll tell her. But don't you worry, I'm taking good care of her."

I could just imagine. She was going to be real ready to get back to work.

"What did he mean you don't have any food left?" Green asked.

"Not that it's any of your business, but most of my food got wrecked in the break-in last night," I said.

"You telling me they actually dumped boxes, broke open food packages, stuff like that?"

"Yeah, is that important?"

"Well, it could tell us something about what they were looking for. Like maybe it was something small enough to be hidden in a cereal box."

"I just assumed they really got into a ripping and tearing frenzy, and they didn't stop to discriminate."

I told him about Banana and then wished I hadn't when my eyes filled with tears. He handed me a handkerchief from his shirt pocket. I glanced at it first and then felt guilty when I saw it was clean and ironed.

"It's really creepy having someone touch all your stuff, huh?"

"Is that what they teach you in cop school?"

"No, that's how my wife and I felt when we got robbed a few years ago."

"You got robbed? Wait a minute, you have a wife?" I'm not usually so rude, but I couldn't imagine a wife letting her husband go around in polyester and ties that were so short. Plus, any woman would make him wash what was left of his hair a little more often.

"Yes, and not anymore. What? You think cops never get robbed? I don't post a sign in the yard that says 'Beware of Cop.'

"When I was married, we lived in a little house in Beaverton. We had a dog door into the garage. Someone squeezed through it and found the door from the garage to the house unlocked. Wanda wasn't home, so they cleaned us out.

"We were on a cul-de-sac that backed up on one of those urban wetland areas. They came and went from the back. Trampled all the plants the school kids had planted. The neighbors saw nothing. They took all Wanda's jewelry and the fly-tying equipment my dad left me when he died. Insurance covered it all. I could of got new fly-tying stuff, but what was the point? I don't tie flies."

"I guess I was lucky, then," I said. "I didn't lose anything of real value. Just my sense of security."

"Yeah, that's a hard one."

We ate our stew in silence.

"It don't look like Harper's going to show up, so maybe I ought to go ahead and ask you what we wanted to know," he said when we were finished. "We just got back the fingerprint analysis from Mr. Wyzcek's apartment. The ones we took the night of the murder. There are some of his, of course, and a few from Miss Valenta, but the place is covered in prints belonging to Debbie DaMore."

Our Kodak moment was over.

"We been trying to find Miss DaMore," he said. "She don't seem to be anywhere. We thought you might be able to help us out."

"As a supervisor, I've been trained to stay out of my employees' personal lives."

"Yeah, but *trained to* and *do* are two different things sometimes."

"Well, not at Sil-Trac. They really expect us to follow their policies."

"So, you have no idea where she is?"

"Since the plant is closed tomorrow while they search for a bomb, I imagine a lot of my people are out starting their weekend early. You could probably find some of them at The Blue Whale." I was pretty sure Debbie wouldn't be at the Whale, but I was also trained not to start rumors.

"I'll be going, then," he said. "Thanks for the dinner."

"I'll thank Mr. Johnson for you."

"You get any ideas about Miss DaMore, you got my number."

With that, Detective Green went out the back door, got in his car and drove away.

CHAPTER SIXTEEN

I HAD A FEW HOURS TO kill before Noah's plane arrived. I started in his room and cleaned, picked up and repaired everything salvageable. By the time I finished, I had another garbage bag full of stuff.

My garbage cans are beside the garage. I half-dragged, half-carried the bag out the back door. As I wrestled it down the steps, I heard what sounded like a dog barking. My dog barking. I dropped the bag and called his name. All I heard was the sound of canned laughter on a TV program coming from the house behind mine. I decided my ears were playing tricks on me and finished disposing of my garbage.

Noah's best friend is a kid named Chris. Their major bonding point was that they didn't fit in with the other kids in the neighborhood. I called Chris and let him know Noah was going to be home tonight. As I had suspected, Chris asked if he could come over. I decided it might help distract Noah from the Sonny issue, so I said yes.

Noah's mini-blinds were bent beyond repair. I decided to go to the local discount store at 74th and Interstate. If I hit the lights right, I could get there and back in less than an hour.

When I got home, I not only had replacement blinds but curtains for my room and new pillows for the sofa. I never did like the old sofa pillows. They must have repulsed the thief, too. They were one of the few unscathed items in my house. Throwing them out gave me back a feeling of control.

I really like the new shopping concept in America. In those mega-discount stores, you can buy hardware and plumbing supplies and then wheel on over to the ice cream freezer before you check out. I did just that. I figured I deserved a little chocolate ice cream after the day I was having.

I was back home in fifty-six minutes. After I got Noah's blinds up, I headed straight for the freezer. I rolled up two perfect balls of the ice cream then drowned them in chocolate syrup. I've learned to sit at the kitchen table when I'm handling this much chocolate, but not before sacrificing most of the white shirts I own to indelible drips. I could see the light on the answering machine blinking, so I reached over and hit the play button.

The first three messages were the usual "Mr. Spring" communications. Did I want my carpets cleaned? Did Mr. Spring want them to send him a new low-low-interest-rate credit card? Did he want to hear about the latest in window innovations? When Noah was home, he wouldn't write down messages from anyone who didn't know that Harley Spring was female.

The double chocolate fudge ice cream had transported me to a place of pure chocolate bliss. I was barely conscious of the messages when a familiar voice broke my revere.

"Harley, it's me, Debbie. Can you meet me tonight? I just can't do this anymore. I need to talk to you. I'll be at the Whale at twelve-thirty tonight. Can you come, please?"

One of the things I hate most about answering machines is the fact the control freaks in your life can make you listen to their demands without you being able to talk back. Noah's plane didn't get in until eleven. Being at the Whale an hour and a half later would be damned inconvenient. On the other hand, if the police were still chasing her, she might have something interesting to say.

Debbie's problem had to go on the shelf for a while so I could concentrate on how to tell Noah about Sonny. My first idea was to say nothing. I rejected that one when I thought of Noah coming in the house calling for the dog and getting no response. I thought briefly of going for the out-and-out lie: "Sonny is at the vet's." I knew I wasn't a good enough liar to pull off that one. Noah would have lots of questions. And he would worry. Probably even want to go see him.

No, that was no good. I finally decided on the "Sonny decided to take a little vacation" option. I laid out the citation from Multnomah County, which was proof Sonny was alive and well. After all, he'd bitten someone, hadn't he?

Neva Dean would be proud of me.

I felt considerably better as I got the car out and headed for the airport. When I got inside PDX, the monitors showed that Noah's flight was on time so I went straight to the meet-and-greet area. Within moments, people began oozing out of the exit tube, blinking their eyes in the bright lights. Noah must have been sitting in the tail section. I was beginning to think he had missed his flight when he finally came out just ahead of the pilots and attendants.

"Hey, Noah. How's it going?" I asked in my best cheery-mom voice.

"Fine," he mumbled as I hugged his rigid body.

"Was your flight okay?"

"Uh-huh"

"Are you hungry? Should we stop at Mickey D's on the way home?"

"Naw." He walked a little ahead of me, following the crowd toward the baggage claim area. This wasn't going according to script. Noah didn't know about Sonny already, did he?

"Noah, honey, what's wrong?"

"Nothing."

He was right— this probably wasn't the place to talk. I scrapped my plan to tell him about Sonny on the way home.

We got his duffel bag from the baggage conveyor and walked to the car in silence. Things didn't thaw any during the trip home. When we pulled into the drive, I stopped the car without pulling into the garage.

"Noah, I need to tell you some things before we go in."

"What if I don't want to hear it?"

"I'm sorry, that's not an option."

"What a big surprise."

"Look, Noah, I don't know what's bugging you, but whatever it is, it doesn't give you the right to be rude to me. I've gone to a lot of trouble to bring you home for the weekend. The least you could do is be civil."

"Don't do me any favors."

"Noah!"

"I didn't ask to be shipped home, did I?"

"Was something going on at school?"

"Would it make any difference?"

Great. Not only was I bringing him home to a mess, I had probably ripped him out of something at school that would have helped him get adjusted there. I was batting a thousand.

"We can hash this out inside, but I need to tell you what happened before you go in there." I took his silence as a sign to go ahead. "Someone broke in here Wednesday night and pretty well trashed the place — "

"Did anyone get hurt? Did they hurt Sonny?"

"Well, no...not exactly. Mrs. Johnson got hit on the head and tied up, but she's fine. She just got a slight concussion. Cher is fine..."

"What happened to Sonny? What aren't you telling me?"

"Sonny is fine, as far as I know."

"What do you mean? Harley, tell me what's going on."

"I was hoping to find a better way to tell you this, but Sonny is on a little vacation."

"Did you get rid of my dog when you shipped me off to the pen?"

"Noah, get a grip. You are not in the pen, and I didn't get rid of Sonny. He just decided to take a little vacation."

"How can you joke about this?" he yelled, his voice breaking. "He could be lying in a ditch hurt. Have you called all the vets?"

I reached out and put my hand on his arm. "Calm down, Noah. Mrs. Johnson and I have put signs up everywhere. And we have reason to believe he is okay and nearby. He bit someone about a block from here yesterday. Someone probably has found him and will see our signs and return him."

"Can we just go in?"

"Yeah, that's all I needed to tell you."

Noah went to his room to stash his stuff and stayed just long enough that I was beginning to review what options I would have if he refused to come out for the whole weekend. When he did come out, he started calling Cher. She came thundering down the stairs from the attic room.

"Why don't you see if you can get her to sit with you in the living room," I said. "She seems to be avoiding the places where the intruders tore things up. She basically hasn't come out of the attic since it happened. I finally moved her food and water up there, but I really don't want to move her kitty pan. I've been carrying her down to use it, then she runs right back. Maybe she'll be so thrilled to see you, she won't notice the change in scenery. You could just kind of sit there with her."

"Is that what you thought about me? I wouldn't notice if you moved me to a prison?" Noah's dark eyes flashed.

"Noah, I don't think it's a good idea to rehash this when we are both so tired, but I've told you more than once this military school idea wasn't mine. I would have been happy to have you right here, but your dad wants you to have an education he didn't think Portland Public Schools could provide."

"He could have sent me to private school here. Or home school me, like Chris."

Chris was a high-tech whiz kid. He and Noah had been in a Boy Scout troop that met at one of the electronics companies in town. One night while Chris was waiting for his turn on a CAD system, he wandered into a designer's cubicle and, seeing a circuit with what he perceived as a flaw in it, he left a note on the designer's desk saying how it should be corrected. It turned out a team of engineers had been working day and night trying to solve the problem.

After they tracked Chris down and talked to him, they contacted his parents and volunteered to underwrite his education from that point on. Now Chris worked with tutors half the day and designed circuits at the company the other half.

"I'm not saying you're not smart, but Chris is a very special case, a computer and electronics genius. By the way, did I mention I called him and he's coming over tonight?"

"Why would you suddenly start telling me anything?"

"Noah, it's going to be a long weekend if you keep on like this."

Before we could go any farther, there was a tap on the door. Chris let himself in. The boys went through some hand-slapping, hip-bumping routine known only to each other.

"Chris, just so you know, since the break-in I've been arming the alarm even when we're home, so be careful. Make sure someone knows you're coming in."

"Don't worry, I know how to disarm it if no one's here."

Somehow, this news didn't cheer me up. If a fifteen-year-old boy can get around my system, how safe should that make me feel?

"Listen, guys, I need to go out for a little while. Will you be okay here alone?"

They both looked at me as if I was speaking in a foreign tongue.

"I thought you dragged me home so we could spend some 'quality time' together," Noah said. "I haven't even been home an hour and now you're leaving?"

"Do you boys want me to stay here and visit with you?"

"Not really. I just wanted to make sure I had the picture," Noah said. "You were feeling guilty so you sent for me. You didn't really care about seeing me."

"Noah, I promise you, we are going to talk about this. Just not now."

I checked the clock in the kitchen. It was ten minutes before midnight. If I didn't waste time, I would just make it to the Whale in time to meet Debbie.

My plan would have worked if I hadn't chosen to cross the river on the Burnside Bridge. I had just driven up the approach when the flashing lights went on and the barrier went down. It was hard to imagine why they needed to raise the bridge at midnight, but raise it they did. By the time they finished and traffic was able to cross again, it was twenty minutes past midnight.

There was plenty of time as I waited at the bridge to contemplate why Debbie Dayshift wanted to see me after midnight on a Thursday night. None of the options was real good. You couldn't escape the fact she had been at Mike's apartment during the window of time when he was shot. On top of that, it was possible she was working for one of the direct competitors of Sil-Trac. Debbie didn't seem sophisticated enough to be an industrial spy, but you never know.

When I was finally on the highway headed for the Whale, another possibility occurred to me. The timing of this meeting could have something to do with the fact that a bomb was supposed to be going off at Sil-Trac tomorrow. Debbie didn't fit my image of a mad bomber, yet here I was meeting her in the middle of the night before the blast.

I just can't do this anymore, she had said. But what couldn't she do?

The Whale stays open until two or three in the morning. I pulled in to the parking lot at twelve-fifty. Debbie's battered red pickup truck was parked near the door. She must have been pretty sure I would show up. Either that, or she was drowning her sorrows at the bar and didn't notice I was late.

A car that looked vaguely familiar was parked beside it.

❧ ❧ ❧

"I can't believe you're still here, Skip," I said.

"Me? What are you doin' here after midnight? This ain't your end of town."

"Have you gone home since the last time I saw you?"

"Sure, what do you think? Andy don't know the law? I go home for at least seven, eight hours a day."

"Which means you're working sixteen hours a day? You know, there are limits to how many hours a guy is supposed to work in a day."

"Yeah, but this ain't work, now, is it?"

"Good point. Have you seen Debbie DaMore tonight? She called me and asked me to meet her here."

"Yeah, she's here somewhere." Skip looked around through the smoky haze, squinting at the lighted pool table area. "I don't see her, but I know she's here. Maybe she went into the powder room. Hey, Ralph," he yelled across to the drunk maintenance man, who was slumped over one of the tables in a booth. "You seen Debbie?"

It was pretty clear Ralph hadn't seen anyone in the last few hours. He barely moved his head at the sound of his name.

"You aren't going to let him drive like that, are you?" I asked.

"Harley, I'm hurt," said Skip with mock indignation. "I cut him off about an hour and a half ago. I'll let him sleep another two hours and then wake him up and start pouring coffee down him. He ain't gonna feel great by closing, but he will be able to drive."

"I'm going to go check out the ladies room. If she shows up before I come out, tell her I'm here."

Some of Skip's patrons went for regular trips out to their cars to indulge in substances not sold in the Whale. I didn't think Debbie was part of that crowd, but you never knew.

The bathroom of The Blue Whale is much like any other tavern bathroom. They must sell a special air freshener just for these places. It was a combination of my grandmother's perfume and smelling salts. It could sober all but the truly plastered with one whiff.

I couldn't hear anything but my own breathing as I looked at the three stalls. The doors to the first two were open. When I got to the handicapped stall, the door was closed; but then again, they usually are, since they open the opposite way from the other stalls. I bent down to look under the door and saw Debbie's feet, the soles facing me. She must have passed out in the stall.

CHAPTER SEVENTEEN

I REACHED UNDER AND wiggled Debbie's foot. She was sitting with her back against the rear wall. Her foot was limp, and the motion caused her torso to slump sideways to the floor. I couldn't stifle my gasp when her face came into view. Her skin was waxy and pale blue. A neat hole, like a third eye, stared at me from her forehead.

It took me three tries before I could make my hand reach over and touch her neck to feel for a pulse. I didn't find one, but then, I knew I wouldn't. Nobody could look like that and get over it.

I must have been in shock. I felt like I was watching myself from a distance, going through motions but not feeling anything. I saw myself go into the next stall and throw up. I heard someone call to Skip from the bathroom doorway. I didn't recognize the voice, but it must have been mine.

"Geez, Harley," he said, "what's wrong with you? You sick?"

"No, not me. It's Debbie. Call the police."

He started to push past me into the restroom. I grabbed his arm roughly.

"You don't want to go in there."

"If she's sick, I can help her. Believe me, I've done this a few times."

"It's not that, Skip," I said. "We can talk after you call the police."

"What am I gonna tell the police? I got a sick woman in the john?"

"Tell them you've got a dead body in the ladies room."

"Oh, geez," he said as the words sank in. His face turned pale.

He turned around slowly and went to the phone behind the bar. I could hear him make the call, but I couldn't focus on what he was saying. When he put the phone down, he poured himself a shot of whiskey, downed it quickly then set a diet cola on the bar in front of me.

"You ready to tell me what happened in there?" he asked.

"There isn't much to tell. I saw Debbie's feet under the door. I figured she passed out. I wiggled her foot, she tipped over and I could see her face. Someone shot her. Right between the eyes."

"Geez, that's really awful. Are you sure she's really dead?"

"I'm sure, Skip."

There didn't seem to be anything left to say, so we sat in silence until the police arrived.

The paramedics got there in less than five minutes. They quickly pronounced Debbie dead then left the crime scene until the police criminalists could get there. The police told Skip and me to wait at the bar for the detectives. We were still waiting when Tommy Chan came through the door.

"Hey, boss, what's happening?" he asked.

"What are you doing out here at this hour?"

"My dad's cousin has the Chinese restaurant down the road in Cornelius. His son and I went out to the clubs tonight. I was just bringing him home and saw all the police cars. When I got closer, I saw Debbie's truck, Shannon's car and your car. Thought I'd check out the action." He looked around. "Where's Debbie?"

Skip looked at me, and when I didn't say anything he jumped in.

"We got some bad news, Tommy," he said. "Somebody snuffed Debbie tonight."

It wasn't exactly how I would have phrased it, but Tommy got the point.

"You mean snuffed like dead?"

"You got the picture," Skip said. "Shot right between the eyes."

Tommy's face was unreadable. "I can't believe it," he said. "I just talked to her a couple of hours ago. She can't be dead."

"Skip and I were pretty shocked, too," I said. "When you talked to her, did she happen to mention wanting to talk to me?"

"She was mainly talking about Rebecca," Tommy said. "You know she believes Rebecca killed Mike. Maybe she thought of something new about that."

"That's crazy," I said. "Rebecca found Mike, but he'd been dead for hours, according to the police. Rebecca was at Sil-Trac when he was killed. Debbie seemed to be unwilling to accept that fact, but I think this was something else. She sounded like she wanted to unload something."

Tommy shook hid head in confusion.

"Tommy, I want you to tell me something," I was on a roll. "Was Debbie working at MiCorp?"

He didn't say anything for a minute. He shifted on his barstool and took a long, slow drink from the glass Skip had put in front of him.

"I guess it doesn't make any difference now," he said. "Yeah, she was working the night shift there. She was just a regular operator, though."

"Was she passing information to them," I asked. "I need to know the truth."

"No," he said and looked at me with one of those "you have to be kidding" looks. "No, she wasn't doing anything. She just needed more money. I mean no disrespect, but I don't think Debbie was clever enough to be a spy.

"She has a little boy who lives with her ex. She just wanted to get a better place so her son could come spend some time with her this summer. She was only going to do it for a few months. MiCorp is so desperate for workers they're willing to accommodate people with flexible hours. Debbie told them she was going to school."

"You're sure about this?" I asked. "Would she tell you the truth?"

"Debbie and I were tight. She told me everything. She used to come to my dad's restaurant every Sunday night for the buffet. Sometimes I work in the lounge — Skip knows. People tell you anything if you keep the drinks coming."

"Well, I'm glad to hear she wasn't spying. But if it wasn't spying, what would make someone want to kill her?"

"I can't imagine, boss." Tommy said. "Her life was pretty much an open book. Maybe she was just in the wrong place at the wrong time. You know, someone looking for some easy money to buy drugs."

"We don't have them kind of people here," Skip said. Like any good bartender, he did a lot of surreptitious listening, but he couldn't let an insult to his establishment go unchallenged.

The Blue Whale is located beyond the boundaries of the Portland Police, so the two local detectives who came to question us were strangers. Skip was able to verify I had arrived moments before I discovered Debbie, and the deputy medical examiner guessed she had been dead at least a half-hour, probably a little more. Tommy arrived after the fact, and several patrons could verify that Skip hadn't been out of sight all evening. We were given the usual admonitions about being available for further questioning and told we could go home.

The Blue Whale was not designed with security in mind. The short hallway that led to the bathrooms ended in an emergency exit that opened onto an undeveloped grassy area. Skip's boss had disconnected the alarm on it because patrons who couldn't negotiate the two doors into the restrooms used it so often. Anyone could have come and gone unnoticed.

CHAPTER EIGHTEEN

I T WAS ONE-THIRTY WHEN I finally left the tavern. The drive home was uneventful, unless you count the thrill of watching the needle on my gas gauge slip from the white zone onto the orange empty line. I spent most of the drive calculating how many miles I had left to go and comparing that to my recent gas mileage for the one gallon of gas I probably had left. There were no all-night gas stations on my route.

I finally gave up counting and just prayed for the last five miles. North Portland is not the kind of place you want to run out of gas at one-forty-five on a Friday morning. Neighborhoods like mine are islands surrounded by drugs and gangs and prostitutes. We're all hoping that eventually we can get the islands big enough to squeeze out the undesirable elements. For now, we've all just learned to be careful.

I had broken a cardinal safety rule by going out at night with a nearly empty gas tank. All the death I'd seen in the last few days had made me a little careless. I didn't know what I was facing at work. Worse, I didn't know when and where it would end. *My* gangs were at least a familiar danger.

Noah and Chris were in the kitchen drinking hot chocolate — Chris's mom had sent a thermos along with a plate of chocolate chip cookies. I guess everyone on the block had heard about my break-in. They were my kind of people. When in doubt and no matter the occasion, send chocolate.

"I told Chris he could spend the night," Noah said, laying down the challenge.

"I figured he would," I countered. I made a quick decision not to tell the boys what had happened tonight. "Since we don't have any food yet, how about I take you boys out for pancakes in the morning? We could go to the Original Pancake and Steak House on Powell."

Noah had to think about that one. OP-and-S was one of his favorites. Chris looked at him.

"I guess we could do that," he said.

Chris let out his breath. "Man, I was afraid you were going to say no."

"I might be mad, but I'm not crazy," he answered and headed for his room.

My sleep was troubled that night. I had dreams filled with dachshunds and dead bodies. The wiener dogs would dig big holes in a yard that was strange yet strangely familiar. When the hole was so deep I couldn't see the dogs, I would suddenly shift perspectives and be looking down into the hole. Debbie was always at the bottom, only a real third eye replaced the bullethole. The eye was blue and lifeless. The eyelid was open, and the eye stared at me. She was clothed in some kind of clerical robe. The kind Roman Catholic priests wear on special occasions. Sometimes, she had large silver coins on her other two eyes. Or all three eyes would be open, and the lower two would look at me as if she was about to speak. I would wake up just before I could hear what she was saying.

It was a relief when daylight finally arrived. The boys were still sleeping and would probably stay that way most of the morning. I had brought copies of the production logs from all my work groups home so I could study the count problem. After yesterday, the count problem seemed small and safe. If I could solve that, I could regain some measure of control over my life.

I had left the papers in my car, so I went out to the garage. When I opened the trunk, the Black Madonna stared at me. My car was not a great place to keep a religious icon. I took it inside along with my papers and the package of smoked fish Neva Dean had sent to Cher.

Noah and I never used the hidden safe Sam had installed behind the electrical box. It was our way of saying we didn't really believe the cloak-and-dagger story that was his explanation for being a flake. He had taught me how to open it before he left the first time. As soon as he was gone, I'd opened it and surveyed the contents. It held a couple of sealed envelopes marked "open only if I'm dead." A couple of larger bundles looked a lot like stacks of cash. Up to this point, I hadn't opened any of the packages. I didn't want to support his psychosis.

I took the back off the picture frame and removed the old canvas. I wasn't sure how you were supposed to handle such an item, so I layered paper towels over it and put it in a big brown mailing envelope. I put this package in the safe, replaced the Black Madonna in her frame and returned it to the trunk of my car. I put the fish in the refrigerator.

The production records were in a big archive box. I brought them into the living room and spread them out on the floor according to area. I had just finished organizing them by date when the boys got up.

"Wow, what's all this?" Chris asked.

"It's a big headache from work," I replied. "The count of our product is off from area to area and we have a big inspection of our records coming up that's real important to our customers."

"You must mean ISO nine thousand," Chris said. I tend to forget that, despite his tender age, he spends a lot of time in the adult world of manufacturing.

"Noah's really good with numbers. Maybe we could look at it for you."

Noah glared at Chris, who just shrugged.

"I don't want to impose," I said. "If you don't want to, just say so."

Noah had been into fractal geometry before he left. I had only the slightest grasp of what fractal geometry was. The books he read all had *chaos* in the title, though. Somehow, it seemed appropriate for this task. Chaos came to my mind a lot when I looked at the lab records.

"Well, maybe we could look," he said. "There's nothing else to do here. Don't expect anything, though."

"Great," I said in a voice that sounded false even to me. "Let's go to breakfast first."

"We want to look first and get it over with," Noah replied. He looked at Chris to see if he would object.

"Fine."

I showed the boys how the stacks were organized then went into the kitchen to make tea. After about a half-hour, Chris came in to ask a question about how things were recorded in the scribe area, the point where each wafer containing multiple die is broken into individual pieces. I told him the count multiplies up to a die count from a wafer count.

"I know that much," he said. "What I need to know is how you count broken wafers."

I explained our procedure. Officially, we didn't process broken wafers, but I knew there were times when we made exceptions. Chris frowned at this news and went back to the living room.

Noah came into the kitchen an hour later. I was up to my elbows in clean-up activities.

"Are there any of those cookies left from last night?" he asked. "You know they don't let us have sweets at the prison."

I looked up and saw just a brief flash of the old Noah.

"How's it going in there?" I handed him the half-filled plate of cookies.

"Don't get your hopes up, but I think we're on to something." He turned and went back to the living room.

I fooled around in the kitchen a few more minutes. I tried to think of a good reason that would take me into the living room. In the end, I just barged in.

"I can't stand it. I have to know. What have you found?"

"If you'll take us to breakfast, we'll tell you," Noah said.

"You drive a hard bargain."

"I learned it from you."

CHAPTER NINETEEN

HE DRIVE FROM NORTHEAST to southeast Portland is a pretty one if you take the neighborhood streets. There is a sense of permanence in older gardens. No amount of bark dust or carefully placed river rock can recreate the elegance of hundred-year-old Douglas fir trees.

Even the streets have become riots of color and style. English-style botanical gardens with their tall clumps of perennials are stem-to-stem with natural yards planted in Oregon grape with azaleas and rhodies, or formal beds of roses waiting for the annual festival that is their namesake.

There were daffodils blooming in almost every garden. I didn't see any of it. I drove with both hands on the wheel and eyes straight ahead. Chris and Noah decided it would be too hard to explain their theory unless we were sitting down and they were full. I intended to accomplish this in record time.

The boys enjoyed my agony; and once we got to the Original Pancake and Steak House, they took their time ordering. Both boys started with stacks of fluffy pancakes and sides of crisp bacon. They moved on to those big waffle creations that are covered in fruit and whipped cream. They washed it all down with big glasses of orange juice followed by Cokes. A teenager's stomach must be like a pregnant woman's womb. There seemed to be no end to the quantity Chris and Noah were able to stuff in without apparent pain.

Noah finally took mercy on me.

"Are you ready to hear what we found?"

A thousand quick comebacks came to mind. "Yes," I said. "Tell me what you have."

Chris laid a chart and some of the lab log copies on the table. "We were looking at all the yield rates — " he began.

"Someone is robbing you blind," Noah jumped in.

Chris glared at him. "That's only one explanation."

"What other one makes sense?" Noah shot back.

"You're right, but I thought we were going to play it cool and see if Harley came to that conclusion on her own."

"We were, but she was getting too nervous." Noah looked at me.

"Could someone tell me what's going on?"

"Show her the chart, Chris," Noah said.

Chris reshuffled the papers and produced the requested chart. He blocked a part of it with his napkin.

"Notice there is a line for each of your areas," Noah continued. "Each area except one has a random pattern of yield loss. If you notice, we plotted the daily yields. From week to week and month to month, you have a consistent line. It slopes up a little, which must mean you're improving with time. That's how the computer gives it to you.

"But we looked at the daily numbers and charted them. Look at this one. They had ninety-five percent one day and eighty percent the next and ninety-three the day after that. If you follow their line for months, you never see the exact same yield pattern two weeks in a row."

"What's the punchline?"

Chris moved the napkin aside. The line he revealed was as regular as the cornrows in my garden. Each day was different for three weeks, but then the pattern repeated itself. Again and again. I stared at it.

"We thought that looked a little weird," Noah said. "By itself it could mean several things."

"Yeah," Chris joined in. "Like maybe it reflects a particular combination of products that go through that area, or maybe there's some environmental influence, like when they service machines or clean filters."

"But we couldn't figure out how that would result in this kind of line," Noah said. "And why it didn't affect any other area the same way."

"That's when my man here got a brilliant idea," Chris said. He put his arm around Noah's shoulders. Noah shrugged him off.

"It wasn't that brilliant," he said. "It was mostly just dumb luck."

"Anyway," Chris continued, "Noah said we should look at the yield by wafer from start to finish. It doesn't look like you always track it by wafer, but someone did for a couple of months. At least in some of the areas."

"And we had to guess a little," Noah said. "Your workers seem to have a little trouble counting. But their errors are usually just one or two here or there."

"And so...?"

Noah took up the story again. "This sounds crazy, but listen. It looks like some of your lots grow a bunch in the middle of the process. Wafers that are noted as being broken in the photo area yield one hundred percent at the finish end of things."

"That's impossible," I said and sank back against the wooden booth.

"We think we know how it was done," Chris said, "on paper, anyway. It looks like someone adds in a couple of wafers at the second step in the process, but they don't get recorded like normal. Then, just before the end, they sprinkle a few in to fix the yield, and the rest of the extras just disappear."

"You think they're being stolen?"

"What do you think?" Noah asked.

"I think you sound like a therapist," I said. "It's hard to believe anyone would go to such trouble just to make their yield chart look pretty, though."

"Don't you read the trade rags, Harley?" Chris asked. "Chip thefts are an epidemic in California."

"The key word there is California." I said.

"There have been a few here," Noah said. "Remember that one a couple of years ago. I think it was in Tualatin. Our teacher talked about it in current affairs class. She said a couple of million dollars-worth of stuff was taken."

"I can't believe it," I said.

"Well," Noah said, that defensive tone creeping back into his voice. "It's the only thing that makes sense."

I reached across the table and put a hand on each boy's arm.

"I don't mean I don't believe you guys. I mean I'm just kind of shocked. A lot has gone on in the last couple of days." My head was spinning with all the new possibilities. "Guys, promise me you will not say a word to anyone about this until I tell you it's okay.

"Oh, right," Noah said. "Like we know a lot of people who care."

"Please, this is serious," I said. "Both of you promise."

They each held up a pinkie finger and hooked them into mine.

"Pinkie swear," they said in unison.

CHAPTER TWENTY

WE GOT BACK INTO THE CAR and pulled out of the driveway.

"Do you boys mind if we make a quick stop at St. Stanislaus Church on the way home?"

"Do we have a choice?" Noah asked.

"Yes," I said. "Despite the inconvenience, I could drive you all the way home and then go back."

"Are you sure you aren't Catholic?" Chris asked. He was convinced I was the only human on earth that knew how to lay on guilt better than his mother did.

"Could we stop at the comic book store on the way home?" Noah asked.

"You got a deal," I said and headed for the church.

When we got there, Noah and Chris took one look at the neighborhood and decided to come into the church with me. We went in a side door. Only the daylight coming in through the unadorned windows lit the hallway. There was a door at the end of a passageway. Incandescent light spilled into the hallway from a room attached to the door.

"Let's go down there," I whispered to the boys.

"Why are you whispering?" Noah asked in a normal voice.

Chris jabbed him hard in the ribs.

"Ouch," he said.

Chris gave him a dirty look.

A woman in a floral cotton dress and no makeup stepped through the doorway.

"Can I help you?" she asked.

"I'd like to get some information about religious icons. Is there

122

anyone here I could talk to?"

"It depends on what you want to know," she said. "I can tell you about icons in general, and I'm familiar with most of the well-known pieces held by the Catholic Church. I'm not an appraiser, but I have studied a little art history. What is it, exactly, you wish to know?"

"I've got a friend who is coming here from Poland. She has an icon that has been in her family since the late fifteen-hundreds. Being destitute, she is wondering what value it might have."

The woman covered her mouth with her hand and looked into the distance.

"I couldn't give you an accurate guess without seeing the piece, of course," she said. "But if it's in good condition, and it's more than a few centuries old, then it would be priceless. As an icon ages it moves beyond its value as a religious item and gains value simply as an antiquity. Your Nikes will be priceless after a few hundred years. If you keep them in good condition, that is."

"Thank you," I said, "That's what I wanted to know."

I turned to go.

"If your friend truly has such an object, she needs to insure it right away against theft, before anyone knows it's here," the woman said. "As soon as she does that, she should take it to the art museum and get them to assess its preservation needs."

An image of the painting rolled up in paper towels flashed through my mind.

"What kind of needs might those be?"

"I'm not an expert," she said, "but humidity and temperature control are important as well as light exposure."

"Thanks for the information," I said.

We both knew I wasn't telling the whole truth. I didn't want to risk having that said aloud while we were in church.

"What was that all about?" Noah asked as soon as we cleared the building. "Did we get some new art I don't know about, too?"

"Noah, this is going to be a long weekend if you keep on like this," I said. "And no, *we* didn't get any art. One of my workers asked me to hold on to something for her. I just wanted to know what it might be worth."

"Is it really from the sixteenth century?" Chris asked.

"Maybe," I said.

"You mean you lied to a church woman?" he said. "You're bad, Harley, really bad."

"It *might* be that old, so it's not a total lie."

"Only you would see that distinction, Harley," Noah commented.

We got in the car and drove to Noah and Chris's favorite comic bookstore on northeast Sandy Boulevard, the so-called Hollywood district. The area showed signs of becoming the kind of yuppie hangout that Hawthorne and northeast Broadway had become. I felt sorry for the locals.

I was trying to gain parenting points, so after I bought the boys each a handful of comics, I swung the car into the drive-thru window at McDonalds. I wasn't surprised when they both ordered full meals.

The drive home was silent, except for the muffled sounds of boys consuming hamburgers. When we arrived home, I parked close to the garden hose at the side of the house.

"I wouldn't want to impose," I said. "But if anyone wanted to wash the car I wouldn't mind."

"I should have known there would be a price to pay for the comic stop," Noah complained.

"Lighten up a little," Chris told him. "I'll get Mr. Chang's hose from next door. We can have a duel like we used to."

The boys were still talking as I got out of the car.

"Guys, hush a second," I said. "Do you hear that?"

They were silent for a minute.

"I don't hear anything," Noah said.

"Me, either," Chris chimed in.

"I was probably just hearing things," I said. I shut my car door and headed for the house.

"What did you hear?" Noah asked.

"Nothing," I said. I could see the muscle in his jaw twitch. "Okay, I thought I heard Sonny barking. It was faint, but it sounded like Sonny."

"I think you're losing it, Harley," Noah said.

We stood staring at each other. I felt helpless. I couldn't do anything to make things better for him. I didn't like this feeling.

Chris opened the garage door and grabbed a couple of sponges from the workbench. He threw one at Noah.

"Come on. Let's wash the car before it starts raining again."

I glanced at the blue sky and went in the house.

The light on my answering machine was blinking, so I kicked off my shoes and pushed the play button. Detective Green's voice came growling out of the machine.

"Harley, the forensics people found something you ought to see at Debbie DaMore's apartment. I'll come by in a while and see if you're home. Oh, and, uh, by the way, it's noon and, uh, this is Green."

I looked at my watch; it was after one. I wondered when "in a while" was. I didn't have to wonder long. I reorganized my kitchen desk and then looked out the window to check on Chris and Noah. Detective Green was talking to them. It looked like he was showing them the finer points of bug and tar removal.

I opened the back door and waited. He looked up and saw me, finished his demonstration and came to the door.

"What was so important it required a personal visit," I said.

"Good afternoon to you, too," he said.

I stood in the doorway.

"Do you think I could come in a little?"

"Oh, yes. I'm sorry. Come in. Would you like some tea?"

Green grabbed a chair and bellied up to the table like it was an old friend. "That sounds great."

I filled the kettle with hot water and put it on the stove to boil. I set two mugs on the counter and got out a box of tea bags.

"Is Earl Grey okay with you?"

"Sure, sounds great."

We didn't speak. I poured the hot water into the cups when it boiled. I turned around and set the two cups on the table. Green grabbed his and wrapped his hands around it as if he were cold.

"Okay, Detective, you've got your tea. Can we get to the point? Why are you here?"

"Geez, lady, are you always this friendly?"

"I'm sorry, it's been a tough week. Look, we aren't friends, and correct me if I'm wrong, but this isn't a social call, is it?"

"You're right, it's not a social visit, but we don't have to be enemies, do we?" He held his hand up when he saw a protest forming on my face. "The reason I came by in person is to ask you a favor."

"What?" I asked. "You called and said you had something to show me just so you could ask a favor?"

"I do have something to show you. Actually, the original is in evidence. I have a copy to show you, if you can lighten up."

"All right, talk. What do you want?"

"Here, I'll show you what I've got."

He pulled several folded sheets from his coat pocket. I took the papers and glanced at each sheet. There was no need to read them in detail. I'd seen them before. They were the sexual harassment claims filed against me.

"You found these at Debbie DaMore's house?" I asked.

"Yeah, we did. And another one was in her computer ready to go."

"I can't believe it," I said. "Debbie DaMore was trying to frame me for sexual harassment? Oh, my God." I sat back in my chair. The possibilities wrapped themselves around my brain.

"This woman was framing you for sexual harassment, pretending to be her ex-boyfriend who happens to get himself killed and then she gets herself killed. And they both work for you. Somehow, I think you know something you aren't telling me. Like the way you never mentioned about the sexual harassment claims. Course, I guess it would have been awkward to bring it up at the scene of his death, huh?"

"I didn't know about it then," I said, a bit too quickly. "They date-stamp all paper that comes into the Human Resource Department at Sil-Trac. The first claim didn't come in until after Mike was killed."

"That makes no sense," Green said. "Could it have been stuck in the mail?"

"My contact says it was hand-delivered to the office. With Mike dead, there would be no point. I don't understand why Debbie would want me out of the picture. She wanted Mike back and hated Rebecca, but I was the one who promoted her to lead operator."

As I said the words, I felt a knot in my stomach. If Noah and Chris were right, Debbie might have a good reason to want me out of the way. Maybe I was getting too close to solving the count problem. Or maybe Mike was. Or maybe he was part of the theft ring. I found it hard to believe.

"Hello," Green said. "You just went somewhere else. You want to tell me about it?"

"I just can't believe Debbie was filing the sexual harassment claims. Frankly, I didn't think she had the brains for something like this."

"Apparently, she didn't. If you're right, she waited till he was dead to turn the claim in."

We drank our tea for a moment in silence.

"What was the favor you wanted?" I asked.

"I understand there's a private memorial service for Mike tonight at his uncle's place."

"You're half-right. There's a service, but it's tomorrow night."

Green pulled out a tattered spiral-bound book and scratched a few words down.

"You think you could get me an invite?"

"People don't generally invite total strangers to their private gatherings," I said. "Especially when they're homicide detectives."

"They do if the stranger is dating a friend of the family."

"You have got to be kidding."

"Don't flatter yourself, honey," he said. "You aren't my first pick for Friday night bowling, either."

"I don't suppose I have a choice."

A slow smile spread across his face.

"Meet me here at five-thirty tomorrow afternoon. And by the way, if you want them to think you're my date, try to wear something from this decade."

I stood and went upstairs.

CHAPTER TWENTY-ONE

WATCHED GREEN FROM THE upstairs window. He paused by my car and inspected the bug-and-tar removal job Chris and Noah had done. He must have said something. Both boys grinned.

He slapped Noah on the back and walked toward his car. They must have called after him. He turned, said something, smiled and waved before finally getting in and driving away. How dare he charm Noah?

I went back to the kitchen. The boys finished washing the car and came in.

"Who was that dude?" Noah asked.

"That guy that was just here?"

"No, the guy that was here last week," Noah answered. "Of course, the guy that was just here. Who is he? You have a boyfriend you 'forgot' to tell me about?"

"No, I don't have a boyfriend. If you must know, he's a police detective."

"Have they found out who robbed you?" Chris asked.

"No, he was here for something else."

"Come on, Harley, spill." Noah said. "Why is a detective calling on you if it isn't about the break-in?" His face clouded. "Did you already know about the chip thefts? Were you just giving us busy work to keep us out of your hair?"

"If you'd be quiet a minute, I could tell you." I thought briefly about how to describe what had happened in the last few days.

"He came to ask me to take him to a private memorial service for one of my employees." I continued, "The man I had working on the count problem went away for the weekend, and when he came

128

back, someone killed him."

"Geez, did he figure out about the thefts?" Noah asked. "Is that why he was killed?"

"I'm not really sure. He had some family problems. There is no indication in his notes that he was on to anything unusual with the counts."

Chris's eyes were as big as silver dollars. "Do you think they'll come after us?"

"I really doubt our count problems have anything to do with Mike's death. All we have are suspicions, anyway. There's no hard evidence. You boys don't pose a threat. You don't even know who works at Sil-Trac."

"Is that supposed to make us feel better?" Noah asked. He turned and started for his room. I grabbed his arm and pulled him back to face me.

"Wait, there's a little bit more."

He rolled his eyes to the ceiling.

"Isn't there always?" he said.

"Last night, after I picked you up, when I left?"

He nodded.

"One of my employees, the dead man's ex-girlfriend, left a message for me to meet her at a tavern out near work. When I went there, at first I couldn't find her. When I did find her, she was dead."

"Did she kill herself?" Noah asked.

"I doubt it," I said. "Why would she bother to call me out there if she wasn't going to be alive to talk to me?"

"You didn't ask if she killed herself?" Noah said. "I can't believe you didn't ask. She probably killed him in a fight over the money they got for the stolen chips or maybe 'cause he dumped her, then when she had time to think about it, she felt guilty and snuffed herself."

He was getting into this.

"I hate to burst your bubble," I said. "But I don't think it was anything quite so dramatic. I really don't know the details, but it seems she was working for another chipmaker at the same time she was working for me. The police think maybe she was stealing secrets."

"You don't think that's true, do you?" Chris asked. "An operator would have a hard time getting her hands on anything of value."

"I tried to tell them that, but nobody wanted to hear it."

"So, if she was stealing secrets, and he was involved somehow, then why did someone break in here?" Noah asked. "What did they think we had?"

"I think the break-in was unrelated to the murders."

"Harley, the mathematical probability of this much crime happening around one person and the incidents not being related is infinitesimal," Chris said.

I could feel my face turning red. "I'm sure you're right."

"Yeah?" Noah asked. "Why do I get the feeling there's more?"

Bright children are a curse. You spend their childhood teaching them to be inquisitive and to question everything, then you spend the teen years trying to take it all back.

"Remember that piece of art I was asking about at the church?"

Both boys nodded.

"It's kind of complicated. A woman who works for me asked me to keep a picture for her. She's keeping it for a family friend. The friend's brother lives in Portland and seems strapped for cash. They're from another country where the customs are a bit different. I think he may have come here looking for the picture."

Detective Green's words flashed into my head. I pushed them aside. It made more sense that the thieves were looking for the icon. Even though it was a large and fairly obvious object.

"This just keeps getting weirder," Noah said. "Did you tell the detective all this, or are you keeping him in the dark, too?"

"Why do I get the feeling you're on his side? He's a virtual stranger."

"He seems like a cool guy," Noah said. "You know, honest."

"The police can't deal with guesses. They only want to hear about facts. I've told them all the facts I know. Detective Green hasn't been real interested in those, I might add."

"I'll bet you didn't even show him our numbers and graphs, did you?" Noah asked. He looked at me. "Oh, my God, you don't believe us, do you? You don't think anyone is stealing chips, do you?"

I tried to think of a way to explain exactly what I thought about it.

"C'mon, Chris, it's obvious we're not appreciated here."

The boys went up to Noah's room. Before I could figure out a good way to explain my thoughts about the possibility of high-tech thieves operating in my clean room, Chris's mom called and invited Noah to join Chris and his family for dinner. He was only too eager to go. They left almost immediately.

The house seemed empty. I had cleaned a lot of the damaged stuff out of the living room, but it would take a few days to get the insurance money. Then who knows how long it would take me to find replacement stuff?

I gathered up all the records from work and the graphs and notes the boys had made, and I went upstairs. I figured I owed it to them to go over it again and see if there was something to it.

Numbers aren't my best area, but I felt a swell of maternal pride as I flipped through the pages. Noah had organized them into groups. I recognized his neat script marking the sequence. They had used different-colored highlighters to follow individual lots.

The boys had studied the most recent lots that had been through the clean room. I took a few pages from three months ago. If they followed the same pattern, and assuming I could figure it out, it might convince me.

I had just laid all the pages from the boy's work and all the pages from three months ago on the floor in sequence when the doorbell rang. I thought about ignoring it, but I was afraid Noah had come back for something and had forgotten his key.

The doorbell rang again as I came down the stairs. I opened it with a little more force than I meant to. The angry comment I was going to make about laying off the doorbell died on my lips when I saw who was standing on my porch.

"Andrush, what are you doing here?" I asked in a higher voice than I intended.

"I believe you have something that belongs to me," he said.

He put his hand on the handle to the screen door. I flicked the lock into position before he could pull the door open.

"I wouldn't be so hasty if I were you," he said.

"And just why is that?"

"As it happens, I have something of yours, also."

"I can't imagine what that could be. Now, if you don't mind, I've got work to do." I started to shut the door.

"I have your son," he said in a quiet voice.

I didn't like the look on his face. "Don't be ridiculous," I said. "He's at his friend's house."

"I'm in no hurry," he said. "Call his friend. I think you'll find they don't know where he is."

The hair rose on the back of my neck. My brain was saying one thing, but my gut said another.

"I'll be right back." I went into the kitchen and dialed Chris's house. His mom answered after three rings. "Could I speak to Noah?" I asked. "They aren't there? When are they due back?...I see...Could you have him call me when they get back?"

I went back to the door.

"Was he there?" Andrush asked.

"Just because he wasn't there doesn't mean you have him," I said with more conviction than I felt.

"I'm a patient man." He turned and started back down the porch steps.

"Wait a minute. Where are you going?" I asked.

"If you won't let me in, I'll leave. As I said, I'm a patient man."

I knew I shouldn't let him in, but I couldn't take the chance. I unlocked the screen.

"Very well," he said. "I was not wrong. You are a smart woman. We can do business." He came up the steps and into the house. "I propose a simple trade," he said. "You give the picture to me, and I will return your son."

"Pardon me, but nothing is simple with you. First of all, I didn't say I had your picture. Second, if I did have your picture, I wouldn't hand it over without seeing Noah first."

"Let's not play games," Andrush said. "I do a little janitorial work at the church. I was there when you stopped by."

"Then you know I made a few inquiries on behalf of a friend. I said nothing about having an icon in my possession."

"My sister had the icon, now she does not. I know it came to America."

"America's a big place."

"Don't be coy, Miss Spring. It's not becoming. You either have the icon or you have access to it."

I was about to deny it again when he stood up and started taking books off my bookshelf.

"You don't mind if I satisfy myself that it is not here," he said.

"Yes, I do mind," I said.

We both knew there was nothing I could do to stop him. He was bigger than me. I watched with a growing sense of rage as he dumped my books onto the floor then moved toward the remains of my sofa. He bent over the torn cushion. He slipped his arm up to the shoulder into the slit in the seat.

Seeing him like that enraged me. I felt like I was being defiled all over again, only this time I was forced to participate. Before I had time think about it, I grabbed one of the soapstone Buddha statues and hit him on the head. He slumped facedown against the ragged stuffing sticking out of the sofa cushion.

I dropped the statue. "I can't believe I just did that," I said to no one. "Oh, God. Now I'll never get Noah back."

Cher chose that moment to come investigate. She walked over to Andrush's limp form and sniffed it. After a moment, she turned her back on him and began that air scratching cats do in imitation of their cat pan behavior.

It took me three tries to make my hand touch Andrush's greasy skin. I felt for a pulse and found one. I turned his face to the side so he wouldn't suffocate. Then I got mad all over again. I backed over to the door to my bedroom without taking my eyes off him. I reached into my dresser drawer and pulled out the first thing I came to, which turned out to be a scarf. I was afraid to move him too much so I tied his free hand to his ankles. If he woke up and pulled his arm out of the cushion, he could untie himself, but it would slow him down.

With him somewhat secure, I hurried to the kitchen and put a call in to Detective Green. The officer who answered said Green had just been called out and he didn't know how long he'd be gone. The best he could do was to page Green and wait for him to respond. As I talked to the officer, the implications of what had gone down in my living room played through my head.

I went back to the living room. Andrush was still out cold. He seemed to be breathing easily enough, so I decided to let sleeping dogs lie. I sat down on the rug near his unconscious form to ponder my options.

If I called 911, they would revive him. I couldn't say he broke in, because I did, in fact, let him in. He was looking for a lost possession, which I did, in fact, have. If I told anyone he had Noah, and he did have him, I might never see my stepson again. I didn't want to revive him until I had control of the situation. I just wasn't sure how that was going to happen.

The sound of the back door slamming made me jump.

"Harley? Are you here?" called Mrs. Johnson.

"In here," I answered in my loudest whisper.

"Why are you whisp — Oh, my God! You've killed the gas man," she said as she walked through the dining room and into the living room.

"This is not the gas man," I said. "And he isn't dead. He's just...resting."

"I know that kind of rest," Mrs. Johnson said, rubbing her head. "He came here earlier today. I stopped by to make sure my Henry cleaned up his mess. My Henry can cook, but he's not so good at the clean-up part."

"About the gas man?"

"Oh, yes. This fella said he was from the gas company, and he said was a leak in the neighborhood. I didn't want to let him in, but he said the house would explode. I'm sorry."

Mrs. Johnson's face had permanent smile lines etched into its surface. When she wasn't smiling, they made her look all of her seventy-three years. I decided a lecture on security could wait.

"Don't worry," I said. "This guy is a con man of the highest order. He's a trained actor, among other things."

"What are you going to do now?" she asked.

"That, Mrs. J, is a very good question. This guy claims he has Noah. Chris's mom says the boys went to play basketball at the park but are overdue. He probably just saw the boys on his way here. Of course, that doesn't explain how he even knows I have a son, much less what he looks like."

Mrs. Johnson's face reddened. "I think I know how that happened. When he was here looking for the gas leak, he saw the picture. You know, the one on your desk of Noah in his school uniform and the ones in the hall of you and Sam at Hagg Lake."

I knew the picture of Noah she was talking about. It was my only picture of him.

"I'm afraid I prattled on a bit about how proud we are of him being in military school and how he's home visiting. I've really made a mess of things, haven't I?" Her shoulders slumped.

I put my arm around her. "There's nothing wrong with being proud of Noah. You had no way of knowing what a viper you were dealing with. Besides, he's very resourceful. If he hadn't talked to you, he would have found some other opportunity."

We sat in silence for a moment.

The ringing phone startled us both. I went to the one on my desk in the kitchen and glanced at the caller ID unit that sits beside it. Anonymous, it read.

"Some help you are," I told it.

I picked up the phone and Noah's voice greeted me. I almost dropped the receiver.

"It's Noah," I mouthed to Mrs. Johnson, who had followed me into the kitchen. "What? Say that again," I said to Noah. Then, I said goodbye and hung up.

"What did he say? Is he all right?" Mrs. Johnson asked.

"He's better than all right. He's with Detective Green, and they're on their way here right now."

"That's great," Mrs. Johnson said. "What are you going to do with the guy in the living room?"

"Oh, God." I put my hand on my forehead and closed my eyes to think. "We can't carry him out to his car. The neighbors would see. We could put him in the bathroom, but if someone wants to use it, how would we explain it?"

"Why don't we put him in the garage?" Mrs. Johnson suggested. "Leave the door open and put him out of sight, behind the car. He'll probably wake up soon. If he sees the police car, he won't come back into the house. I can watch from the kitchen. I have groceries to put away."

"Mrs. Johnson, you are a genius," I said. "Are you feeling well enough to help me drag him out there?"

"It'll take more than a little bump on the noggin to lay me down," she said. "Let's get him moved before your detective friend gets here."

It wasn't a great plan, but nothing better came to mind.

CHAPTER TWENTY-TWO

HE WAS MOANING AS WE laid him down in front of my car. Mrs. Johnson opened the big garage door just in time to see Detective Green pull into the driveway.

"There's my Noah," Mrs. Johnson boomed as Noah got out of the car. "Come have some cookies. I made some ginger cookies this morning, just for you. You, too, Detective, come have some cookies and milk."

She grabbed Detective Green's arm and guided him to the steps that went up to the kitchen door. She looked back over her shoulder at me and followed the man inside.

I went to the side door of the garage, which was still open from us dragging Andrush through it. He was starting to move around. I shut the door as quietly as I could and locked it.

Mrs. Johnson had Noah and Detective Green installed at the kitchen table with glasses of milk and a big plate of her spicy ginger cookies.

"Harley," Noah said, "you'll never guess what happened to me and Chris."

I glanced at Mrs. Johnson, who was doing a better job than I was at looking calm and collected. She gave me an encouraging smile.

"Tell us, Noah," I said, in a voice that sounded foreign to me.

"Chris and I found a lost kid in the park, right where we were playing hoops."

"So, what did you do?"

"Well, we were afraid if we took the kid anywhere he might start screaming or something, and then people might think we took him, so Chris stayed with the kid and I went to the gas station down the street and used the phone to call Detective Green. Only, when Detective Green showed up a bigger kid came up and said it was his brother. He didn't have any ID on him, but they both spoke the same language and they looked alike, too."

I'll just bet they did, I thought. I was willing to bet Mrs. Johnson and I knew someone else they looked like.

"That was very responsible of you, Noah." I said. "I'm sorry the boys had to bother you, Detective Green. I imagine you have more important things to do than chase after lost children."

"Hey, it's no problem," Green said. "I told Noah and Chris they could call me anytime."

"That's nice of you, but with two murders in the last few days, I'm sure you have more important things to worry about. By the way, have you made any progress in either case?"

"No, we're still interviewing people. You know, police work isn't like they show it on TV. Breaks come because of hard work. We're waiting for results from some of the tests we asked for. Other than that, Harper and I are just talking to a lot of people.

"I'm hoping to learn something at the memorial service tomorrow night. People rarely get snuffed by strangers so chances are if it's a friend or relative they'll turn up at the memorial."

"That's a comforting thought."

"Hey, you ain't got nothing to worry about," Green said. "You're gonna be with me."

I went to the sink and drank a glass of water I didn't want so I could look out at the street. The car Andrush had arrived in was gone. I said a small prayer of thanks for his timely escape and turned back to the table.

I said, "I'm picking up Mike's neighbor at six. If you aren't here before I leave, I'll go get her and check back here on my way to the service."

"Don't worry, I'll be here," he said. "I wouldn't miss it."

"I just thought you might need some flexibility, in case another crime happens or something."

"Harley, you gotta stop watching so much TV," Green said. "We got more than one or two detectives on the force. Don't you worry. I'll be here."

I was beginning to dread having to introduce him as my date.

I'd rather explain Harper as my date. I hoped he would be called away and have to skip the memorial service.

"I'd like to stay and eat more cookies," Green said, "but I gotta follow up a few more leads." He looked at Noah. "You call me again anytime, you hear?"

Noah blushed and averted his eyes. "Yes, sir."

"The same goes for you," he said to me. "You need anything or hear anything, you call me. Okay?"

He didn't wait for an answer. He took his plate and glass to the sink, kissed Mrs. Johnson on the cheek and went out the back door. She stepped onto the back porch and watched until he pulled out.

"He's gone," she said, and breathed an obvious sigh of relief.

I collapsed into the chair Green had just vacated. "I was afraid he was going to leave too soon," I said.

"What's going on here?" Noah asked.

"Nothing that concerns you."

His face darkened. "How did I know you were going to say that?" he said. "Maybe I'll just call Detective Green and ask him."

"Noah," Mrs. Johnson said with a glare, "Harley said it was none of your business, and that's what she means. Is that what they teach you at that fancy-schmancy school? How to talk back? What happened to my sweet Noah?"

He blushed but didn't say anything. He took his plate and glass to the sink and went to his bedroom.

"He has quite an attitude," Mrs. Johnson said. "You want me to talk to him?"

"No, he's just angry because I can't get Sam to let him come home. He can't direct it at Sam because, as usual, Sam isn't here. When I talk about it with Sam, he won't even listen. He says Noah has to go to military school and for me not to waste my time trying to discuss it with him."

"That still doesn't make it okay for him to be so disrespectful to you." She began loading the glasses and plates into the dishwasher.

"I just wish Sonny would come home," I said. "That would cheer him up."

"You know, Harley, when I came here today, I could have sworn I heard Sonny barking. Just for a moment and from a distance, but it sure sounded like his yippy little voice."

"I thought I heard him the other night, too. I think it's just wishful thinking. I could have used his help today. I'll bet Andrush wouldn't have come in if Sonny had been here." I grabbed a diet cola from the refrigerator. "I'm going to go up and study the numbers Noah and Chris prepared," I said. "Maybe if I'm not down here, Noah will come out and talk to you."

I went back up to the papers I had so carefully laid out what seemed like an eon ago.

❧ ❧ ❧

Chris had returned when I came back downstairs an hour and a half later. Both boys sat at the table with Mrs. Johnson. They were all laughing. There were empty food dishes on the table.

"Ah, Harley," Mrs. Johnson asked, "you finished with your papers? I brought some of my sauerkraut with a little sausage. It's good. You want to try some?"

"No, thanks, I'll have some later. I need to ask the boys a few questions."

"Now I suppose you believe us, huh?" Noah started out on the offensive.

"You guys seem to know about this stuff. If someone is taking chips out of the lab, where do they sell them?" I asked.

"California," they said in unison.

"Is that the only place?" I asked.

"California is the distribution center," Noah said. "They repackage them then ship them all over the world. We studied this stuff in economics at school last term."

"How do people typically get things out of the factory?"

"Every way you can think of," Chris answered. "At my company, they caught a guy hiding them in his knee brace. Turned out he wasn't even hurt. He just wore the brace to smuggle whole tubes of IC's out of the area."

"How did they catch the guy?" I asked.

"I guess he got sloppy," Chris answered. "Someone saw him without his brace at the grocery store. He didn't even limp. The security guard made him take it off on his way out a couple of days later and out fell a tube of parts."

"So, practically anyone could be taking them," I said, thinking aloud. "People don't take anything personal in or out of the lab, but I suppose if they are willing to steal in the first place, they probably are willing to break the clean room rules and open their

139

bunny suit to access their pockets."

"No duh," Noah said.

"I just find it hard to believe that Mike and Debbie were stealing parts from our area," I said. "After their breakup, it's inconceivable they would work together on anything. And I can't believe Mike would work so hard trying to figure out our count problems if he knew what the problem was all along."

"Didn't you say he was the nephew of Andrush?" Mrs. Johnson asked.

"Good point," I replied. If the boys were curious about who Andrush was, they didn't say.

"The real question is, who is the third person or persons?" Noah said. "Do you have any idea who that would be?"

I looked at him. "You're right. There must be a partner. Someone who got tired of sharing."

"That could be anyone," Chris said. "The third person could be the out-of-state partner. Maybe they just work a situation for a period of time and then move on when things start getting too hot."

"Were the two people acting different?" Noah asked. "You know, really nervous or anything?"

"Mike was just like he always was— argumentative— but he's been that way ever since I've known him. Debbie was acting a little strange there at the end. Detective Green thinks she was the one who was sending sexual harassment claims against me."

"Someone claims you were harassing them?" Noah said. "Get real."

"I guess someone wanted you out of the way, huh?" Chris asked.

"That's what I'm thinking," I said. "It's kind of weird, though. The claims were all sent in ways that made them very easy to disprove. Almost as if Debbie wanted Sil-Trac to know they were false. It just doesn't add up."

"Have you searched through their stuff?" Noah asked.

"I went through his bedroom the night of his murder," I said. "I didn't find anything revealing. Just the logs and notes from work. The pages you have copies of."

"Do your workers have desks or lockers?" Noah asked.

"All of them have lockers. A few have desks. Usually, the desks are shared by several people, though."

"Has anyone searched the lockers?" he asked.

"Not that I know of. We had a bomb threat, so everyone had to leave the building Thursday and stay gone until Monday."

"Let's go search their lockers for clues," Noah said.

"Yeah," Chris chimed in.

I hesitated. It was against my better judgment, but in a selfish moment, I said "Yes." The look on Noah's face was worth it.

"You mean, yes, we can go look?"

"That's what I mean."

"Cool."

"Chris needs to call his mom for permission, and I need to talk to her."

"You aren't gonna tell her what we're doing, are you?" Noah asked. I could hear the defensive tone creeping back into his voice.

"Of course not," I said. "I just want her to know there was a bomb threat at Sil-Trac yesterday so she can make an informed decision about whether she wants Chris to go there."

The boys paced around while I talked to Sheri. I assured her Sil-Trac had done a thorough search, including bringing in a private company with bomb-sniffing dogs. It was probably the safest place on the planet right now.

We were all shocked the first time Sil-Trac had a bomb threat. The local police evacuated the building and waited until the appointed hour to see if the building blew. Since then, the company had developed its own response protocol. We have since received something like a dozen bomb threats, and not once has a real bomb been found.

Sheri decided Chris could go as long as the boys stayed right where I was. I thanked her and hung up.

"Are you sure you want to go now?" I asked. "It's kind of creepy there at night. We could go first thing in the morning."

"Are you kidding?" Noah protested.

Mrs. Johnson wiped the table with a dishrag and threw the cloth to the sink. "I'm going to go check on my Henry, and then I'm coming right back. Harley, you take my little black phone with you. You call me every thirty minutes so I know you're still okay. Don't forget. You don't call, and I'll call that detective fella, right away."

Noah looked at Chris. "Cool, we get to take Mrs. J's cell phone."

Mrs. Johnson handed him the phone and made him call our

number so she could verify that everything was working and Noah was adequately trained. He went out the door then stopped abruptly, causing a chain reaction with Chris and me that nudged him down the first step.

"Be quiet," he whispered.

We listened.

"I don't hear a thing," Chris said.

"What do you think you heard?" I asked.

"Oh, of course, I just think I heard it," Noah said. "It can't be real if you didn't hear it."

"Geez, Noah," Chris said, "I didn't hear anything, either."

Noah poked him and a mock fight ensued, carrying them down the stairs to the car door. They were acting as if this was a trip to the park, but I knew otherwise.

They climbed into the backseat of the car; I got in and backed the car out of the driveway.

Noah spoke up. "I thought I heard Sonny barking," he said, "just for a second, when we first stepped out the door. It sounded far away, but I'm sure it was him."

I stopped the car. "I had that same thing happen yesterday. It just didn't go on long enough to get a fix on where it was coming from."

"Do you think Sonny is running around in the neighborhood and can't find his way home?" Noah asked.

"He knows where his food comes from," I said. "If he was able to, he'd come home."

I glanced in the mirror and could see a worried look on Noah's face.

"Do you think he's somewhere hurt?" he asked.

"No, if that's him and we can hear his bark, he can't be hurt very bad," I said. "He's probably going to turn up at the pound in a day or two. Someone probably found him and doesn't know where to return him."

We discussed which radio station to listen to and how loud we would play it; then the boys settled into their own world. I could hear their voices, but they kept their chatter just low enough I couldn't eavesdrop.

Night fell as we drove to Sil-Trac. The parking lot was nearly empty. In addition to a few workers' cars, the company kept one or two late-model American-made sedans for use by Japanese visitors. Sil-Trac also had a round-the-clock security guard and a round-the-clock maintenance technician on duty.

I parked in my normal spot, three rows back. Noah and Chris offered the opinion I was nuts but got out when it became obvious I wasn't going to move any closer.

The guard nodded as we walked in. Supervisors often work nights and weekends.

"Hey, Ozzie, how's it going?"

"Fair to middling, Miss Spring, fair to middling."

"Are we your only customer today?"

"Land sakes, no," he replied. "Been a bunch of you supervisory types, a few lead people, one of the maintenance crew. The maintenance crew came early. Mostly everyone was making sure the bomb people didn't disturb their turf. I 'spect that's what you're doing, too, huh?"

"Yeah, something like that."

I led the boys through the maze of cubicles. Only the emergency lights were on, casting eerie shadows over the walkways. A door slammed, and both boys jumped. I don't think either of them took a breath until we reached my cubicle.

I noticed the light flashing on my phone, indicating I had messages waiting. Out of habit, I dialed the sequence to play my voice messages. There was the usual one from Mary telling me there would be a mandatory meeting for supervisors first thing Monday to debrief about the bomb scare. There were calls from two of my workers who were going to be gone Monday. Geneva had developed appendicitis and was in the hospital. I grabbed a notepad and wrote a memo for Mary to send flowers. Truc called to say his grandmother in California had a heart attack, and he had to drive his mother there. He assured me he would be back as soon as possible.

After the last message, there was static. I was about to hang up when Hieu's voice came on the line.

"I have figured out the count problem. I hope you check your messages a lot because I don't have your home number. Call me as soon as you get this. I'm going to Sil-Trac to confirm my suspicions. If I'm right, Harley, this is really big. Here's my number..."

I copied down the number. According to my voice mail, he had called about an hour and a half ago. I hadn't noticed his car, but that's not unusual. I don't relate to cars. He could be parked behind the building or on the other side of the company cars.

I dialed Hieu's number even though I knew it wasn't likely he could have made the round trip that quickly. His wife answered and said he was at work.

"Boys, I need to go in the clean room to see if Hieu is in there. He says he's figured out the count problem."

Noah looked at the darkened cubicles around us. "Can we come with?" he asked.

"I guess that would be okay. You have to follow my instructions exactly, though. Can you do that?"

"Yeah," the boys said in unison.

"Call Mrs. Johnson. Tell her we're fine. Let her know the guard is here, so she doesn't have to worry."

Noah called Mrs. J. She insisted we call again in a half-hour anyway.

"We have a special way of taking objects in and out of the clean room," I said.

I took them around to the pass-through in the wall. The pass-through is a clear plastic box with a door on the inside and a door on the outside. We opened the door on the outside, put the phone in and closed the door.

"Are you just going to leave it there?" Noah asked.

"Just until we get dressed in our bunny suits. We'll retrieve it on the other side."

I led the way into the air shower and guided them in the suiting-up procedure. We went through the inner air shower and into the hallway. Noah went to the pass-through and started to open it.

"Don't touch it yet," I yelled. "In addition to particle contamination, we have to worry about sodium contamination. You have to take a clean room cloth from that dispenser." I pointed at a box on the wall. "Grab the bottle of alcohol from the top there and wipe the phone with alcohol. Then you take that air gun and hose it off, all before you take it out of the box."

"This is crazy," Noah said.

"Well, crazy or not, it's what we have to do to avoid contamination," I said.

I walked to the intercom on the wall and set it to announce in all rooms. I paged Hieu several times. We waited, but only voiceless static came from the speaker.

"He might be by one of the laminar flow hoods."

To keep any particles of dust away from the work, we have these big filters above our work areas that clean the air and direct the flow toward the floor. If we do have any particles, we want them to be below surface level.

"If Hieu is working at one of the laminar flow hoods, he might not be able to hear us," I said. "I'm going to look in the test room. That's the area where he would most likely be working. Why don't you boys look in the packaging room next door?"

Noah gave me one of those "are you nuts?" looks. "Which room is the packaging room?"

"Right down there," I said, stepping down the hall a few steps and pointing.

The boys followed.

"What's that on the floor?" Chris asked. He pointed at a dark-looking puddle on the floor outside the photolithography room.

"I don't know," I said. "They use photo resist in there. It's a photosensitive plastic they mask the wafers with."

I knew Chris knew, but Noah was too proud to ask.

"It's reddish-brown. It looks a lot like blood. The people who work in there always look like they just came out of the emergency room. A machine hose probably popped off. I'll go check real quick."

I stepped into the black revolving door that protected the room's yellow-lit interior from white light contamination. For a moment, while you spin the opening from the hall to the room, you are in total darkness. When the door lined up to the room side, I stepped one foot out.

It touched something that wasn't the floor. As my eyes adjusted, I looked down and screamed. My foot was on someone's bunny suit-covered leg. The mask was pulled to one side. The hood was pulled over the face. All I could see was black hair sticking out where a face should be. A few inches below there was a new opening cut in the fabric.

Whoever was in the bunny suit had just had their throat slit. Blood was still trickling from the gaping wound.

CHAPTER TWENTY-THREE

HARLEY, WHAT'S WRONG?" Noah called. I could hear the boys beating on the back of the door tube. I pulled my foot back in and spun the door. When the boys came into view, I stumbled out into the hall. I leaned against the wall.

"Harley, what's wrong?" Noah asked again. He put his arm around me. "Harley, say something. You're scaring me."

"The–There...There's a body in there. Oh, my God. I need to check and see if it's still alive."

Somewhere deep in my brain, I knew no one could have a wound like that and survive, but I needed to check. I straightened and stepped back into the door tube.

"Call nine-one-one then call the front desk and tell Ozzie what happened. The number's on the phone."

I realigned the door with the lab and stepped out over the body. I kneeled down and gently pulled on the hood to the bunny suit. Whoever this was had been cut so deep there could be no possibility of survival — it appeared the hood was the main thing keeping the head attached.

The door spun, effectively locking me in with the body. Before I could think, it spun again. I looked up. Someone in a white suit stepped into the room.

"Tommy," I said, "what are you doing here?"

"Hieu called and asked me to meet him here," he said. "He said he had something he wanted to show me. When I came through the air shower, two kids said you were in here with a dead body. Oh, my God, is that Hieu? Is he dead?"

I looked back down at the body. "Oh, Hieu, not you, too."

Without seeing his face, I couldn't be sure, but you develop the ability to recognize people by the way their bunny suit fits. I'd bet my next paycheck this was Hieu.

"Come on, Harley," Tommy said. He pulled me up and put his arm around me. He walked me over to a chair on the opposite side of the lab and eased me into it. "Stay over here. You can't help Hieu now."

He went over to the chemical shower. The Process labs used a variety of caustic chemicals; emergency showers are required in every room. The first time we had to use the shower at Sil-Trac, we stripped the poor victim out of his bunny suit and street clothes, pulled the curtain and showered them with cold water for ten minutes as required. Everything went according to plan until we tried to get the person out of the shower and realized we had no clothing or towels.

We remedied this by putting paper clothes and blankets by every shower. Tommy pulled a blanket from a bag on the side of the shower. He stepped back over to the body and covered it.

"We should call the cops," he said.

"My son did that," I whispered. "They should be here any minute."

"What are you doing here, anyway?" Tommy asked. "Did Hieu call you, too?"

"He called me, but I didn't get the message until I was already here. I just came to do a little work." I stood up. "Noah. I need to talk to my son and his friend."

I stepped in a wide arc around the body and went to the door. The boys were huddled by the air shower entrance where the phone was.

"Before anyone gets here, I want to talk to you guys," I said. "If anyone asks, I don't think we should spell out exactly what we were planning to do here tonight. I don't think the police appreciate people trying to help them with their investigations."

"So, what are we supposed to say?" Noah asked.

"I don't think anyone will ask you, but if they do just say I had some work to do and you guys came along for the ride."

"Won't that be lying?" he asked.

"Let's not get technical, okay?"

"Just checking," he said.

Ozzie brought the police to the clean room. It was almost painful to watch as the two uniformed officers passed through the second air shower in street clothes. I couldn't think about the implications right now. We could deal with the contamination later.

"You the one that found the body?" the taller officer asked me.

"Yes, he's right in here," I said. "You have to go in one at a time." I demonstrated how the door worked. "Be careful, he's lying right inside the door."

"You know who it is?" the second officer asked. His name badge said Clark. "You said 'he.'"

I explained why Tommy and I thought it was Hieu. We were still talking when a couple of paramedics arrived. They quickly entered the photolithography room and formally declared that Hieu was beyond help.

Clark asked us everything we had done and seen. After we told him the same thing the third time through, the boys and I went out to my desk to wait. It was a good fifteen minutes later when Tommy appeared.

"I'm going to go now," he said. "I talked to the police, and they agreed to let me go with their people to tell Hieu's wife. She shouldn't hear this from strangers."

He pulled a cell phone from his pocket and pushed a sequence of numbers. He spoke rapidly in Vietnamese.

"His wife's mother will be told and brought over to help," he told me. "Here's my cell number." He handed me a printed card with a number on it. "Call me if you find out anything."

Chris and Noah looked at each other.

"Mrs. Johnson," they said at the same time.

Noah grabbed the phone at my desk and started dialing.

They were talking to Mrs. Johnson when Ozzie paged me. I went to the front desk and saw Detective Green leaning toward him. Green had on his usual motheaten sport coat and polyester pants.

Both men laughed. Green's face became serious when he caught sight of me.

"Mrs. Johnson called me and said you were in some kind of trouble," he said, turning towards me. "She asked me to check on you. Judging from the number of police cars and the ambulance parked out front, I'd say she wasn't far off the mark."

He looked at me expectantly. When I didn't say anything, he continued. "Would you like to explain what's going on here?"

I tried to think of a way to describe what I had just seen. Every time I started to speak, nothing would come out. In the end, my eyes filled up with tears, and it was too hard not to cry.

"Oh, geez," Green said. He put his arms around my shoulders and pulled me toward him. I could feel the skin on my face reacting to the scratchy wool of his sport coat where it rested on his shoulder. I pulled back and dried my eyes on the handkerchief he handed me.

"Until this week, I'd never seen a dead body. Now, three people I care about have died violently, almost before my eyes."

"If you weren't shook up, I'd be worried," Green said. "Do you think you could tell me what's going on here?"

"Can't you just talk to the police who are here?"

"I don't have jurisdiction out here. Besides, I'm more interested in hearing what you have to say."

It did actually help to talk about it. I told him everything that had happened. He asked a few questions I couldn't answer, like which cars were in the parking lot. I wasn't much help. Like I said, I don't relate to cars. The subtle nuances, like the difference between Fords and Chevys, escapes me.

"I thought you technical types paid better attention to details than that," Green said.

"I didn't develop a sudden interest in cars just because I went to a technical school," I said. "I wasn't interested in them before, and I'm still not. It wasn't a prerequisite at the school I went to."

Green held his hands up. "Whoa, there. I didn't mean anything. It just would be good if you could remember anything about who was parked outside when you went in."

"I'm sorry, there were a few cars. That's all I can say for sure."

"Tell me again about the victim."

"Hieu," I said. "His name is Hieu."

"Okay, tell me what Hieu did here."

I explained again what lead operators do.

"So, isn't that what the woman did?" Green asked.

"Actually, both Mike and Debbie were lead operators. Mike was more senior than Hieu and Debbie, but they did the same job."

"Are there other people in the same job?"

"Of course," I said.

Green seemed unable to grasp the rather simple structure common to many manufacturing companies.

"There are lead operators in every area for every product in the company. There must be twenty or thirty of them at this plant alone. And then some areas have assistant lead operators. There's a whole crew on swing shift with their own lead person, too."

"What about your area?" he asked. "Do you have more of them?"

"I've got two more. Tommy is in charge of the die prep and test, and Shannon is in the packaging area."

"You got a phone I can use?"

"You don't think they're in danger, do you?"

"I don't know, but I'd like to talk to them and maybe put a safety plan in place for each of them, just in case," he said. "You know where I can find them?"

"Tommy left just before you came. He went over to Hieu's house to tell Hieu's wife what happened and help organize support for her. I have Shannon's address in my file at my desk. You can use the phone there, too."

Green followed me through the maze back to my desk. We could hear Noah and Chris talking before we got there.

"Geez, did you see that guy when they took him out?" Noah said.

"Yeah, somebody really did a number on him," Chris replied.

"Let's show a little respect, you guys," I said. "That guy, as you put it, was a loyal worker, and he was my friend."

"Geez, Harley, you don't have to blow a gasket."

My mouth opened to reply, but Green's firm squeeze on my elbow killed the words before they came out.

I got Shannon's phone number and address for him and, after a brief argument, called her. No one answered. I left a message explaining about the protection without telling her about Debbie or Hieu. Green called his precinct and set up protection for both Tommy and Shannon. He also arranged for a community service officer to visit and give them instruction on personal safety.

I was talking to the boys when I heard him mention my name.

"I'm going to be staying with Harley tonight, but I'd like someone to take over tomorrow morning at about eight."

"You'll do no such thing," I said.

Green finished his conversation and hung up. He turned and

faced me.

"This is not the time to pull any liberation crap," he said. "Someone is killing a lot of people close to you. Until we figure out who and why, we have to assume you're in danger."

I glanced past him and could see the smile leave Noah's face.

"We have a security system," I said. "Can't you just follow us home and tuck us in? You could come back first thing in the morning."

"Let's not argue," Green said. "I got a job to do here." He looked at Noah. "I need you to sleep at Chris's house until you go back to school."

"Sure," Noah said without enthusiasm. "You're the man."

I could feel the heat rise up into my face. "How dare you banish my son from his own home?"

"Did you forget your home was trashed?" Green asked. "Someone knows where you live."

"That doesn't mean it was the murderer."

"I don't think Noah is a target. As long as he stays out of the crossfire, he'll be safe."

I hated to admit it, but what he said made sense. I wasn't looking forward to explaining all this to Sheri, however.

"Let's go see if the local boys in blue will let you leave," Green said.

We went back to the clean room. Yellow crime scene tape was strung across the hall leading up to the first air shower. When Officer Clark saw us, he came over.

"Who would you be?" he asked Green.

"A friend of the family," Green said. "The boys called me. We were wondering if it was okay for Harley and the boys to leave."

"Not yet," Clark said. "We have a few more questions for Miss Spring."

He ducked under the tape and walked down the hall a few steps. I went with him. When Green started to follow, Clark held his hand up to stop him. I wasn't sure why Green didn't identify himself, but if he wasn't going to neither was I.

Clark asked me to describe the sequence of events leading up to the discovery of Hieu's body again. He listened intently.

"As far as you know, no one found the body before you?"

"No, Tommy came up from the hallway after I was in the room.

I didn't hear anyone else. With the HEPA filters going, you can't hear a lot anyway."

The air in all parts of the clean room is filtered continuously. The filters create a constant background hum. When you work here, you get used to it. The only time you really notice it is when you have to turn your radio up to almost full volume to hear it.

"Why are you asking? Isn't it obvious? He had just died when Tommy and I found him."

"We found a couple of footprints around the body. Looks like the person was wearing those boot covers you guys wear." He glanced down at my ample foot. "It doesn't look like it matches either of you."

"Don't you think it might be the murderer?" I hated to state the obvious.

"I might, except the prints are pretty small," he said. "I would be real surprised if someone with feet that small was able to inflict the damage that was done to the victim. He was pretty big for an Oriental."

"I can get a list of all the people who wear extra-small booties, if you need it. Not until Monday, though."

"Good," he said. "Tell your boyfriend he can take you home now. Just don't leave town without letting us know, okay?"

I bit my tongue and walked back to Green and the boys.

"Let's go."

CHAPTER TWENTY-FOUR

NOAH CALLED MRS. JOHNSON and told her the plan. She said she would still be there when we got home. Green said he would follow us home and then take the boys over to Chris's house.

I spent the drive home trying to convince the boys they were safe and that nothing else was going to happen. It was a hard sell, especially since I didn't believe a word I was saying.

When we walked in the door, I could hear Cher meowing. It sounded like she was upstairs.

"What's got her so riled up?" I asked Mrs. Johnson.

"Oh, I don't know. Maybe she smells a mouse," Mrs. J said.

We both knew Cher had lived a pampered life. She wouldn't recognize a mouse if it bit her. Mrs. Johnson was putting dishes into the sink as she spoke. She picked up the dishrag and swiped at the table, wiping the whole surface. Noah went to his room and packed his backpack. After he finished he stood in the doorway to the kitchen for a minute.

"Are you too big to give an old woman a hug goodbye," Mrs. J asked in her booming voice.

He came over, and she smothered him in her embrace. When she released him, she gave him a less than subtle shove in my direction. He gave me an awkward hug.

"I'll call you," I said.

"Don't go to any trouble on my account," he said.

"Come on, boys," Green said. Then, to me: "I'm going to swing by my place and feed the cat after I get the boys settled. Then I'll be back. Save me a couple of those cookies," he said with a wink to Mrs. J.

Mrs. Johnson looked stricken. As soon as Green closed the door, she headed for the stairs to the attic room.

"You can come down now," she called. I heard footsteps, followed by a very pale tearstained Shannon. "I'm going to my house to get more cookies," Mrs. J said. "I fed yours to this young lady. My Henry is waiting in the car just around the corner."

She was getting into this cloak-and-dagger stuff.

"Shannon," I said, "what are you doing here?"

She shrugged as tears began rolling down her cheeks.

"Come on in and sit down," I said, motioning toward the nearest chair. She walked over and collapsed into it. She put her arms on the table and rested her head on them.

"Shannon," I said again, "I know you were there. Now, tell me what you saw."

She cried for another minute and then sat up. I handed her Detective Green's handkerchief. He'd never know the difference.

"Shannon," I tried again, "we don't have much time. Detective Green is coming back. Tell me what you know."

"Did you see me?" she asked. "I didn't see anyone. Except Hieu, of course."

"Just tell me what happened, please."

"I went to the clean room," she said. I could see the tears building in her eyes. "I went to the clean room," she repeated. "I just wanted to make sure they didn't contaminate anything when they were looking for the bomb."

I decided this wasn't the time to give her the real info on the local bomb squad.

"Which part of the room did you go into?" I asked.

"At first I went into my room," she said. "I looked around. Nothing was disturbed that I could tell. Then, I started looking at the logs again. Before I knew it, a couple of hours had passed." She stopped and dabbed at her eyes. "I thought I was starting to see a pattern, but I just couldn't quite make sense of it. I thought I'd do something else for a while. You know, let my mind rest. I decided I should do a wipe-down of my area. When I went to get a bottle of alcohol, I couldn't find a full one."

She stopped again and blew her nose in Green's handkerchief. I made a mental note to get rid of it before he came back.

"I knew Debbie Dayshift had filled a bunch of new squirt

bottles, and I didn't think I should try to refill mine with no one else there."

My people were notorious for swiping each other's supplies. None of them wanted to be the one to refill bottles or get clean room paper or pens issued to them.

"So, that's when you went into the photolithography room?" I said, trying to encourage her to get to the critical part of the story.

"Yeah," she said. "I went into Debbie's room, in the back where she hides her extra squirt bottles of chemicals. I heard the door turn, twice. I knew it couldn't be Debbie, and I didn't want to be caught taking her bottles. I crouched down behind the aligner.

"I could hear two people talking. I couldn't see them. It was too noisy to tell who it was. From where I was, I could see the edge of the door tube. When I saw it spin, I waited another minute and then I came out."

Her eyes filled with tears, and her shoulders began to shake.

"Shannon," I said firmly, "this isn't going to help Hieu."

She snuffled loudly and took a deep breath.

"I came out from behind the aligner, and he was lying there. I went closer. No one could survive a cut like that." She stared off into space.

"What did you do next?" I asked. "I was there right after it happened. Why didn't I see you?"

"He was just staring off into space, so I pulled on his hood until it covered his face. Before I could do anything else, I heard the outside air shower. I was afraid. I thought whoever did that to Hieu might be coming back for me. So, I went to Debbie's chemical pass-through cabinet. I moved one of the cans out of the way and crawled out. I pulled the can back in place and shut the doors on both sides."

"Ozzie didn't say anything to the police about anyone going out."

"I waited until he got a phone call. He bent over his switchboard, and I just walked out."

I could guess why he didn't look up. He was probably talking to Noah.

"Did you call the police?" She didn't answer. "Shannon, I have to tell you, the police aren't going to like the fact that you ran. I'm not sure I like it. If you didn't do anything wrong, why didn't you call the police? Or try to get help for Hieu?"

"You didn't see him," she said. "It was obvious there was nothing to be done for him."

"It was probably me that was coming into the clean room when you ran. He was still bleeding when I came in. Maybe if you had tried to help him when you were there, he could have been saved."

I didn't really believe that, but it made me mad that she hadn't even tried.

"I didn't know it was you. I thought you were the killer." She began sobbing again.

"Okay, okay, maybe I would have run, too." I patted her back. I wasn't good at this kind of stuff. When people at work cry, I usually just hand them a box of tissues and continue with whatever it was that was making them cry in the first place. This was a little different from the usual "she stole my boyfriend, how can you expect me to work with her" kind of stuff I have to deal with.

"Shannon, don't you think you should tell the police what you saw?"

She looked at me like Bambi staring down the barrel of a shotgun.

"They'll think I did it," she said, and started crying again.

CHAPTER TWENTY-FIVE

T TOOK A FEW MINUTES TO get Shannon calm enough to talk again. I knew if she was this upset there had to be more to the story.

"Shannon, tell me why you think the police will believe you did this?"

"It's a little complicated," she said.

"I don't think things can get any more complicated, so why don't you just tell me what's going on."

"I met this guy," she began and then stopped to wipe her nose. "We've been seeing each other for a few weeks," Her face softened. "He's so sweet and gentle. He really cares about me. We like the same kind of music and wine, and he's not like the guys around here." She blushed. "We met at the art museum."

"And so?" I prompted. "I'm glad you've found someone, but what does this have to do with Hieu?"

Shannon's eyes filled with tears again. "I'm coming to that," she said. "Everything has been wonderful with Robert. We've seen each other every night. He calls me at lunchtime just to see how my day is going."

She gazed at a point in the distance, then her eyes flashed with anger. "Debbie can't stand to see anyone happy. She had to try to ruin things between Robert and me."

"Why would she do that?"

"She's unhappy and wants everyone else to be, too. Or at least she did." She started to cry again.

Mrs. Johnson had left a box of tissues on the table before she

157

left. I pressed a wad into Shannon's hand.

"I'm confused. How does this all relate to Hieu?"

"Debbie told me that Robert got Hieu's daughter pregnant," she said. "I know he wouldn't have done anything like that. Hieu's daughter is fifteen. She's still in high school. I don't know why Debbie always has to spoil everything. Just because Mike broke up with her doesn't mean she has to make everyone else miserable."

"What did Robert have to say about it?"

"He said their families pray at the same temple. He told me that Hieu's daughter has a crush on him, but she's just a kid. She isn't his type, anyway. She wears those big baggy jeans and has pierced eyebrows. He gave her a ride home once, but he says that's all, and I believe him."

"Did you talk to Hieu?"

"Oh, yeah, no thanks to Debbie D. She couldn't leave things alone. She had to go tell Hieu I was dating Robert. Hieu went ballistic. He came storming over to my room. He was like a crazy man. He told me Robert was the lowest scum on the earth. He insisted I had to stop seeing him immediately. He said Robert slept with his daughter and got her pregnant, and when she told him he tried to force her to get an abortion."

"I take it you told Robert what Hieu said."

"Of course, we talk about everything. He said she made the whole story up. He said she's been sleeping around since she was thirteen. He said she hangs out with gang members."

It obviously hadn't occurred to Shannon to ask how Robert would know that.

"Harley, it was awful. Robert and I met at The Blue Whale last night. Debbie was there. She came over and was totally rude to him. She'd been drinking. She asked him how many other teenyboppers he had impregnated and how many bastard children he had running around. She told him to quit trying to pretend to be something he wasn't. It was so embarrassing."

"So, what did you do?" The image of Debbie in the bathroom stall was still fresh in my mind.

"We just left. Robert said to ignore her, she was just a drunk. He is so mature. He doesn't sink to the level of most of the people we work with."

"So, you don't know anything about Debbie?"

Shannon blushed and looked down. "I tried to call her this morning," she said softly. "I thought she would be more reasonable when she wasn't drunk. Her sister answered and told me what had happened."

Tears flowed down her face again.

"Okay, you know about Debbie and you know about Hieu. That brings us back to why you're here."

"I'm here because I didn't know where else to go," she said. "You always know what to do..."

She trailed off and looked at me.

"I still don't understand why you think the police are going to suspect you," I said. "Nothing you've said makes sense. If anything, Hieu had good reason to want Robert dead, not the other way around. I don't think the police are going to believe you killed Hieu and Debbie because they called your boyfriend names."

"You think I should talk to the police?"

"I can't tell you what to do, but I can tell you this — if you do nothing, you'll be talking to Detective Green. He'll be here in a few more minutes."

"God, Harley, I don't know what to do. I'm pretty sure I was the last one to see Debbie alive, and I was there when Hieu died. Everyone heard Hieu and me yelling at each other. And the fight with Debbie, too."

"If I were you, I'd be more worried that whoever is doing this is going to find out you were there and start thinking about what you might know."

Shannon's face lost its color. "I hadn't even thought about that."

"The police want to keep an eye on you. Why don't you just let them?"

She got up and started pacing.

"Look," I said, "I don't know what's going on, and I understand you don't trust the police to do the right thing. I'm not sure I like Detective Green, but I think he's honest. Why don't you just try telling him the truth about what happened and see what he says."

"The truth has nothing to do with anything," she shouted. "I've got to get out of here and think."

We heard a car pull into the driveway. Shannon froze.

"I've got to go. Can I get out the back?"

I grabbed her arm and guided her to the back door. "How did

you get here? Did you drive?"

"My car is on the next street over. I didn't want anyone to know I was here."

"There's a gate in the back corner, you can cut through the neighbor's yard."

Mrs. Johnson came in the front door and then into the kitchen. I watched Shannon cut across the yard and leave through the gate. As I shut the door, I heard what sounded like a muffled bark. I stepped onto the back porch and listened, but all I heard was the distant noise of an engine starting and a car driving away.

Mrs. Johnson set the plate of cookies she was carrying on the kitchen table. "You hear the little dog again?"

I nodded. "He sounded faint. Like he's getting weak or something."

"You don't even know if that was him," Mrs. J said. "He's probably fat and happy in someone's kitchen. They found him and don't know where he belongs."

"I'm just afraid the longer he's gone the less likely it becomes we'll ever see him again. And if we don't find him, Noah will never forgive me."

"Yes, he will," she said. "Noah cares for you more than he shows right now. He's a smart boy. He knows what side his bread is buttered on."

I wasn't sure what that meant, but somehow I took comfort from her words.

"Here." She handed me a warm gingersnap. "Sit down and I'll make you a nice cup of Earl Grey."

I was on my third cookie and second cup of tea when the doorbell rang.

"That's probably your detective friend," Mrs. Johnson said.

I took the hint and got up to answer the door.

"I'm looking for the slumber party," Green said when I opened the door.

I stood aside and let him into the living room. He was carrying a faded blue duffel bag with a peeling white Special Olympics logo on it. He had a plastic suit bag draped over his shoulder.

"Where do you want me to put my stuff?" he asked.

"Mrs. Johnson," I asked, "which of the guest rooms did you prepare?"

Mrs. Johnson took a sip from her mug and gave me one of her looks.

"Okay, it's like this," I said. "I'm sleeping upstairs on the futon, because my bed is ripped to shreds. The sofa down here has a torn cover, but is mostly in one piece, or you can use Noah's room."

"Actually, Noah offered his room when I took him to Chris's house. I just wanted to make sure you were okay with it."

"Why should I care?"

"You tell me," he said. "You're the one that gets tense whenever he and I talk."

I turned and walked back into the kitchen. Green carried his stuff into Noah's room. Mrs. Johnson poured me another cup of tea.

"I'm going to be floating before this night is over if you keep up this tea routine," I told her.

"Will you tell him about the young lady who was here?"

"I don't know," I said. "She didn't ask me not to tell anyone, but I'm sure she was expecting the same privacy rules that apply at work would govern our relationship here. Besides, I think she was being a little melodramatic. I can't see her being involved in anything other than a poor choice of boyfriends."

"You need to trust somebody," Mrs. Johnson said. "This detective fellow seems like a good place to start."

"Anyone I know?" Green walked back into the kitchen and sat down at the table.

"Who?" I said.

"Do you always answer a question with a question?"

"Stop already, you two," Mrs. Johnson said as she placed a plate of cookies on the gray Formica tabletop in front of Green and then got a mug from the dishwasher. "I'm going to fix you a cup of tea, and then I want to know just what you're going to do to keep Harley and Noah safe."

Green ate his first cookie in silence while Mrs. J went through the ritual of heating water and steeping tea. When she finished, she put the mug next to the plate on the table then sat in the chair opposite him.

"So?" she said. She stared at him.

"What?" he said, smiling.

"Don't play dumb with me, young man. I want to know what you're planning to do to protect us."

Green's face became serious. "It would help a lot in finding the perpetrator if we could come up with a motive for these crimes. The only thing all three of the victims have in common so far is their job." He tilted his chair back on two legs. "Without a motive, we might as well pull names out of a hat. It'd be as accurate."

He looked at Mrs. Johnson. "I'm going to be honest with you. If we can't figure out why these killings are happening, we're going to have a hard time protecting anyone. We have a team of detectives working round-the-clock on this case. I'm confident we'll get a break soon. Until that happens, I plan on making sure you and Noah and Harley are not targets."

I looked at Mrs. Johnson. "Noah has an idea that might provide a motive," I said quietly. "We have a big inspection coming up at Sil-Trac. Our recordkeeping has to be very accurate. So far, my numbers don't match. Mike was working on the problem when he disappeared. No matter how we look at it, the numbers don't add up. All my people have been trying to figure it out.

"I had Chris and Noah take a look at the problem. You know, a fresh set of eyes. It looks like they found an answer. They think the books don't agree because someone is stealing chips from the lab."

I looked at Green to see his reaction. His face had lost its customary smile. He was looking intently at a point on the table in front of my mug. When I didn't say any more, he looked up at me.

"What do you think?" he asked. "Is that possible?"

"I've been through their numbers, and I can't find anything that would refute their idea." I paused for a moment. "No, I'm not being fair. Theft would explain a lot. And not just a single theft. It's apparently been going on for several months."

Green looked up and locked his eyes onto mine. "Tell me more about what's been stolen," he said. "And who would have access to this stuff."

"It's kinda complicated. It appears that extra wafers are being started that aren't on the books. They're removed sometime after the die are cut up. We wouldn't have known if the person or persons hadn't gotten greedy. Someone used some of the extra parts to improve the yield numbers. It's unclear if they took out raw chips or if they had them packaged."

"Don't you keep track of what gets processed?" Green asked.

I didn't say anything. I couldn't. Trying to explain how hard it is to count large quantities of small things when many workers are involved was difficult.

"What?" Green said when I didn't answer.

"It's hard to explain. Our product flows through the work areas in a pretty continuous manner. Each area has to keep track of how much stuff goes through each day by lot number. Sometimes people miss the transition when one work order stops and another one starts. Also, we have test wafers go through with work orders sometimes. People are supposed to keep them straight, but it's difficult."

"Go back to what you said about someone getting greedy. The part where they added something to something. Who benefits from that?"

"Unfortunately, we promote teamwork big time. Everyone's bonus is based on the end result. They only get their bonus if the end yield meets their target."

"So, no one benefits more than others?" Green asked.

"No, it's an all-or-nothing deal. If anyone wanted to insure they got their productivity bonus they would have to figure a way of getting more product out to the end of the process."

"Who would have the access to get these chips out of the place?"

"Have you ever seen an integrated circuit?" I asked.

"I'm sure I have, but why don't you remind me," Green said.

I got up and walked to the built-in desk in the kitchen. I picked up a clear resin paperweight and carried it back to the table.

"Look in here." The paperweight had several unpackaged chips imbedded inside. All the supervisors in my division had been given these paperweights to commemorate the first hundred-thousand parts sold from our factory.

Green turned the cube over in his hand and looked at the small shiny squares inside.

"This all there is to it?" He held his finger up beside the cube. "These are smaller than my fingernail."

"You're beginning to see the problem," I said. "If the parts were taken before they were packaged, all someone would have to do is keep them clean and wrap them in a conductive wrapper. They could be put in a pocket, a notebook— almost anywhere."

"What do you mean 'keep them clean?'"he asked.

"Integrated circuits can be damaged by contamination in two

ways. You need to keep big hunks of dust and dirt off them. That's what we call particulate contamination. Even a little speck of dust is a big deal when you work at this level of miniaturization. The second problem is ionic contamination. If the salt from a person's skin gets on these devices, it wreaks havoc on the performance of the chip.

"The people in the fabrication labs wear bunny suits to prevent particulate contamination and surgical gloves to prevent ionic contamination. In addition to all that, once the chips get their metallization, they are sensitive to static electricity at a level well below what would cause you to feel a shock."

"So, what does all that mean?" Green asked. "What would a package of these chips look like?"

"If the parts were in their final package, ready to use? Only static would be an issue. They'd be stuck in antistatic foam. It looks like a dense black sponge. If they were really bold, the parts would be in shipping packages, which could be plastic tubes or trays. I don't think anyone would do that, just because it would be recognizable to anyone.

"If someone is taking chips and packaging them elsewhere, it gets trickier. We have little chip trays with snap-on lids that would keep the parts clean. Plus, they're conductive, which means static wouldn't be an issue. Those could be smuggled out in the palm of your hand. Or a person could put them into any number of holders— a glass vial, any plastic box. All they'd have to do is add a small layer of foil to make it conductive. A lot of everyday ordinary items that get carried in and out of the lab could have chips hidden inside."

Green leaned his chair forward and put his elbows on the table. "This is starting to make a little more sense. Someone was looking for something small when he ripped this place up. They wouldn't have taken the time to dump the cereal boxes or to cut things up so much if they were looking for something like a book or a briefcase.

"That means you must have intercepted some evidence. Maybe even a shipment."

"That's a great theory," I said. "Unfortunately, I haven't brought anything but papers home from work lately."

"Do you carry a briefcase?" He asked.

"Her briefcase is at the luggage shop having its handle stitched,"

Mrs. Johnson said.

"All I've been carrying back and forth is my Daytimer." I got up and went back to the kitchen desk. My leather-covered schedule book lay open on the cluttered surface. I picked it up and shook it. A receipt for gas fell out onto the floor. "Nothing unusual here."

I paged through the calendar pages. There was nothing but a bunch of blank days.

"I have the copies of the log book pages I brought home, but the boys have been through them. They separated each page when they were figuring out the problem. I'm sure they would have noticed something that supported their theory, like the lost chips."

Green looked at Mrs. Johnson. "Has she always had such an acid tongue? Or is it just me?"

"How can you joke at a time like this?"

"The guys that can't laugh at times like this don't last in this business."

"So, if robbery is the motive," I said, "then Mike and Debbie and Hieu were killed because they figured it out?"

"Something like that," Green said. "Either they figured out who was doing it and confronted them or they caught them in the act. They might have just stumbled into the wrong place at the wrong time."

"But Mike and Debbie weren't killed at work."

"I don't want you acting like a mother bear with her cubs threatened, but there is another possibility."

"What's that?" I asked. I could feel my face turning red, and I didn't even know what he was going to say yet.

"It's an inside job, and they were all in on it."

"That's not possible," I said a little too quickly.

"You just think about it," he said. "It would answer a lot of questions. I'm betting the black market for these things is overseas. They probably are routed through San Francisco or Seattle. Some guy comes to town, gets a couple of your people involved and milks it for as long as he can. When you start getting on to him, he ties up the loose ends by killing the people involved."

"I just can't believe it," I said. "Maybe Debbie, but not Mike and certainly not Hieu. Mike and Hieu both grew up in communist countries. I know they both felt strongly about living in a free country. Hieu was against corruption of any kind. He used to talk to the young people in the group about it. Mike was very involved in his church. He lived by himself. He didn't have to go to church; he went because he wanted to. He used to talk about it once in a while. It was one of his and Debbie's problem areas when they were dating."

Green stood up and carried his plate and cup to the sink.

"Maybe it will turn out different this time," he said. I knew it was for my benefit.

"I'm gonna call my Henry to come get me," Mrs. Johnson said.

"I'm going to take a look at your yard and the back of the house," Green said. "Harley, when I come back in, I want you to show me where all the windows are and where the alarm system control is."

Mrs. Johnson left, Green checked the yard and I gave him the requested tour of my windows. He checked each one and then asked to visit to the basement. We ended up at the foot of the stairs, where the security system master control panel was located. I reached my arm past his head, and he ducked.

"Relax," I said and showed him the rather impressive cobweb he had walked into. "If I'd known we were coming down here, I would have cleaned."

"Liar."

"Well, I would have tried harder to get you not to come down here."

"This place is like Fort Knox," he said.

"You wouldn't listen. I tried to tell you we would be safe here."

"I'm curious," he said and paused. "Why do you need such a sophisticated security system? And how did the people who tore the place up get past it?"

"We don't usually put the system on during the day when we're home. Mrs. Johnson was here. The burglar just walked in and hit her on the head. As for the system, Noah's father is more than a little paranoid about security issues."

"That's putting it mildly. The President of the United States could stay here in safety. And, no, I'm not going home."

I smiled. He was a mindreader.

"If someone got in once, we aren't going to take chances. These high-tech types you work with might know how to get around even this system. Besides, someone has been here once and had a look at it."

"Did you have to tell me that right before bedtime?"

"You got nothing to worry about tonight," he said. "I'm here."

His assurances did nothing to calm my fears. I went to bed anyway and fell into a dark and dreamless sleep.

CHAPTER TWENTY-SIX

THE SOUND OF HAIL BOUNCING off the attic skylight woke me early on Saturday morning. It was soon replaced by torrential rain. I glanced at the travel alarm I had set by my bed and was surprised to see it was past eight. The dark clouds made it seem much earlier.

Ordinarily, on a Saturday morning, I would have changed into exercise clothes. Or my version of them, which consists of a pair of faded cotton Lycra tights and a one-size-fits-all T-shirt Sam had brought home from a "business trip" he made to Disneyland a couple of years ago.

With Green downstairs, I didn't want to risk the dash to my bedroom to get them. I was still waiting for the miracle body transformation promised by my exercise video. Until it appeared, I did my workout in the solitude of my dimly lit attic. I wasn't about to do it with him watching.

I had just finished the last of three hundred leg lifts when I heard the phone. I was still in my pajamas, so I grabbed the plaid kimono I use for a bathrobe and dashed down the stairs. The phone stopped ringing as I hit the bottom step. I opened the door at the foot of the stairs and looked into the kitchen. Green had gotten it.

"Hang on a second, I'll get her for you," I heard him say.

He looked at me as I walked toward him then turned his attention back to the phone.

"None of your business," he said. I looked at the caller ID on my desk. "Anonymous" was its contribution.

Green covered the phone with his hand. "It's Sam. He says he wants to talk to you."

I grabbed the phone from him. "Hi, what's up?"

"What the hell were you thinking?" Sam asked. "What in God's name possessed you to drag Noah to a murder scene? I told you I didn't want his picture in the paper. I was thinking of school photos or things like that. I had no idea you were going to take him from the safety of his military school and involve him in a front-page murder case. The boy seems to like you, but if you can't act responsibly and in his best interest, we may have to make a different arrangement."

"What on earth are you talking about?" I asked.

Green held up the morning edition of *The Oregonian*. On the front page was a picture taken at Sil-Trac yesterday. It showed Hieu's body being carried out on a gurney. Noah and Chris were in the background. Noah was standing sideways, as if he were whispering something to Chris. You would have to know Noah to recognize him in the picture. BRUTAL MURDER AT LOCAL HIGH TECH FACTORY the headline read.

"You tell me," Sam said. "All I know is that Noah is on the front page of *The Oregonian* at the scene of a murder."

"I didn't take him to the scene of a murder," I said. "I took him and Chris to work with me to get something. They wanted to come into the clean room with me. I had no idea one of my workers was in the lab dead."

"I don't understand why he isn't at school," Sam said. "If he was where he is supposed to be none of this would have happened."

"What, exactly, do you think happened?" I asked. "I found the body. The boys didn't go into the room with the body. They saw the body covered with a blanket from a distance."

"I don't give a shit if they saw ten bodies," Sam said. "I thought I made myself clear. Under no circumstance is Noah to have his picture taken. Not for school, not for ID cards and not for front-page news stories. If you can't do this one simple thing, I'm going to remove you as the kid's guardian."

"Maybe if you told me why you're so paranoid about pictures it would be easier to make it happen."

"Look, lady, I don't have to tell you anything. Noah likes you. He wants to spend time with you. But understand this. I can't have you broadcasting his picture. This better not happen again. If I even think you are letting someone take his picture that will be the end. You will never see Noah again."

I heard a click. I slammed the receiver into its cradle and I stared at the ceiling in silence for a moment.

"God, he is so impossible."

"Sounds like he's got a thing about pictures, huh?" Green asked.

"That's not the half of it," I said. "Sam is one of the most paranoid people I've ever met. He sees conspiracy everywhere."

"That's kinda unusual, don't you think?"

"Bizarre is more like it. Ultimately, it's what broke us up. I couldn't live like that, constantly looking over my shoulder, taking circuitous routes everywhere and never having a picture of Sam or Noah. Except for Noah's school ID picture and one I took of Sam when he was sleeping he doesn't know about."

"How long were you married?"

"Five years," I replied. "And, no, he wasn't always like that. The first couple of years were fine. He was a little mysterious about what kind of work he did. Said he was a consultant. He always had money, and he did send in tax returns, so I assumed he earned it lawfully. Other than that, he was your average guy.

"It all changed when he brought Noah home. He said Noah was his child from a liaison he had when he was working in the Middle East. From the time Noah came to live with us, Sam began to change. Eventually, it was impossible to live with him.

"He traveled a lot. Each time he came home he would act strange for a longer period of time. When I tried to talk to him about it, he just said I was right and he was being selfish. He said he was putting Noah and me in jeopardy by living with us.

"Then he just left. I received divorce papers a few weeks later. Included in the envelope were papers granting me legal guardianship in Sam's absence. Child support was deposited automatically into my checking account."

"What's Noah got to say?" Green asked.

"He doesn't know anything," I said. "He just remembers living with a series of 'aunts' and 'grandmothers' when he was a little boy. First in the Middle East and then in New York. He says the women who raised him were harsh and encouraged him to keep his questions to himself."

"What do you think it all means?"

"What it means is I don't have enough information to figure it out. In the end, it didn't matter whether Sam was some kind of international spy or just some paranoid head case who did too many mind-altering drugs in the sixties. The end result was the same. I couldn't live with him, and neither could Noah. There was a time when I loved the guy, now I just feel sorry for him."

"Wow, that's really tough, huh?"

Green had stepped closer to me while we were talking. I looked down at my hands.

"I'm sorry. I don't usually ramble on about my personal life like that,"

He put his fingers under my chin and tilted my face upward. My cheeks flamed as he looked directly into my eyes.

"You got a raw deal," he said. "There's no reason to be embarrassed about that. You're supposed to feel bad when people dump on you. Besides, you didn't ramble. I asked. "

I was spared further embarrassment by the ringing phone. Noah called to ask if he could come home yet, and if not, could I bring him some things. By the time I finished with him, Green was nowhere to be seen. I could hear the shower running and assumed he was in it.

The water I had put on the stove for tea had just begun to steam when the phone rang again.

"Hello?" I said.

"Harley?" Tommy asked. "Are you going to the service at Mike's uncle's house today?"

"Yeah, I'm planning on it. Why?" I asked.

"My dad said I could bring some food and champagne from the restaurant, but I wasn't sure if that was okay. What do you think?"

"I think that would be very generous of you. His uncle doesn't have a lot of resources. I think he would appreciate the gesture."

"Do you know how to get hold of him?"

"Do you want me to call him?"

"Could you?"

"Uncle Andrush isn't my favorite person, but I guess I could tell him."

"Thanks, Harley, you're the best."

Best or not, I was having second thoughts about talking to Uncle Andrush. As a supervisor, I walk a fine line. I have to remain professional and detached and follow the letter of the law.

At the same time, I'm the interface between management and the workers, so it's also my job to be the human face of the corporation. If Mike was an innocent victim, it was my job to make Mike's family feel like Sil-Trac cared about their loss. If he was involved in a theft ring, it was my job to help the police find his partners and keep a cool distance from his family.

I was pondering my options when the phone rang again. It was Shannon.

"Harley?" she asked. "I'm just calling you to let you know I'm okay. I've decided I'm just going to stay out of the way until the police find the killer. I'm not going back to my apartment."

"Don't you think it would be safer to tell your story to the police and let them protect you?" I asked. "You could tell them what really happened and then take a lie detector test if they don't believe you."

"You can't be that naive, Harley. They can make those tests say anything they want. They could make it look like I killed Debbie and Hieu, and then the real killer would get away."

"I think you're making a mistake. But I guess you have to do what you have to do. Are you going to Mike's memorial tonight?"

"I have to," she said. "He was my friend. I couldn't let them bury him without saying goodbye. I'll just come for a while."

"Could you do a big favor for me?" I asked. I felt a brief stab of guilt for using her in this way. She had enough problems without me helping her. "Tommy's parents are sending some food and champagne to Mike's Uncle Andrush for tonight. Someone needs to call Andrush and tell him."

"That's no problem," she said. "I was going to call and ask if they needed help anyway."

She rang off, and I felt a little less guilty. My relief was short-lived.

"Was that anyone I need to know about?" Green asked as he walked into the kitchen, rubbing my purple towel on his wet hair.

"No," I lied. "Just one of my workers calling about Mike's memorial."

I told him in detail about Tommy's call and his parents' offer. I even filled him in on my call from Noah. If Green noticed how chatty I was, he didn't say anything.

I felt bad about the fact I hadn't warned Shannon that Green was coming with me tonight. I kept telling myself she wasn't my problem. A small voice in the back of my head insisted I should be telling Green about Shannon. In the end, I decided the best route was to let them both be at the service and see what happened. There are times when being spineless is the best option.

"I've got to get out of here," I said. "The phone is driving me crazy."

I braced myself for a protest from Green, but he surprised me.

"I think that's a good idea," he said.

I looked at him and didn't make a move.

"What?" he asked, looking back at me with a grin.

"What's the catch, that's what," I said.

"There's no catch. You can go anywhere you want, except to see Noah, of course."

"What aren't you telling me?" I asked. "And I want a straight answer."

"Okay," he said, suddenly serious. "That's fair. I want you to go out so I can have you followed. I'd like to see if anyone is tailing you. I want to know how serious these clowns are."

"So, I'm going to be some kind of guinea pig? Or is it more like a worm on a hook?"

"I don't like that you are in this situation, but you are. If you sit home, whoever bashed Mrs. J could came back and try again. If there was someplace I could take you, keep you safe and make this all go away, I would. But, lady, that ain't reality." He closed the distance between us until he was staring into my face, no trace of his smile left. "The reality is some nutcase is killing people. We don't know who and we don't know why. And we for sure don't know who else is on the list. My job is to stop this clown before anyone else gets killed. I'm gonna use everything available to do that, including you."

He took a step back and looked away. "I'm sorry if that hurts, but if I don't do my job someone else is gonna die."

"Well, I'm glad we got that cleared up," I said and started straightening the papers on my desk. "What about Noah? How am I supposed to get his stuff to him?"

"Get his stuff together. I'll take it to him after you leave. I'll have someone watching you. No one will follow me. It's you they're after."

"Thanks for the words of comfort," I said.

"Hey, you're the one who wanted straight answers. What's the matter? Is the truth a little too ugly for you?"

I turned and went out of the kitchen. I didn't stop until I got to Noah's room. I was used to dealing with difficult people, but Green was something else. He seemed to take great pleasure in irritating people.

I took my time getting Noah's stuff together. I put it into an old purple gym bag I found in the closet. I started out of his room when I spotted Banana. I unzipped the bag, grabbed the monkey and put him between the sweatshirt and the video games. Noah would understand.

My mood was better by the time I came back into the kitchen. Green sat at the table drinking instant coffee out of my favorite cup. The jar of Folgers was on the counter, surrounded by spilled grains of coffee.

"Harley," he said when he looked up, "I'm sorry for being so blunt earlier."

"You don't have to apologize, Detective Green. I asked for the truth, and that's what you told me. I understand you have a job to do. I get that you have to be here, but I don't have to like it and I don't have to like you."

"Jesus, lady, don't you have to be even a little bit charming in your line of work?"

His last comment didn't rate a reply. I dropped Noah's bag on the table and went to my room. Or what was left of it.

CHAPTER TWENTY-SEVEN

HEN I CAME OUT OF THE bathroom after my shower, Green was gone. Noah's bag was gone, too. There was no note, so I assumed whatever tail was on me when I left didn't require my participation.

I needed to do several errands, but I found myself driving to Neva Dean's house instead.

"Come in, dear," she said from her doorway as I walked up her sidewalk. She grabbed my arm and guided me into her living room. "I thought I might see you today."

"What made you think that?" I asked. "I didn't know I was coming here until I turned on your street."

"The angels, honey, the angels. They've been all a-twitter this morning. They get that way when we're going to have company," she said in a conspiratorial whisper. "You just sit yourself down for a minute while I make some tea."

The fragrance of orange peel, cloves and a spice I couldn't quite identify came wafting into the living room, where I sat in a chintz-covered overstuffed chair. I could hear the clinking sounds of cups and silverware and then the muted whistle of Neva Dean's teakettle. I must have dozed off— the next thing I knew was Neva Dean gently shaking my arm. She had set a tray with the tea supplies and a plate of warm chocolate chip cookies on the ottoman between our chairs.

I wondered briefly how it was that women like Neva Dean and Mrs. J always seemed to have a fresh batch of cookies coming out of the oven. What did they do with the cookies on the days when no one showed up unexpectedly? Did they have a premonition that drove them to stir up a batch of dough before someone came? Or did they compulsively bake cookies day and night, hiding the excess in unexpected places?

Neva Dean interrupted my pondering. She handed me a gold-rimmed china cup and filled it with the spicy blend she had brewed for this occasion. We drank our tea without speaking for a few minutes. Neva Dean watched from her chair in silence until I put my teacup down.

"Now, you tell Neva Dean what the problem is. Whatever it is, I'm sure it'll seem better if you tell me about it."

"It's that damn picture we found," I began.

She looked shocked. "You mean that religious painting?" She leaned over to me and whispered, "Honey, the angels don't like that kind of language when you're speaking of religious things."

"I'm sorry. Tell them I'm sorry."

"Honey, they can hear you. You can speak to them yourself."

"I think I'd be more comfortable if you could handle the angels. okay?"

"I'm sorry, honey, of course, I'll take care of them. Sometimes I forget not everyone is used to dealing with them." She pointed skyward.

I was glad we had that settled. I was also beginning to wonder why I was here. Perhaps so I would feel normal by contrast.

"Neva Dean, I don't know what to do with the painting. Uncle Andrush forced his way into my home looking for it. He wants to sell it, probably at a fraction of its worth. Mike's mother sent it from Poland, so I assume she doesn't want me to give it back. She probably had enough trouble getting it out of there once.

"Since Mike had it and kept it hidden, I'm guessing his mother didn't want Andrush to get his hands on it. Andrush has made it clear he's willing to do almost anything to get the painting back."

I stopped talking and looked at Neva Dean. Instead of the encouraging look I expected, she looked uncomfortable.

"Neva Dean," I said, "tell me what you're thinking."

"Now, honey, I don't want to offend you." She looked at a spot above my left shoulder. "Okay, all right," she said.

I was pretty sure she wasn't talking to me.

"Harley, Mike told me he thought you were a pretty good supervisor. Even when he didn't agree with you, which I gather was pretty often, he still thought you were fair."

I was beginning to wonder if I knew anyone who could make a point without circling it four or five times first.

"What I'm trying to say is," she finally continued, "I'm trying to say that I think you're a good decision maker at that big factory, but I'm just not sure this is your decision to make."

She looked at me to see how I was going to react to her news.

"But I have the picture — " I started.

Neva Dean held up her hand to quiet me.

"Honey, you have one idea of the situation. I know you don't like Andrush. I'm not saying you don't have good reason, but you're not dealing with a full deck."

"I beg your pardon."

"I don't mean it like you think. I just mean you don't have all the facts. You can only make decisions based on what you know. Right now, I'm not sure you know enough about the situation."

"I take it you have more information?"

"Well, let's take Andrush, to start with. First of all, I know he's done some things that aren't kosher."

"You can say that again," I said.

Neva Dean gave me a stern look. "As I was saying, just because Andrush isn't likable, it doesn't mean Mike's mother is a saint."

I felt my face heat up. I was guilty as charged. I could tell I was about to hear things I probably wasn't going to like about Mike's mother.

"Mike's mom is involved in Polish politics. She belongs to, by Mike's account, a radical group that isn't happy with the slow pace of reform. They're willing to use violence if it aids their cause. Mike told me his dad died when he was about twelve. His mom remarried, a man who was involved in this political group or some such thing.

"Mike said the guy was thrown in jail after a skirmish with the local police a few years ago. He said his mother gave all the money he would send her to the stepfather or the group. He wanted his mom to have a better life. I guess she couldn't see anything but her cause."

Neva Dean was right. Things were definitely not what they seemed.

"So, are you saying I should give Andrush the painting?"

"Honey, I didn't say that." She paused a minute. "Why, I'm not sure I know just what you *should* do with the painting. I don't believe it's your problem to solve. Each person has a reason to have it. At least, in their own mind they do."

"But, Neva Dean, it *is* my problem as long as I have possession of the picture."

"Well, why do you have it? You have it because Rebecca asked you to keep it for her. Why don't you just do that?"

"You mean hold on to it until she asks for it?"

"She came to Mike's to get the painting," Neva Dean said. "The only reason she gave it to you is because the police showed up. I'm not sure she expected you to do anything but keep the picture until she got free of the police. After all, she didn't tell us about the real painting. Has she asked about it?"

"No, she hasn't, and I haven't called her about it, either. You're right, though. Rebecca asked me to keep it, she didn't ask me to get involved with it. I think maybe I should just bring it to the memorial service. I'll give it to her with the Black Madonna showing. She can do whatever she was going to do before the police showed up."

I felt a lot better having a plan worked out. How I was going to get the picture to Rebecca without alerting everyone else in the place was another problem, but I decided I would take mine one at a time.

Neva Dean walked me out to my car. She nodded toward a man pulling weeds in a garden strip across the street.

"He's been weeding that one little patch for the last three hours. I hope he isn't being paid by the hour."

I looked at the man, but he had ducked his head, obscuring his face from view.

"He doesn't look very dangerous," I said. "I think you're bigger than him. Just in case, keep your panic button around your neck. I'll be back in a couple hours to pick you up."

I watched Neva Dean go back up the steps to her apartment. The man across the street was still bent over the garden strip. As I grasped the handle on my car door, a sweaty hand clamped over mine. I jumped like I'd been shot then immediately got angry. It was Green.

"What are you doing?" I demanded.

"Checking up on you, of course. I said you'd be followed. What's up with Neva Dean?"

"Nothing," I said, trying not to look guilty about my lie.

"Why are you here, then?" he asked.

"I didn't know I had to have a reason. Or your permission, for that matter."

"Don't get your knickers in a twist," he said. "I get this feeling there's more going on here than you're telling me."

You don't know the half of it, I thought.

Green looked at me as if he expected a response. He didn't get one.

"I *will* find out everything in the end, you know," he said.

"If I come across any information you need to know, I'll tell you," I said. "Not everything in my life is related to...this," I said, for lack of a better way to describe what had been going on.

Green looked down and shook his head. He looked back up with a smile. "You want to go get a bite to eat?"

"Do I have a choice?"

"Sure. We can go together, or we can go together separately."

"Fine," I said. I didn't have a plan for how I was going to spend the time before the memorial service, now that Noah was not an option. "Where do we have to go?"

"You tell me. I'm the one who's doing the following."

Green looked like a meat-and-potatoes guy.

"How about sushi?" I asked brightly.

"Just say where," he said.

I described a sushi place right off the corner of Broadway and Burnside. They served on color-coded plates that traveled on a conveyor past all the patrons, who sit on stools at a long, U-shaped counter.

Green climbed in.

"I'll have the surveillance team pick up my car. I left it a couple of streets over."

We drove across the Willamette River in silence. I found a parking spot on a side street, and we walked the two blocks to the restaurant. I guided Green to a stool at the counter. He looked uncomfortable.

"What do you recommend?"

"Any of the raw fish ones are good," I replied. "Tuna is my

personal favorite."

I pointed to a picture on a laminated card, which featured photos of the offerings.

Green watched as I took a small dish and poured in a splash of soy sauce. I took a pair of chopsticks from a container on the counter and used them to add a chunk of wasabi, the hot green horseradish that is essential for the consumption of sushi. I stirred the mix and then added a few pink slices of ginger. With my preparations complete, I selected a dish of three tuna-topped pieces of sushi from the conveyor. Green was still watching when I dipped one of the pieces in my sauce mix and then popped it into my mouth.

He watched the dishes go by, looking at each new offering, but not choosing any.

"Is there a problem?"

"No," he answered. "I'm just waiting for the right one."

I was eating my third piece of tuna when I saw him reach for a plate. He had chosen a sushi that had cooked crab and fresh avocado as the main ingredients. He popped a piece in his mouth.

"That's what I call good," he said. "I don't know what the orange powder on the outside is, but this is great."

Finally, the moment I'd been waiting for. I was just about to deliver my knockout punch when his pager sounded. He glanced at it, jumped up, dropped a quarter in the pay phone and had a hasty conversation. He flashed his badge at the attendant and dropped a twenty on the counter as he walked back to me.

"Let's go," he barked.

I jumped up and followed him, almost running to catch up to him. My revelation about fish eggs would have to wait.

I finally caught up and grabbed his arm.

"What's going on?"

"Get in the car, we're going back to Neva Dean's. Someone just tried to break in."

CHAPTER TWENTY-EIGHT

WHAT?" I CRIED.

Green grabbed my keys from my hand and got behind the wheel.

"Get in," he said and started the car. He was back on the Burnside Bridge before I got my seatbelt buckled.

"Neva Dean heard a noise and hit her panic button. Nine-one-one alerted our surveillance team. They ran around behind the building and saw a perp running down the street. He was dressed in black from head to toe. He jumped into a waiting car and sped away."

"Is Neva Dean okay?"

"We'll know soon enough."

He turned a corner and parked in front of Neva Dean's apartment. There were white Portland police cars in the street in front, and the front door was open. A policewoman leaned against the doorjamb.

Green had pulled his badge off his belt and held it up. The policewoman stood up abruptly and backed out of our way. We walked into Neva Dean's living room.

She sat in one of the overstuffed chairs talking to a tall young patrol officer. I went to her chair and kneeled beside her.

"Are you okay?"

"Heavens, yes, girl. It takes more than a little window rattling to scare Neva Dean Willett."

"What happened?" I got off my knees and sat in the same chair I had occupied scarcely an hour ago.

Neva Dean stood up. "Let me get us a little cup of tea, and I'll tell you all about it," she said.

The police officer started to protest, but Green held his hand up to quiet the guy.

Let her be, he mouthed.

Neva Dean set the kettle on the burner, turned the knob and ignited the gas flame. "Now," she asked, "who all wants tea?"

Green and I agreed to cups. The patrolman excused himself and went out to his car. From a cabinet above the sink, Neva Dean got heavy mugs that looked hand-thrown.

"My sister Ozie gave these to me back in the seventies," she said to no one in particular.

The kettle boiled, and she poured water into a teapot. She had placed a mixture of tea and aromatic herbs into the pot while the water boiled. When she completed her preparations, she loaded the tray and carried it back to the living room.

She looked at Green and then at me. "I suppose you want to know what happened."

We looked at her intently.

"You probably won't believe me, but I'm going to tell you what took place. I was sitting in my chair." Her hand absently caressed the smooth fabric of the arm. "I was just getting ready to watch a program my friend Hazel had recommended. One of those British comedies, I think. I was searching the channels trying to find the show when the angels just purely went crazy. They were downright frantic.

"Well, I knew something was wrong, but they can't tell me exactly what the nature of a problem is. I have to figure that out myself. I was listening carefully to see if I could get any idea when I heard the bedroom window rattle. When I heard that, I pushed my button right quick. The rattling stopped, and the police were here in no time."

Green took Neva Dean through her story three more times, but she couldn't add anything else. The angels alerted her, and she alerted the police.

"When was the last time you spoke to Mike?" Green asked Neva Dean.

Neva Dean looked down, as if she were thinking real hard. "Why, it was right before he went to his aunt and uncle's house. He wanted to let me know Rebecca would be coming and going, feeding Lech. When Debbie and he went places, he would ask me to feed the cat. Debbie did it if he went by himself. I guess he wanted to let me know Rebecca was taking over Debbie's job."

"Did he give you anything to keep for him?" Green asked.

"Honey, he gave me things all the time," Neva Dean said. "His aunt and uncle in Eugene grow herbs. Every time he goes there, he brings me some back. I give him special spices and such to take to them. His Uncle Andrush sends stuff over for me, too. He sent me some fish he had smoked that day. He also sent me a jar of jelly his wife made. I'm sure he didn't expect to get those things back."

"Can I see the fish and jelly?" Green asked. "Also, anything they were wrapped in."

"You think the missing chips are in a smoked fish?" I asked.

"I'm not saying that," he said. "All I know is someone is looking for something. They must want it pretty bad if they're willing to break in, in broad daylight." He turned to Neva Dean. "You did good, Neva Dean. You keep that buzzer around your neck. I've got people nearby, all you need to do is call. I'll have Officer Haynes stay with you until we come get you tonight, okay?"

"Don't you worry about me, honey," she said. "I've seen worse days than these. Besides, I've got my angels to warn me if any trouble is coming."

"Yeah, well, whatever. You need me, you know how to find me."

I could see Green wasn't buying into the angel routine. I wasn't sure I was, either, but I wasn't going to let Neva Dean in on my doubts.

Green went out to the patrol car and brought back a woman officer. She would stay with Neva Dean. Another officer was given the task of questioning the neighbors.

"You want to finish lunch?" he asked.

"I'm not hungry anymore," I answered. "I think I just want to go home."

"Okay, drop me at my car, and I'll follow you home."

"God, I hate this."

Green got in the passenger seat and handed me my keys. We drove to his car in silence. I wished I could stop this merry-go-round and get off. I wanted Noah back home where he belonged. I wanted to spend my weekend pulling weeds in my flowerbed instead of attending memorial services. And I didn't want a roommate.

Saturday wasn't one of Mrs. Johnson's regular days, so I was surprised when I turned into the driveway and saw her car.

"What are you doing here today?" I asked when I got inside.

"I missed so much time with my bump on the head I had to come," she said.

We both knew that wasn't true. Getting hit on the head was the most exciting thing that had happened to her in the last ten years. I think she wanted to be near the center of the action in case anything else came up.

She asked what had I'd done today. I'd just finished telling her when Green arrived.

"Sit down, I'll make you a sandwich," she said. "You must be starving." She pulled out a chair at the table for him. "You, too, Harley. You need a snack."

I protested, but it did no good. Mrs. J layered smoked turkey and Jarlsburg cheese on thick-sliced dark rye for Green and topped a bowl of romaine lettuce with leftover chicken breast and Caesar dressing for me. He ate like a starving man. I picked at mine, wishing this day was over.

We finished eating, and Mrs. Johnson whisked our dishes away like a waiter at closing time.

"The way I see it," Green said, "the thief thinks either you or Mrs. Willett has the missing circuits. Chances are he's going to keep looking until he finds them. All we have to do is find them first."

"Oh, is that all," I said. "It sounds simple. In fact, I only see one problem."

"What would that be?"

"I don't have the damn chips," I said, exasperated. "Mike gave me nothing. We had no contact before he left. He has never been to my house. I have taken nothing home from work except papers, which have been gone through."

"Well, someone seems to think otherwise."

"Tell you what. You just feel free to look all you want. I'm going to lie down for a little while before we go to the service."

I didn't wait for a reply, just went upstairs. My head was pounding. I meant to just lie down on the futon and shut my eyes for a few minutes.

※ ※ ※

The next thing I knew, Green was sitting beside me on the futon, gently shaking my shoulder.

"Wake up, sleepyhead," he said.

I slapped his hand away before I was awake enough to recognize who he was.

"Sorry," I said.

"Hey, I'm used to people resisting my requests. It's part of my job."

I guess he was attempting cop humor. I didn't say anything. I did look at the clock.

"Why didn't you wake me sooner?" I asked. "We have to pick up Neva Dean in twenty minutes."

He didn't move. "You needed the sleep. Besides, I didn't think you were the kind of gal that required hours to get ready."

"I don't. I mean, I'm not. It would have been nice to have fifteen minutes, though."

"You look fine," he said. "I'm going like this." He held out his arms. He had on an outfit very much like the one he'd had on the first time I met him. It aged him about ten years and thirty pounds.

"On you, it looks fine," I lied. "But I don't think polyester is my look. If you'll wait for me downstairs, I'll freshen up and be down in a minute."

Green looked at me without moving. I couldn't believe I'd hurt his feelings. Surely, the polyester pants and short tie had to be an effect he was going for. Finally, he gave me a kind of half-smile and got up without saying a word.

When I came downstairs after a quick freshen-up, I was wearing a pair of black twill pants and a black-and-white print silk blouse. I wasn't sure what proper mourning wear was in Poland, but this would have to do.

Green was feeding Cher — the cat must have given up her post upstairs while I was asleep. She was on the counter, rubbing her head on his arm as he scooped kitty tuna into her dish. I silently branded her a traitor.

Seeing the cat food gave me an idea. Sonny liked cat food better than almost anything else. He went to great lengths to subvert whatever system we came up with to protect Cher's food from him. He could get around childproof latches to get to her bag of dry food. He was able to climb up onto the counter somehow when we fed her up there. Finally, Sam built a special shelf on the stairwell that only she could manage. It was a bit tricky for me to reach, but I wasn't willing to argue with success.

All of us thought we had heard Sonny barking somewhere nearby in the last few days. I decided to set a trap. I took a hand-painted bowl from the closet, one of the few dishes that wasn't damaged in the break-in. I poured it full of dry kitty food and then opened a can of kitty tuna and put it on top.

"What's the matter, didn't I give her enough?" Green asked.

"This isn't for Cher." I carried the dish to the back porch and set it on the step. "It's a summons. If Sonny is anywhere within smelling distance, he'll find his way here. He loves Cher's food more than life itself."

He raised his eyebrow but stayed silent.

"Could you see if my coat is in the trunk of my car?" I asked.

I tossed him my keys from the kitchen desk. He went without comment. I immediately went to the electrical panel/safe and flipped the series of circuit breakers that were really the controls to the safe. The door popped open, and I brought the painting out. I grabbed a coat off the hook on the stairwell and stuffed the rolled-up painting in the sleeve. I would deal with the frame later.

"I didn't see a coat in the car," Green said as he came back inside. "Are you are sure you put it in the trunk?"

"Now that I think of it, I dropped it back at the cleaners. I'll just take this one." I took the keys as I walked past him. I was careful to keep the coat away from his prying gaze.

"Well, let's go," I said. I went out the door. Green followed.

"Don't you need to set your alarm?" he asked.

"I'll do it from the car."

I showed him the small remote control I had pulled from my purse. I walked around the car and opened the trunk. I put the coat in quickly and shut the lid before Green could get a good look.

"Has anyone ever told you how strange it is to carry your coat in your trunk?" he asked.

"Not once," I said and got in the car.

Green made small talk on the way to Neva Dean's place. I didn't pay attention. I was too busy trying to plan in my head how I would get the picture back to Rebecca without the whole party knowing about it.

If Neva Dean was affected by her afternoon excitement she didn't show it. The red in the Yves St. Laurent scarf draped across one shoulder of the black silk suit she had on was a perfect match with her lipstick.

"Neva Dean," I said, "I love your suit."

"This old rag?" she said. "I've had it for a hundred years. I got it at that resale shop down on Ninth.

"Well, you look great, doll," Green said.

"And you look so handsome in your suit," Neva Dean reciprocated.

If I didn't get out of there I was going to be sick.

"Can we go?" I asked.

They both agreed. With only a moment's pause for last-minute instructions from the angels, we were on our way.

CHAPTER TWENTY-NINE

THERE WERE CARS IN front of Andrush's house, so I drove past and turned around to park on the opposite side of the street. Before I could turn the engine off, one of Andrush's sons came over and directed us to park in the driveway.

"So Mrs. Willett, she doesn't have to walk so far," he said. "Papa says I should tell you."

I wasn't going to argue. It could only help my "return the picture" scheme.

The kid waited for us to park then guided us into the house through the kitchen door. The smell of cabbage rolls was so strong it took my breath away. We walked past several women in white aprons over cotton dresses. They were stirring things at the stove.

"Miss Spring, come in," Andrush said. "Welcome to my home." He spread his arms wide. I couldn't help feeling like he was putting on a show.

"Come meet my sisters." He put his arms around Neva Dean and me and guided us to a long sofa. Two women sat at one end. You could see a resemblance to Mike in both their faces. Mostly around the eyes. They both had weathered skin that spoke of time spent outdoors.

"This is my sister Ruta," Andrush said. "She is Mike's mother."

I took her offered hand in both of mine.

"I'm so sorry about Mike," I said. "We were all shocked."

Ruta looked at Andrush and listened as he translated for a moment. When he finished, she dipped her head and said, "Thank you."

Tears welled in her eyes. She took out a worn handkerchief and dabbed at their corners.

"And this is my sister Ana." Andrush finished his introductions.

"I'm so sorry we are meeting under such tragic circumstances," I said and looked to him to translate.

"Nothing prepares you for the death of a child," Ana replied. "Especially after you think they are all grown up."

I was surprised. Obviously, this woman had spent a substantial amount of time in America. You couldn't speak English that well if you hadn't, could you?

"I can see from your face you are surprised," she said. "I worked for my government when I was young. They taught me the English language. I returned to Poland many years ago, but I've worked to keep my English."

"You speak the language very well," I said.

Andrush repeated his introductions with Neva Dean. When she had finished offering her condolences, Green stepped forward.

"This is my friend...Mr. Green," I said. Only at that moment did I realize I didn't have a clue what his first name was.

Green filled the awkward space after our condolences with questions about the women's flight and inquiries about Poland's weather. Neva Dean worked her way back to the kitchen and appeared to be in deep discussion with a woman who could only be Andrush's wife. The wife was offering Neva Dean tastes from various pots. She looked totally at ease. I was the only one who seemed out-of-place.

I was studying the glass figurines on a knickknack shelf in the living room when Rebecca and her parents arrived. The parents gave me a nod and went into the kitchen. Rebecca came toward me. I could see her stiffen when she saw Green.

"What is he doing here?" Her eyes were dark with anger.

"It's a long story," I said. "He's my date, sort of. He says he's protecting me."

"He doesn't belong here," she said defiantly.

"Rebecca," I said, not believing what I was about to say, "Green is not the problem here. He's just doing his job. Three people we know have been killed. He's trying his best to make sure none of us are next."

Her pale face turned even whiter, if that's possible. "Three?" she said through stiff lips.

"Oh, God, I'm sorry. Haven't you seen today's paper?"

"Who?" was all she could get out.

"Let's sit down," I said and quickly guided her to an upholstered chair.

"Who?" she asked again as I pushed her down into it.

"Hieu," I said. "It was Hieu. Someone cut his throat. He had gone back to work yesterday."

A single tear slid down Rebecca's porcelain cheek. "When will this end?" she asked in a weary voice.

"I wish I could answer that. We don't know what's going on. All I know is three people I knew and liked are dead."

I hesitated a moment. My management training said you don't pass on gossip and you don't involve your employees in idle speculation. The managers' guidebook didn't have a chapter on murder, though. I had a feeling I was way off the edge of the map.

"Rebecca, we think we might know a reason why someone would want to kill people at work. Maybe you've heard something that could help."

"What is the reason?" she asked.

"Please don't tell anyone about this," I cautioned.

She gave me one of those "You've got to be kidding" looks. She was right. With the exception of Mike, she hardly spoke ten words a day to anyone at work. She was really going to miss him when she came back. That is, if she came back.

"There is evidence that someone has been stealing die from the lab. At this point, we don't know who is involved."

"Mike would never steal," Rebecca said. The color came rushing back to her face. "I know him. I know his family. He could never do such a thing. He would never steal anything."

She crossed her arms across her chest.

"Rebecca." I put my hand on her crossed arms. "No one said Mike was involved. It's possible he knew something and someone found out he knew it."

After dealing with Andrush, I wasn't quite as sure as Rebecca was about Mike's purity, but I wasn't about to discuss it with her.

"Did Mike ever mention anything to you about the counts being off?" I asked. "Did he mention anything about what he thought the problem was?"

"He didn't talk about work very much," she said. "He just said he had to work on his papers. He didn't tell me what kind of papers."

"Hi, Harley. Hi, Rebecca, sorry about Mike," Shannon's voice came from across the room. It was not the way I would have offered my condolences, but I hadn't been on the lam for the last twenty-four hours like she had.

Andrush greeted her at the front door. She handed him a small package. I couldn't see what the package was, but Andrush's face lit up. She gave him a hug. He turned and walked across the living room then disappeared down a hallway. Shannon came over to Rebecca and me. Clearly, this was not her first encounter with Andrush.

Green had gone into the kitchen before she arrived. I was not looking forward to their meeting.

"How's it going?" Shannon asked.

"How do you think it's going?" I asked. Her perkiness was not only inappropriate, it was getting on my nerves. Rebecca just stared past her as if she wasn't there.

"What's with her?" Shannon asked in a stage whisper.

I grabbed her by her skinny arm and pulled her toward the door.

"We're going to look at the flowers," I said over my shoulder to Rebecca as we walked outside.

"What's going on?" I asked Shannon as soon as we were safely out of hearing range of the house. "Are you on drugs?"

She looked at me. A tear formed at the corner of her eye and hovered there, bulging, not quite full enough to spill over and run down her cheek, but it was a tear, nonetheless.

"I just haven't had any sleep since I...I mean since...you know."

"You mean since you found Hieu's body," I said. I wasn't a cruel person by nature, but Shannon's theatrics were getting very tiresome. "Why don't you go home? Get some rest. I'm sure you'll get a little perspective if you get some sleep."

"You don't know everything, you know. Being a boss doesn't mean you're God."

"What are you talking about?" I asked her. I leaned a little closer so I could get a good look at her eyes. Surprisingly, her pupils looked normal. I tried subtly to sniff for the odor of alcohol or marijuana. She smelled faintly of gardenias. That only left one option. She must have suffered some kind of mental breakdown because of Hieu.

"I tried going home," she said. "When I got there, someone was waiting for me. They would have had me, too, if my landlord hadn't clued me in. I stopped by the mailboxes in the lobby of my building to get my mail. I was getting my little key out when Mr. Vaughn said I didn't need to check my mail. I asked him, did I forget a holiday? He said no, it was just that my brother-in-law had checked my mail earlier and then taken it back to the apartment with him. Harley, I don't have a brother-in-law. I'm an only child."

"So, did you call the police?" I asked. I saw the expression on her face. "Don't tell me you still haven't talked to the police. Are you crazy?"

I wished I hadn't put it that way as soon as the words were out of my mouth.

"I already explained to you about the police. I'm just not sure I'm ready to talk to them yet. They won't understand." Shannon must have seen the doubt on my face. "Besides," she said and dropped her head until her chin was nearly on her narrow chest. "Robert asked me not to. He said, if I talk to them they would ask him about Hieu's claims about his daughter. Robert said they would try to throw him out of the country."

"Shannon, you didn't fall for that line, did you?"

She didn't say anything.

"They don't deport a person because someone's dad accuses him of fathering a child."

"But she's a minor."

"I thought you said he was innocent. And even if they convicted him of statutory rape I don't think that would get him deported. Is he a citizen?"

"He said he is." She didn't look up.

"Does Robert have a key to your apartment?"

She just nodded. Her attempt to conceal her tears was futile. They ran in a steady stream across the side of her nose then onto the tip, where they fell silently to the new-turned earth in Andrush's garden.

I patted her on the back and looked over her bent head to the window on the side of the house. Green was standing there watching us. I tilted my head slightly, hoping he would read my signal. He disappeared from sight and, in a moment, came out the front door and crossed the wet grass to where we stood.

He looked at me without speaking. Shannon hadn't noticed his arrival; I tapped her shoulder to get her attention. She dropped a wad of tissues as she looked up. Green immediately bent to pick it up.

"Shannon, this is a friend of mine..." I hesitated.

"Frank Green," he said and extended his hand.

"I think he might be able to help you," I said. "Frank works with the police."

His given name felt strange coming off my tongue.

Shannon's eyes widened. She took a step back. "You're that detective, aren't you? You came with that woman to ask questions at Sil-Trac. Didn't you?"

"When Shannon got home, there was someone in her apartment," I said.

"Are you aware the police have been looking for you?" Green asked. "We'd like the chance to protect you. See if we can keep you alive until tomorrow, you know? That okay with you?"

"Isn't the important point that she's here now? And she's willing to tell you everything she knows." I looked at Shannon, silently daring her to protest.

"Miss King?" Green asked. "I'm gonna need to ask you some questions. Will you come with me?"

She nodded silently then turned to go with him. He looked back at me.

"Don't you go anywhere until I get back," he said.

They strolled out the front gate as if they were looking at the flowers along the border of the yard. They continued past and on down the block. I saw Green reach in his pocket for his radio. He probably had a patrol car in the area.

Neva Dean was visible through the living room window. I decided to go in and check on her. As it turned out, she was doing fine. She was deep in conversation with Ana. Mike's aunt was gesturing with both hands. Neva Dean was smiling. I decided not to interrupt them.

I stood around for a few minutes. I wasn't anxious to talk with

Rebecca again. Tommy had arrived while I was outside. He was carrying a case of bottles that looked like champagne. Debbie Red was with one of Andrush's sons looking at CDs in a tall, skinny rack by the shelf that held the stereo unit. A few other people I didn't recognize arrived. Andrush's wife took shawls and hats and hung them on a rack by the back door.

I looked down at my hands. There was a green streak across my left palm. I must have picked up something from the garden. Maybe when I touched the daffodil. This never seems to happen to Martha Stewart on TV when she stops to smell the roses. I only had to step into someone's garden and the dirt rose up and attached itself to me.

Andrush's house was the square shape that was common to its era. The living room was across the front of the house, and the kitchen and dining area were behind that on either side of a central hallway. One of the three doors at the end of it had to be the bathroom. I spotted Andrush in the kitchen as I passed by on my way to the hall. He was busy opening a bag of plastic champagne glasses and attaching the plastic feet. There was no evidence of the package Shannon had handed him.

My best guess was that the doors on my right and left were bedrooms and the one I was facing was probably the restroom.

The door to my left was slightly ajar. My curiosity got the best of me. I looked back to see if anyone was watching. No one was. I nudged the door with my foot. It opened. I could see a blond bedroom suite. A heavy crocheted cover in off-white was draped over a lavender quilt. Several crystal figurines were arranged on the top of the dresser. I pushed the door farther and froze.

Along the windowsill above the bed was a neat row of plastic boxes. They were round and flat, made of a familiar semitransparent plastic we called by the trade name Nalgene. I threw the door open and walked around the bed. It no longer mattered who heard me.

I grabbed the first box I came to and twisted the top. That instant, I saw, or rather felt, a flash of lightning in my head. The lights went out.

CHAPTER THIRTY

WHEN I CAME TO, IT WAS DARK. I could feel something wet running down from the corner of my eye. It was impossible to tell whether it was blood or tears. I tried to reach up and assess the damage to my skull, but my left arm was pinned under my body and my right arm ran into something hard when I tried to raise it. I attempted to roll from my side, and the hard barrier moved a little. I pushed with my knee, and it moved more.

I turned facedown into a large dust bunny and pushed myself up onto my knees to escape it. I sneezed. Pain radiated through my skull, and I collapsed.

Whoever had hit me had evidently pushed my body over the far side of Andrush's bed. I was on the floor, wedged between the wall and the bedframe. The bed had moved enough to allow me to attempt standing up. I was not successful. I slid back down onto the floor and lost consciousness again.

The second time I woke I was on the bed, and Green was leaning over me, waving a vile-smelling capsule.

"What happened?" I asked.

"I was hoping you could tell me," he answered. "I couldn't find you. I gave your friend over to a patrol car a couple of blocks from here. I wasn't even gone fifteen minutes. Neva Dean was worried about you. She wasn't making any sense. Something about angels. You sure made a mess in here."

I raised my head slowly. I could see all the plastic cases open and strewn about. There were colored contacts all over the top of the dresser. My head throbbed with the effort of looking.

"I didn't do that," I said. "I did come in here. I was planning to

195

see if my missing chips were in those boxes."

"I guess someone else wanted a look, too."

"Your deductive powers are staggering."

"Your head must be feeling better. You think you can get up?"

"No." I closed my eyes.

Green waved the evil capsule again. "Don't you even think about passing out, lady. We've got to get you upright and out to the car. So far, I don't think anyone has noticed you're missing, but if we're both gone they might get ideas."

"Don't flatter yourself. How do you propose I get out of here without attracting a crowd? I can imagine what I look like."

"I'll get a washcloth from the bathroom. You just promise me you won't pass out while I'm gone."

I watched him crack the door open and look out before he stepped across the hall to the bathroom. He was back quickly with a warm, wet towel.

"They're passing champagne around. They're about to start the speeches."

"I'll be okay. Just help me sit up a minute."

He put his arm around my shoulders and lifted me into a sitting position. A wave of dizziness hit me, and my grasp on reality slipped for a moment.

"You're in no shape to go out there," he said. "Why don't I get you out of here?"

"No," I said, with more conviction than I felt. "I have to go out there. For Mike. I'll be fine." I sat up under my own power. "Just stay by my side, in case I get dizzy."

For once, he didn't make a wisecrack; instead, he helped me stand up. I leaned heavily against him as the shock of being upright reached my head.

"You wait here," Green said. He put my hand from his arm onto the dresser by the door. "I'll get Neva Dean to create a distraction. I'll come back for you."

He didn't wait for a reply.

I heard the background rumble of voices from the living room; then Neva Dean's voice rose above the crowd.

"Oh, my poor angel..." She was playing her part well.

The door popped open, and Green took my arm and led me out as quickly as he dared. He shoved a cell phone into my hand.

"If you're through with your phone call, I think Neva Dean needs you," he said, loud enough that the people closest to us could hear.

"Thanks," I said and handed him the phone. He stayed close, his arm supporting my waist without being obvious as he guided me across the room. I sat down next to Neva Dean on the sofa. I handed her a handkerchief that was pressed into my hand from a silent Polish woman. At least, I assumed she was Polish. She had the same shapeless black cotton dress that seemed to be a uniform with the older crowd.

"Mike was more than my co-worker," Tommy was saying to the gathering of mourners. "He was a true friend."

He went on to tell a heart-wrenching story about how Mike cleared three trees that had fallen into Tommy's parents' yard during a storm when Tommy was sick with the flu. Apparently, no one had asked him. He knew Tommy was sick and saw on the news that Tommy's parents lived in a hard-hit area. He showed up, chopped wood all day and left without asking for anything. When Tommy asked him why he did it, he shrugged and said that was the way they did things where he was raised.

Tommy was very eloquent. Other guests in turn told their memories. I hoped they wouldn't think I was rude but standing in front of the group was not an option.

The memory session ended when Rebecca got up to talk. She started out okay but quickly disintegrated into a sobbing heap on the floor. Mike's mother went to help her up. Rebecca's own mother was a little slower to come to her rescue. One could only guess that, memorial service or not, she was somewhat immune to her daughter's theatrics.

Green walked up to Neva Dean and me. "Give me the keys, and I'll get the car. Let's get you out of here while everyone is distracted."

"Who put you in charge?" I asked.

Neva Dean patted my hand. "Honey, I don't think this is a good time to argue with the nice detective. I'm not meaning any insult, but you aren't looking yourself just now."

I had to admit I wasn't feeling that great just now, either. My head hurt too much to think up a better plan, so I handed over the keys. The Polish clan was still tending to Rebecca. It looked like she wasn't ready to relinquish the stage anytime soon, so it should be pretty easy to escape.

"That lady with the midnight-blue crocheted shawl," Neva Dean said, nodding toward the woman in question. "She says she was engaged to Andrush when they were young. Mike's mom said that was wishful thinking on her part. Andrush only had eyes for his wife, they say. I do have to say I find that hard to believe, knowing Andrush, but this poor gal has followed him halfway around the world in the hope he'll leave or outlast his wife and finally come to her."

In a few minutes, Neva Dean had learned more about these people than I had learned in my three years as Mike's boss. She was a gem.

"Harley." Tommy was standing next to Neva Dean. He leaned across her and looked into my face. "Are you okay? I don't want to be rude, but you aren't looking well. You want me to drive you home or something?"

"Thank you, Tommy, I'm fine. All this is just catching up to me, with Mike and Debbie and now Hieu." I feigned a tear and dabbed at my eye. I did feel a bit overwhelmed by the deaths, but I had more immediate problems. "I'm here with friends, but thanks for your concern."

"Have you seen Shannon?" he asked. "She was going to find out about Debbie's funeral from Debbie's sister."

I looked up. "I think she left," I said truthfully. "She was taking this all pretty hard."

"All of us are," Tommy said.

Neva Dean scooted over, patted the sofa and motioned Tommy to sit between us. I saw Green come back in from the kitchen. I started to get up, but he raised his hand in a stay-where-you-are gesture. He worked his way through the crowd, neatly sidestepping Rebecca and her audience. He put his hand on my shoulder.

When Neva Dean and Tommy finished their discussion about the essential difference between Vietnamese and Chinese names, Green softly requested my presence in the kitchen. Tommy asked if he needed help with something, and Green assured him it would help most if he would stay with Neva Dean.

Green grabbed my arm as I started to get up, supporting my weight and pulling me to my feet at the same time. The lights dimmed for a moment, but the pain was a little less than it had been. He gave me a hug as I wobbled.

"If you make like you're enjoying this, your friends might have an easier time believing we're a couple and not a cop and a semi-conscious victim of a beating."

I put my arm around him. "You have no idea how much this disgusts me," I whispered in his ear.

"I guess you're feeling better," he said as he guided me to the kitchen and out onto the back step. "There was a little problem with your car."

"Define problem"

"Whatever these clowns are looking for..." He paused. "...they decided to try looking in your car."

He caught me as I slumped and helped me to sit on the step.

"Is it ruined?"

"Pretty much," he said in a voice that was almost cheerful.

"Couldn't you work up a little sympathy?" I asked.

He grinned. "I can't help it. We may have our first break in this case. The lab guys lifted at least three sets of prints off the trunk. Noah hasn't been home since the boys washed the car. One set of prints is probably yours, but with luck, at least one of the other prints will match our perp."

"My car is ruined?" I repeated. I could feel a tear forming in my good eye.

"What's the problem?" Green said. "You got insurance. If you're lucky you'll get a new car out of the deal."

"I don't want a new car. I like my car. Just the way it is."

"Well, get over it, 'cause it's never gonna be the same."

Green had just helped me to my feet when the back door was thrown open with a bang.

"What is going on here?" Andrush demanded. "Why is police car in my driveway?"

He was about a foot from my face. Green grabbed him by the elbow and guided him down the steps away from me.

"There has been a little problem with Miss Spring's car. Someone broke into it. We didn't want to interfere with the memorial, so we took care of it. If you will lower your voice, no one will be the wiser."

Andrush pulled his arm free and stormed over to my car. Ana

appeared at the door.

"Andrush," she called, "we need you..." She stopped mid-sentence. "What has happened here?" She walked over to the car.

Andrush was at the back of my car. The thieves had left the trunk open.

"You!" he bellowed and pointed at me.

I had followed the party down the steps and was standing by Green.

"You've had the painting all along. You lying little witch."

Green turned to look at me. At the same time, I was attempting to keep him between Andrush and me. We circled each other for a moment.

"I can explain," I said softly.

He took a long look at me then turned back to Andrush. Andrush took that moment to lunge at me, both hands extended.

"Okay, that's enough," Green said. He grabbed Andrush's right arm and neatly twisted it up behind his back. He had handcuffs on Andrush's wrists before anyone realized what was happening.

"God, you're good," I said.

He looked at me, all traces of humor gone.

"What is going on here?" Andrush sputtered, his face a dangerous shade of red.

"That's what we're going to find out," Green said. "But I think we'll leave the bracelets on for now." He pulled a black wallet out of his pocket with one hand and flipped it open, exposing his shield to everyone's view. "Detective Green, Portland Police. Now, start talking."

Mike's mother Ruta came out and joined her sister by the trunk of my car. She stared into it. Her hand came up and covered her mouth. She was saying something softly in what must be Polish.

"Harley?" Green asked.

"She is a thief!" Andrush bellowed. "She has my picture."

"Not your picture," Ruta yelled back in surprising clear English.

A heated shouting match ensued in Polish, Ruta's face inches away from Andrush's. Ana spoke softly in Polish. Ruta and Andrush fell into a stunned silence. Ana turned to Green and me.

"I tell them the painting here is a — how do you say? — fake."

"Fake," I repeated.

"Yes, that's it. It is fake."

For once, Andrush was speechless.

"Perhaps you can explain what's going on here," Green said to Ana.

"Of course," she said. "A very long time ago, one of our ancestors was a monk. He did many good works for his church. He was a healer. He helped the poor, was widely known. Before he died, an icon was painted of him and presented to the family for their private chapel. The family had better fortune then.

"It has been in the family ever since. We lost our land and our fortune, but always we kept the icon. Hundreds of years the Wyzcek family has protected it. Its worth cannot be expressed in dollars."

She paused.

"That thing?" Green asked, peering into the trunk.

The painting had been removed from the toweling and looked like someone had taken a knife to it.

"No, not that thing," Ana said. "This is what I am telling you. Always the Wyzcek family has understood the value of the icon. It is our history. Always they understood, until Ruta and Andrush. All Ruta can think is political cause. All Andrush can think is move to Hollywood and be actor. They just think 'How much can I sell it for?'

"Before he die, my father tell me to protect the icon for the family. He knew Mama could not resist Andrush's charms or Ruta's causes. So, I did as Papa asked."

"What have you done?" Andrush said in an anguished voice.

"After Father died, I went to Petr and asked him to paint a copy. When he finished, I switched the two."

"Where is icon?" Ruta demanded.

"In a safe place where everyone can enjoy it," Ana said. Her mouth turned up slightly on one side. It occurred to me she had been waiting for this moment for a long time. She seemed to be enjoying it.

"It's funny almost," she continued. "Ruta, you were so clever to use Rebecca and Mike to get the fake icon to Portland. I did the same thing. Rebecca's mother carried it when she visited me when I lived in Washington DC. We were few years before you."

"But that was twenty years ago," Andrush sputtered.

"That's right." Ana did smile now. "All this time you have dreams of riches from the icon, it is safe in Washington museum."

"Museum?" Ruta and Andrush said at almost the same time.

"Yes, it is safe in museum. All Wyzceks can see it, and it will be safe. It is how Father wanted it."

Andrush crumpled to the damp surface of the driveway. I could see tears glistening on his cheeks.

CHAPTER THIRTY-ONE

GREEN WAS ABLE TO REMOVE the handcuffs from Andrush without incident. Ruta and Ana had further words, but in the end, Ana shrugged and said in English, "It was what Father wished."

Andrush's wife summoned the group back into the house. Green and I were left standing by the car.

"My car," I groaned.

He put his arm around my shoulders. "Hey, kid, I know a good repair shop."

All of a sudden, I was tired. It seemed like too much effort to repel his attempt to comfort me.

"Just tell me how we're getting home," I said. "I can't think anymore."

"Let's go back inside. You can make your goodbyes and I'll call us a cab."

I had to admit I was ready to go home. Neva Dean still sat with Tommy. They were laughing as if they were old friends.

"I was just telling Tommy here about that silly cat of mine," Neva Dean said. "He has cats, too. His have their teeth, though."

"Are you ready to go home?" I asked her.

"You aren't leaving yet, are you?" Tommy asked. "We haven't given Mike a proper send-off."

"It's been a long week, Tommy. I don't want to make a big scene, but someone has broken into my car. I'm going to have to call my insurance agent when I go home and arrange to have it towed away from here."

"Geez, that's awful. Can I do anything?" Tommy asked. "My cousin has a tow truck. I could call him, if you want."

"Thanks, Tommy," I said. "Towing is included in my insurance coverage. It means a lot to me that you offered, though."

"Well, you think of anything, you've got my number."

Our goodbyes were awkward after the incident outside. I'm not sure there is any way for goodbyes not to be awkward in such circumstances, but Andrush was obviously hostile toward me. He opened his mouth as if he wanted to say something, but Green walked up, and he closed it again with out saying a word. His wife thanked us for coming and gave Neva Dean a hug.

"Our cab should be here," Green said. "Let's go."

Neva Dean and I followed him out to the curb. Our cab came, and he helped us into the back then joined the driver in front. He made small talk with the driver while we returned to Neva Dean's.

When we got there, he was all business. He took her key and went in before us. He searched all the rooms efficiently.

"Looks good," he said. "Lock the door as soon as we leave and don't open it for anything or anyone."

"What about Fluffy?" Neva Dean asked.

Green looked at me.

"Her cat," I said.

"He comes and goes as he pleases," Neva Dean said.

"Can you keep him in?" Green asked.

"Well..." She paused. "I suppose I could. He won't like it, though."

"He's just going to have to live with it," Green said. "I don't want your door opened for anything until you're ready to go out with family or police. You understand?"

"I'm not simple."

"Okay, you just lock the door."

"Am I going to be locked in, too?" I asked when we were back in the cab.

"You're going to have me," Green said. "I'm going to go check on Noah. I want you to keep the door locked while I'm gone."

Detective Harper was in her car in my driveway when our taxi dropped us off at the curb. She got out and met us as we walked up. She was immaculate, as usual. This time she was in black; a short-sleeved black silk blouse topped narrow black rayon pants. Her tones of black were a perfect match, a feat I had never come close to achieving.

"We're going to check the house here, and then Harper's going to take me to my car. I'll check on Noah, and then be back for the night," Green said. "You wait out here."

Before they could go in, Mrs. Johnson appeared at the door. "Is there a party out here?" she asked.

"What are you doing here?" Green shot back.

Mrs. Johnson looked indignant. She drew herself up to her full six feet. "I belong here," she spat. "What's your excuse?"

"I came to make sure the house is safe before Harley goes in for the night."

"The house is fine. I've been here all evening. No one is here, so you can go."

"I'm sure you're right, Mrs. Johnson," Harper said. "But we're required to check anyway. It's part of the job."

Mrs. J and I sat in the kitchen while Green and Harper searched every room in my house. It felt like a violation. Green came up the basement steps and into the kitchen.

"Everything looks fine," he said. "I'll be back in..." He looked at his watch. "Let's say an hour. Put the alarm on as soon as we go and don't let anyone in until I come back."

"Okay, already," I said. "We got the message."

Harper went to the kitchen door. Green reached around her, opened it and held it while she glided through. Somehow, the gesture seemed more polite when he did it for her.

"You want some tea?" Mrs. Johnson asked. "I got some anise cookies I baked while I was waiting for you to get home."

"Why are you here, anyway?" I asked.

She looked hurt.

"I do appreciate the cookies, but it wasn't necessary."

"I came to wait for Sonny. I knew you were going out, and Noah isn't home. Someone needs to be here for Sonny. Besides, I think it's a good thing I'm here. You look like you could use a little TLC."

I had forgotten how bad I probably looked. "I had a little run-in at the memorial service," I said.

"You sit down and let me look at that bump on your head," she said. She brought a small ice bag out from the bathroom and filled it with crushed ice and water.

"So, you're an expert on head bumps now?" I teased.

"I watched what those young men did when I was under their care. They charge so much to stay in the hospital I asked them for an extra bag. I brought it here yesterday. You see, it's a good thing I did, too."

She screwed the top on and pressed the cold bag against the lump then put my hand on it. "Hold this in place while I heat the water for tea."

I have one of those hot water spouts at my sink that delivers boiling water on demand, but Mrs. Johnson refuses to use it. She declares it to be unnatural. She took my kettle and filled it with fresh cold water from the tap. She stopped halfway to the stove.

"What's wrong?" I asked.

She held her finger up to her lips.

"Shhh," she said. She paused for a moment. "Do you hear that?"

"Hear what?"

"I'll be right back," she said and headed for the door. She was outside before I could say anything.

The teakettle started whistling. I got up, set the ice bag in the sink and headed for the stove. The doorbell rang. I assumed it was Mrs. Johnson, so I didn't look through the peephole. I swung the door open and was on my way back to the whistling kettle in the kitchen, when it registered it wasn't Mrs. Johnson who stepped through the door.

"Tommy," I said, "come in. I was just making some tea. Would you like a cup?"

"No, thanks," he said. "I just stopped by for a minute," He held up a small plastic square. "I found your name badge in Andrush's driveway. I thought you might need it to get in at work."

He followed me into the kitchen and handed it to me.

"You didn't have to make a special trip just for this," I said. I took the badge and set on my desk. "I'm glad you did, though. Eventually, the guard would let me in without it but not before humiliating me and dragging Karen out to the entrance. I've only forgotten my badge once, but once was enough."

I was surprised that Green's forensic team hadn't found it. They had covered the area with the proverbial fine-tooth comb.

"I thought I had looked around pretty well. Where did you find it?"

"It was under the bushes next to the stairs up by the back door."

Green and I had sat on the stairs. There was a rhododendron on the right side. It was old. The foliage at the bottom was sparse, as if someone had tried to do some kind of topiary effect at some time in its past. I remembered looking at the bark dust that Andrush or someone had carefully filled in around its base.

Tommy had on a beautiful black baseball-style jacket. It had an intricate image embroidered in silk on the back. It looked like some type of dragon eating its own tail. I complimented him on it.

"My parents bring junk like this from China all the time," he said. "That friend of yours, what's her name?" he asked, changing the subject before I could ask any more about the coat.

"Neva Dean?" I replied.

"Yeah, Neva Dean. She's a funny lady. Anyway, we were talking, and she said she gave you some fish or something for your cat. Some stuff Mike had given her."

"Yes, she did. I haven't given it to my cat yet. She's off her feed right now. My dog is missing, and she misses him." I wasn't sure why I was telling him all this.

"Well, see, that's what I was thinking. My mom's cat just had kittens, and I was telling Neva Dean about it. She thought maybe you could share some of the fish. I could just take the package, divide it and then bring some back to you."

"Why don't I just divide it now," I said. "I think that would be a lot simpler."

I went to the stove and turned the burner off under the kettle. Tommy followed me. He was a little closer than I like people to stand. He was invading my personal space. I turned to the refrigerator, and when I opened the door, he reached in and grabbed the paper bag with the smoked fish in it.

I grabbed the bag, too, but he didn't let go. "Tommy, it won't be any trouble for me to just divide this."

"My parents have a vacuum machine. I can pack your part in small vacuum packages." He tried to pull the bag free of my grip. I hung on, and it broke.

A lump of smoked salmon wrapped in pink Saran Wrap fell on the floor with a dull thump. It was followed by a small flat black box held shut with a clear plastic clip. It looked a lot like a box of integrated circuit die.

CHAPTER THIRTY-TWO

WE BOTH STARED AT THE box on the floor. Before either of us could speak, the back door opened. Mrs. Johnson walked in with Sonny under her left arm.

"Oh, my God," Mrs. J screamed. "That's her, that's her. The one who hit me. The one who ruined your things."

She was pointing at Tommy.

I looked at her and then at Tommy. I heard Mrs. J gasp and then noticed what caused the gasp. He was pointing a mean-looking black semiautomatic pistol at her.

He bent down and picked up the box of die without moving the gun's aim. He looked at me.

"I'm sorry it had to be like this, Harley. If you had just given me the fish we wouldn't be here now." I could see a thin sheen of sweat on his forehead.

"Exactly where are we, Tommy?" I asked.

"I have to have these chips," he said. "I don't have a choice. I'm just a cog in the big wheel. I've got buyers waiting. They aren't happy they had to wait this long. They need to get out of the country. I'm going to lose money on this deal as it is. My boss docks my profit if my delivery is late."

"Well, Tommy, we all have problems," I said. "What about us?"

"You're a smart woman, figure it out." He pulled his cell phone from his jacket pocket and hit a direct-dial button. He paused. "I got the chips...Yeah, I'll just be a few minutes...Send him to the Whale, I'll meet you there...No, I don't need help here." He said a few words in a language I couldn't decipher. "Let's get this over with," he said.

He motioned with the gun toward the basement steps.

I stepped to one side to let Mrs. Johnson go first, as if somehow I could shield her from what was coming.

"Here, I'll take the dog." I said to her, and I held my arms out. I was trying to calculate how long Green had been gone. I turned to Tommy. "The dog doesn't need to be involved in this, does he?"

Tommy looked annoyed, but he didn't move.

"Can I just put him in his dog carrier? It's in my bedroom. You can come."

"Look, Harley, I got to meet these guys at the Whale or I'm in big trouble," he said.

"Excuse me if I'm not sympathetic right now."

Mrs. Johnson nudged my foot with hers. I looked at her, and she made a very slight no motion with her head. At this rate, I'd never be able to keep him talking until Green got here.

"All right, he'd probably just be in the way," Tommy said. Sweat covered his face. He might be a killer, but he hadn't gotten the cold-blooded part down. His nerves made him even more dangerous. "Put the dog in the bathroom."

He twitched his head in that direction.

I took Sonny; he was growling low in his throat. I looked at Mrs. Johnson and hoped she was ready for what came next.

Tommy sidled to his right. He motioned us to come with him. He stopped as soon as the bathroom was in his line of sight.

"No tricks, or I blow the old lady away right here."

I shifted Sonny so I was holding him with both hands. I started to walk to the bathroom. Just as I passed Tommy, I turned and launched Sonny at him as hard as I could. He staggered back and dropped the gun. Mrs. Johnson fell to the floor and grabbed it.

I plowed into Tommy the way I'd seen football players ram those tackling dummies on TV. My weight pushed him back against the kitchen counter. He attempted some kind of karate move, but Sonny jumped up and grabbed his pant leg, deflecting most of the force away from me. The kick still hit hard enough to knock me to one knee.

He was positioned for another kick when I heard Mrs. Johnson yell "Freeze!" She was holding the gun.

He started to walk toward her with his hand out. "You aren't going to shoot me."

Mrs. Johnson didn't say anything. She just reached up and pulled the slide back, chambering a bullet.

"Stop right where you are, young man," she ordered.

This time he stopped.

"On the floor," she ordered.

He gave her a look of pure hatred, but he sank to the floor.

"Tie him up," she said to me.

I dug in the junk drawer and pulled out a roll of duct tape. I pulled his hands behind his back and taped them together. I taped his ankles tight then flipped him over and ran a strand of tape around his upper arms and chest.

"Come on, Harley," he said as soon as our eyes met. "Can't we talk about this? They're going to kill me if I don't deliver the chips."

I taped his mouth shut.

As soon as he was secure, I picked up the phone and dialed 911. When I finished giving all the relevant information, I asked them to page Green. He arrived at the same time the patrol car did.

He supervised the reading of rights and watched the patrol officer remove the duct tape and replace it with handcuffs. As soon as the tape was off, Tommy started yelling.

"You can't do this. These crazy women kidnapped me. I just came to give Harley her name tag."

"Save it for the DA," Green said.

The police officer took Tommy out and locked him into the backseat of his car.

"You need anything else before I transport?" he asked.

"No, Harper is on her way. We can get it from here, Thanks."

Green came back in. Mrs. Johnson was still holding Tommy's gun.

"I think you can give me that now," he said gently. She held it out to him, and he opened a brown paper evidence bag.

"Green," I said, "Tommy called someone and told them he would meet him at the Whale with the chips."

"Did he give any indication who he was talking to?"

"No, but he called them using speed dial on his cell phone."

"The Blue Whale is outside our jurisdiction. I can't send a patrol car to check it out, but I'll let the High Tech Task Force out there know. Without an ID on who we're looking for, it may not do much good."

The back door opened. Harper came in.

"Look what I found," she said. She pulled a disheveled Shannon in from the porch. "She was stomping around in the flowers. Trying to look in the windows, I think."

"I haven't done anything wrong," Shannon sobbed. "I was just trying to hear what Tommy was saying."

"Let's back up a minute," Green said. "How did you know Tommy was here?"

"Are you going to arrest me?" Shannon asked.

"Should we?" he countered.

"You are under no obligation to talk to us right now," Harper said. "You have the right to remain silent; you also have the right to have an attorney present when you are questioned."

"I think maybe you could clear up a few details for us," Green said, "just kind of informal-like. Here..." He pulled out a chair at the table. "Sit down."

Shannon sat.

Mrs. Johnson made a cup of tea using the instant hot water. She put the cup in front of Shannon. She put a couple of cookies on a saucer and set it beside the teacup. I got a box of tissues and put it on the table. Shannon took one and blew her nose loudly.

"Is that better?" Green said.

She nodded. She stopped sobbing.

"Why don't you start with why you're here," Green suggested.

Shannon took a deep breath. "After I talked to the police, I promised I would go to my parents' house in Gresham. The officer called my mom, and she was home, so they agreed I could leave if I would go straight there. I really did start to drive there, but then I started wondering who was in my apartment. I decided to go back to Andrush's and talk to Tommy. I waited until I saw Harley leave. I was going to go in the back door, but I heard Tommy talking on his cell phone. He was in the backyard. His back was to me.

"I haven't heard from Robert since the day before yesterday, and I really needed to talk to him. When I heard him say "Robert," I listened in. I heard Tommy say Harley's name. When he finished talking, I asked him if he had seen Robert lately. He said no, but if everything went according to plan, he was going to see him later. I asked him if he would ask Robert to call me. He said he would, but he was acting real funny. Kind of nervous. I could tell he wasn't going to remember so when he said he was leaving Andrush's, I decided to follow him. I thought maybe he would lead me to Robert. This is where we ended up."

"Shannon," Green said, "I want you to think real careful before you answer." He paused. "Do you have reason to believe Robert is mixed up with what's happening here tonight or with what happened to Mike?"

"No," she said. Tears started forming at the corner of her eyes. She looked down. "Yes...I mean...I don't know."

"Why don't you tell us what you do know," Green said softly.

"That's just it. I don't really know anything. Robert gets a lot of calls on his cell phone, and he always goes into another room to answer it. And he has to go meet people late at night. But he's so romantic. He loves me." She started crying in earnest.

Green handed her a fresh tissue and patted her back. He closed his notebook. I looked on in disbelief.

"That was a great performance Shannon," I said, clapping my hands. "But it's a bunch of bullshit. You may be fooling Green, but I'm not buying."

CHAPTER THIRTY-THREE

SHANNON LOOKED UP AND glared at me, her tears suddenly gone.

"Why don't you try again? Start with the part where you saw Robert slice Hieu's throat."

Shannon's eyes opened wider. Green had stepped over to the sink to fill a cup with hot water. He froze.

"We both know you were there," I continued. "You just left off the part about seeing Robert."

"I didn't say I saw Robert," she said. "It was Tommy. I saw Tommy."

"You know, Shannon," I said, "Robert isn't going to protect you like this when he's arrested. And he will be, make no mistake. I think you're right. Tommy was there, but it was Robert you saw slit Hieu's throat. That's why you were afraid to go home to your apartment. Robert's been living with you. You had to find out if he knew you had seen him. You knew if he saw you there your life wouldn't be worth anything. Isn't that the real reason you were hiding? You were hiding from Robert, not the police. That's why you've been dogging Tommy, too. You were trying to find out what he knew."

"I think I need an attorney now," Shannon said.

"You have a chance to do the right thing here, Shannon," I said. "Tell Green that Robert is the one who is waiting for Tommy at the Whale. You must know it's over between you two."

She started crying for real.

"I know it's hard." I stepped over and put my hand on her

shoulder. "Honey, Robert used you. That's why he was always so interested in your work. He needed to make sure Tommy was doing his job. You were his spy. You just didn't know it at first. Robert is going to get caught. For God's sake, Shannon, he killed Hieu. And maybe Mike and Debbie, for all we know. Can you live with that?"

I looked at Green. He was still at the sink. I don't think he had breathed the whole time I was talking.

"Maybe if you help Green catch Robert, he can help you stay clear of this mess."

Green cleared his throat. "I can't make any promises, but I think there is a good chance of getting immunity for you if you cooperate fully."

Shannon looked up. "I haven't done anything."

"I'm afraid that's not true," Harper spoke up. She had been standing by the back door all this time, watching the drama unfold. She came over and slowly circled the table as she talked. "You will be charged with being an accessory before and after the fact in three murders. If Robert has been living with you — and that will be easy enough to prove — you will be charged with conspiracy to commit murder. If Robert is wanted, the charge could be harboring a fugitive. And then there will be all the charges related to the theft of the microprocessors. Do I need to go on?"

"But I didn't know about the thefts," Shannon cried. "I didn't know what they were doing. I just knew it was important to Robert."

"Shannon," I said, "you could go to jail as a multiple murderer. Is Robert worth that?"

She put her head down on her folded arms and cried. Her shoulders shook. She finally looked up at me.

"This is for real, isn't it?"

"I'm afraid it's very real."

"Okay, what do you want?" she said in a tired voice.

Harper read Shannon her rights and reiterated the fact she could have an attorney present if she wanted to. Green was making multiple phone calls at the same time, on my phone, his phone and, eventually, Harper's phone, too.

"Here's the deal," he said. "Shannon calls Robert and says Tommy asked her to make a delivery for him. He has a problem he needs to take care of. Shannon will be wired, and the High Tech

Task Force will film it all. When Robert receives the stolen goods, the police will grab him. After it goes down, if Shannon will testify against Robert and Tommy at the murder trial for Hieu, she can probably get immunity for those crimes."

He set it all up like a one-act play. We each had a role. Green and I would go to the Whale first. We would have a drink and talk to Skip. We had already established Green as my date at the memorial service. The way gossip travels through Sil-Trac, I was sure Skip would know about it before we arrived. He tended to be the unofficial town crier for the company, and as such, people reported all news to him first.

Shannon would come in and meet with Robert a few minutes later. Harper would be outside with the task force. They would cover all the entrances just in case things went awry.

Then Green changed his mind. Shannon would not contact Robert before we drove to the Blue Whale. He was afraid Robert would try to change the meeting place to somewhere less accessible for the police if she called ahead. Or disappear, if he was smart.

Green and Harper talked to Shannon all the way to The Blue Whale. A uniformed officer followed us in Shannon's car. Green and Harper drilled her on what she could say and what she couldn't say, what to do if he acted like he didn't know what she was talking about when she approached him and how not to say the words for him.

Green and I played our part. We parked by Sil-Trac so no one would see who came with whom. We crossed the driveway. He draped his arm across my shoulders. He gave me a little squeeze as we approached the door.

"You okay?"

"I've been better. I'm just ready for this all to be over."

"By tomorrow morning this will be a fading memory."

"Maybe it works that way for you, but I don't think I'll ever forget this."

"Well, at least we'll have the bad guys behind bars, and Noah will be back home with you."

"Great, just in time for me to put his angry self on a plane back to the school he hates."

"Let's not go there," Green said.

We walked the last few feet, lost in our own thoughts.

"Hey, boss," Skip called out as I came through the door and

hung my coat up on the rack. "Who's the new gent?"

I introduced Green to Skip, leaving out his occupational title. We walked over to the bar. Skip brought us each a Diet Coke.

"I figure you must be a Diet Coke drinker if Harley is spending time with you. It's her first requirement in a man," he said.

Green raised an eyebrow at me. I glared at Skip.

"You kids call me if you need anything." Skip retreated to the kitchen.

Green and I sat on bar stools. We turned toward each other, as if we were sharing an intimate secret. I looked into the mirror behind the bar.

"That's Robert in the last booth by the pool table," I said. As we watched in the mirror, a slim, leggy Asian girl came out of the restroom and slid into the booth beside him. She tugged on what might have been a skirt if it had been a few inches longer.

"Who's the chick?" Green asked.

"I've never seen her before. She doesn't look old enough to work at Sil-Trac."

The girl in question draped herself around Robert's neck. I looked away when she put her tongue in his ear.

"I'm not liking this complication," Green said. "You think you can get your little buddy to get her out of here?"

"Skip?" I called out. He materialized in front of me. I gestured toward the image of the girl in the mirror. "You letting in jailbait these days?"

"I don't know who that is," Skip whined. "He brings her in through the back entrance. She don't drink, so I don't hassle them."

"Shannon is on her way here, so you might want to, just this once."

"Too late." He nodded toward the door.

Shannon walked in and put her coat on the rack. She smiled at him.

"I'll have my usual," she said.

Skip poured two inches of amber liquid into a glass and put it on the polished surface of the bar. She grabbed it and headed for the pool area. She froze when she saw Robert and Miss Thing.

"You two-timing jerk," she screamed. "I drove all the way out here, just to give you a package from Tommy. Well, I'll give you something all right."

She dumped her drink on Robert and the girl. He quickly slid out of the booth, nearly dumping the girl on the floor.

"Go powder your nose," he said and pushed her toward the restrooms. She looked petulant but went without saying anything.

He pulled a snow-white handkerchief from his pocket and dabbed the front of his black Nehru jacket. "Come on, Shannon, let's talk. This isn't what you think. I don't even know who that girl is. I think she's some kid Skip feels sorry for. He lets her hang out here at night so she isn't on the streets. She comes on to all the guys. You know you're my number one."

I could see Shannon's anger subside. I wanted to scream at her. I bit my tongue instead.

Green and I took our drinks to a booth near the pool tables so we could hear.

"You got a package for me?" Robert asked.

"What's going on with you and Tommy?" Shannon asked. "He was acting really weird."

"We just got some business. You don't need to worry about it. His parents bought some jewelry for my sister. I got to give it to her tonight. Why don't you give it to me?"

"Give him the package, Shannon," Green said under his breath. "Just like we practiced. Hand him the package."

"Tell me who the girl is," Shannon said. "The truth this time."

"I told you the truth," Robert said. "She's no one." He put his arms around her and pulled her to him. He kissed her neck. "You know I only love you."

He whispered something in her ear. She blushed, and I was glad Green and I couldn't hear what he said.

"Tell me what's really in the package, and I'll give it to you," she teased. She rubbed her long body up against his muscular frame. She pulled his head close to hers and kissed him. "I've missed you," she said.

He grabbed her buttocks in his hands and pulled her mini-skirted hips tighter against him.

"Don't worry about what's in that package. It's just some stuff Tommy got for me. I've got to give it to someone, and then we can continue this," he said and kissed her deeply. "Be a good girl and wait for me."

"Maybe your little friend and I can play cards or something

while we wait for you," Shannon said.

He ran his hands up her hips, over her chest, and grabbed her face in his hands. He ran his tongue around her lips and kissed her again. I held my breath.

"I'll be back before you know it. Where's the package?" he asked.

"It's in my car. Come with me," she said and grabbed his hand. They walked out to her car. Green and I got up and went to the door.

Shannon reached into the backseat and picked up the small black package. She handed it to him. He slipped it into the front handkerchief pocket of his jacket. He grabbed her rear end and kissed her one more time.

"Goodbye, Robert," she whispered.

The kiss seemed to last an eternity. My imagination ran wild. I pictured Shannon whipping out a penknife and stabbing him in the gut. Then it was Robert pulling a concealed gun from his pocket and holding Shannon hostage.

In the end, it was much less dramatic. The signal to the police was Shannon saying goodbye. Two undercover police officers wearing faded jeans and flannel work shirts had been bent over the engine of an old truck in the parking lot during their embrace. The taller of the two, a muscular blond in his forties, sauntered toward Robert. He was wiping his hands on a shop rag as he approached. When he got within a few feet, he let the rag fall, uncovering his service revolver. His partner circled around to the side and pulled his weapon from behind his back.

"Don't do anything stupid," the blond said as Robert looked quickly from one officer to another and then to Shannon.

"You bitch," he hissed.

Shannon looked stricken.

"Get her out of here," the blond ordered.

Green moved quickly. He grabbed Shannon by the arm and took her back to his car. Robert was arrested, handcuffed and read his rights. A patrol car hauled him away. The plainclothes officers came to Green's car.

"Okay, miss," the blond said to Shannon, "your turn." He arrested her and read her rights to her.

"Wait!" she shouted. "You said I would get immunity if I helped you get Robert."

She slapped at the hands of the officer trying to cuff her.

"You got to go through the process," Green said. "I told you it wasn't a guarantee. You actually have to testify to get the charges dropped. Until then you're considered an accomplice. I think you should call an attorney as soon as they let you use the phone."

CHAPTER THIRTY-FOUR

Mrs. Johnson was waiting in my kitchen when Green brought me home.

"I thought you might be hungry," she said.

The table was laden with goodies. A plate piled high with assorted sandwiches was the centerpiece. There was a dish of fresh vegetable sticks with ranch dip; a plate of fresh fruit, peeled and cut, ready for consumption and a chocolate pudding cake because Mrs. J believed no meal was complete without chocolate. She had laid out cups and glasses on the countertop, ready to be filled with the drink of our choice. The kettle was heating on the stove.

I took Harper's coat and hung it on the coatrack at the top of the basement stairs. Green washed his hands at the kitchen sink and wiped them on the towel that hung at the end of the counter. His ease in my home made me uncomfortable.

Mrs. Johnson herded everyone to the table and supervised the filling of plates. No one spoke. When she had drinks prepared and distributed, she sat down.

"While you were gone, I talked to Mrs. Parker." She turned to Green. "This is the family who lives behind here. Her children want a dog, but her husband says no. When Sonny appeared in their yard, the children thought their prayers had been answered. They hid him in their mama's garden shed so Papa wouldn't find out. They've been walking him a block from here so Papa wouldn't see. He got loose from them, and he bit the man who caught him.

"So now," Mrs. J said, "you tell me what happened."

Since Tommy's and Robert's crimes spanned several jurisdictions, it had taken several hours to sort out who would charge whom with what. In the end a lot of information was exchanged, and they were both charged with murder and robbery in Washington County, where Sil-Trac is located, and with murder, conspiracy and a host of lesser charges by the Portland Police in neighboring Multnomah County, where Mike lived.

Green took a drink of his hot chocolate. It had been a long day for everyone involved. I could see from his face he was way past tired. He took a deep breath.

"The bottom line is that Tommy and Robert are going to go away for a long time. Probably forever."

Mrs. J looked at him. "Is that little one going to jail for hitting me? I'm willing to testify, you know."

"It may come to that, but more likely they'll drop some of the lesser charges and concentrate on the more serious murder charges."

Mrs. J looked disappointed. "So, what will the big oaf be charged with?"

I glared at her. Clearly, she had forgotten our decision not to trouble Green with our little incident with Andrush.

"She's talking about Andrush," I said. "I doubt he'll be charged with anything, except maybe bad acting. The icon he was so desperate to get his hands on turned out to be a fake. His sister had switched it years ago. His extortion attempt was just a misguided effort to get back to Poland and get the icon. He had no way of knowing Mike had accidentally intercepted the stolen chips when he gathered everyone's notebooks and took them home to work on the count problem.

"Mike apparently hid the chips in the smoked fish he gave to Neva Dean. She innocently passed them on to me. Because of Andrush's scheme, Mike had to lay low while he was supposed to be kidnapped. If he hadn't been hiding, he probably would have brought the chips to work, and maybe he would still be alive."

"I wouldn't be so quick to convict Andrush," Green said. "He probably prolonged Mike's life by spiriting him away to Eugene. If Mike had stayed there instead of sneaking back to get his papers he might still be alive."

"So now it's my fault?" I asked.

"Let's not go there, okay?" he said. "We're all too tired to second-guess everyone's actions and motives. I think Robert and

Tommy were watching everyone pretty close. They were apparently willing to kill anyone that got in the way."

"I'm still trying to figure out how Debbie fits into the picture," I said. "She wasn't the sharpest knife in the drawer, so I doubt she figured out the count problem on her own."

"We know she was working nights at one of Sil-Trac's competitors," Green said. "It's not illegal, but I'll bet it's against company policy. At this point, it's pure speculation, but my bet is Tommy blackmailed her into running the smear campaign against you, hence the sudden run on sexual harassment claims. He was probably trying to keep you tied up until he could move the last batch of chips and cook the books so you could pass the inspection.

"Beyond that, who knows? Maybe she figured out what they were doing. Or maybe she called Tommy's bluff and refused to continue when Mike turned up dead. Either way, she was expendable."

"Hieu must have interrupted them looking for the chips in the clean room," I said. "That must be why they ransacked Mike's and then my place. When they didn't find them either place, they went back to Sil-Trac. They must have been the ones who called in the bomb threat. I know it seems trivial, but an unplanned shutdown like that will cost Sil-Trac dearly."

"Always the manager, huh?"

The phone rang. I looked at the wall clock. It was well past midnight.

"That's probably for you," I said to Green. "No one I know would be calling now."

He got up and answered the phone. "Yeah, It's safe to come home now," I heard him say. "In fact, I think Harley will be happy to see you." He hung up. "I called Noah right after we arrested Robert. I told him he could come home in a few hours if everything went right. Chris's mother is bringing him now."

I took a deep breath and willed myself to stay calm. "My relationship with Noah is complicated. I would appreciate it if you would butt out where he is concerned."

Green smiled. "I know these last few days have been stressful for you, so I won't take that last comment personally. When you've had a little rest, you'll realize what a help I've been."

I was distracted from killing him by Noah walking in the door.

"Hey, how's it going," he said and walked right past me. He pulled a chair over and sat between Green and Mrs. J. "Detective Green, can you tell me everything now?"

I was going to throw Green out, but I could hear the excitement in Noah's voice. I wasn't willing to trade that for silence.

Noah looked back at me. "By the way, Harley, Dad called a little while ago at Chris's. Boy, is he mad at you." He turned back to Green.

So what else was new?

END

ABOUT THE AUTHOR

ARLENE SACHITANO has worked in the electronics industry for twenty-eight years, as a microelectronics process technician, a manufacturing manager and, for the last twelve years, as Director of Training for a high tech staffing service. She has written serial mysteries for a local newspaper and is the author of a proprietary tome on electronics assembly.

Arlene is active in her local chapter of Sisters in Crime. She lives with her husband and their cat Lydia in the Pacific Northwest.

ABOUT THE ARTIST

APRIL MARTINEZ was born in the Philippines and raised in San Diego, California, daughter to a US Navy chef and a US postal worker, sibling to one younger sister. From as far back as she can remember, she has always doodled and loved art, but her parents never encouraged her to consider it as a career path, suggesting instead that she work for the county. So, she attended the University of California in San Diego, earned a cum laude bachelor's degree in literature/writing and entered the workplace as a regular office worker.

For years, she went from job to job, dissatisfied that she couldn't make use of her creative tendencies, until she started working as an imaging specialist for a big book and magazine publishing house in Irvine and began learning the trade of graphic design. From that point on, she worked as a graphic designer and webmaster at subsequent day jobs while doing freelance art and illustration at night.

In 2003, April discovered the e-publishing industry. She responded to an ad looking for e-book cover artists and was soon in the business of cover art and art direction. Since then, she has created hundreds of book covers, both electronic and print, for several publishing houses, earning awards and recognition in the process. Two years into it, she was able to give up the day job and work from home. April Martinez now lives with her cat in Orange County, California, as a full-time freelance artist/illustrator and graphic designer.